A Cattleman's Quest

Book Two of the Fairfax Family Series

Chris Taylor

LCT Productions Pty Limited

This book is dedicated to my children: Angus, Imogen, Rory, Millie, and Madeleine. I love you to the moon and back. Today, tomorrow, forever.
And as always, to my husband, Linden. My heart.

Other books by Chris Taylor

The Munro Family Series
(in order)

The Profiler
The Investigator
The Predator
The Betrayal
The Deception
The Negotiator
The Christmas Vigil (A novella)
The Ransom
The Defendant
The Shooting

CHRIS TAYLOR

The Maker

The Sydney Harbour Hospital Series (in order)

The Perfect Husband
The Body Thief
The Baby Snatchers
The Final Bullet
The Debt Collector
The Lab Test
The Stolen Identity
The Cliff-top Killer
The Likeable Fraudster

The Sydney Legal Series
(in order)

An Accidental Murderer
At the Hand of her Father
A Woman Scorned
Lies and Deception
Ordinary Evil
The Ties that Bind
The Perfect Crime
A Toxic Inheritance
Malicious Love

A CATTLEMAN'S QUEST

The Craigdon Family Series
(in order)

Callum
Joel
Isabella
Nicholas
Sophia
Flynn
Noah
Logan
Elizabeth

The Barrington Family Series
(in order)

Broken Lives
Broken Promises
Broken Bonds
Broken Spirits
Broken Minds
Broken Vows
Broken Hearts
Broken Dreams
Broken Homes

The Fairfax Family Series (in order)

A Cattleman in Disguise
A Cattleman's Quest
A Cattleman's Daughter
A Cattleman's Secret Baby
To Catch a Cattleman
The Doctor and the Cattleman
To Rescue a Cattleman
A Cattleman's Heart
For the Love of a Cattleman

Bachelors and Brides Series (in order)

Matilda
Austin
Farrah
Benjamin
Verity
Denver
Ebony
Tyrone
Willow

Books by Chris Taylor
Writing as
Bella
Christian

This Is Where It Ends Series
(in order)

Jessie's Story
Ryan's Story
Holly's Story
Sarah's Story
Veronica's Story

Love audiobooks? Check out Chris Taylor Books on audio
iTunes   Amazon   Audible   Spotify

Join Chris Taylor's Facebook reader group/fan page and be
among the
first to receive news of book releases, read and review books
prior to release
and other amazing offers.

Join Now!

Chapter One

♥

C ayd Fairfax brushed his hair back off his forehead and
made a conscious effort not to pace. The nerves had
been swarming inside his gut ever since he'd woken that
morning to the knowledge that today three gorgeous, single
women would descend upon his family's cattle station in outback Central Queensland with hopes of winning his heart.
They were due to arrive at any moment.

His red kelpie, Macey, watched him with a bemused expression. Cayd understood exactly how the dog felt. It was right
about now that he questioned the wisdom of agreeing to participate in the TV show, *Outback Bride*. Unfortunately, it was
too late to back out. The TV producer, Lily Calimeris, stood a
short distance away, her brown eyes bright with anticipation
as she stared across the miles of grassed paddocks, seeking
confirmation that the three participants weren't far away.

Cayd had met the women at a ritzy function organized by
the TV station at a property on the outskirts of Sydney. Out

of the hundreds of women who'd applied for the chance to be in the running to win his heart, he'd culled them down to ten. From those ten, he'd narrowed it down to the three who he now awaited with equal parts nerves and excitement.

There was Marissa. A tall, leggy blond. Confident in her good looks. There was no doubt she was stunning, but he wasn't completely sure about the gray matter. Then there was Olivia. A cute, petite redhead. He wasn't sure how she'd do on the farm with her long, painted fingernails and immaculately blow-dried hair, but her cheeky smile had intrigued him, and she'd been as keen as any of the ladies to experience life on the farm. Last, there was Chelsea, with her short, curly brown hair and friendly smile. She was attractive without being head-turning. Her can-do attitude was appealing, and she had experience working on a farm. He wasn't sure if she was already in the friend zone, but he was prepared to give her a go and see how things developed.

"How are you feeling?"

The TV producer's question startled him from his thoughts. He blinked and turned to her with a smile.

"Nervous, excited. I can't figure out which. All this has suddenly become real. I'm starting to wonder what the hell I was thinking when I signed on for this."

"Don't stress. You're not the first farmer to have second thoughts. In fact, this is my sixth season, and I don't think I've ever had a farmer who was entirely at ease with his decision.

You're out of your comfort zone. That's okay. Think of it as a challenge. You want to find a wife, right?"

Cayd shrugged. "I guess."

"And we're going to do our best to find you one. This show isn't called *Outback Bride* for nothing." She grinned.

His gut clenched. Even with only a smattering of makeup, there was no denying the woman was striking. Then again, she was in the TV industry. Weren't they all beautiful? With her long black hair and warm brown eyes framed by impossibly thick long lashes, it was all he could do not to return her grin. She might have been petite—barely coming up to his chest—but everything was in proportion, except for her breasts. They were at least a size or two larger than her slight frame might otherwise have dictated.

Not that he minded. He'd always been a boobs guy, and she had a very nice rack indeed. Too bad she wore an engagement ring. While he was always in the mood to appreciate a beautiful woman, he drew the line at dating another man's fiancée.

And then he mentally shook his head.

Why am I even thinking like this? I have three gorgeous ladies about to arrive any minute. Ladies handpicked by me. Surely one of them will prove to be my match... If things go to plan, I could be engaged myself before the month's out.

The possibility blew his mind. While his primary motivation for taking part in the TV show was to garner publicity for his fledgling farm stay venture, the thought of hanging out with three beautiful women for a couple of weeks sounded like fun.

The idea that one of them might even be his future wife was hard to imagine, but as Lily said, it was a challenge and one he was definitely up for.

"Just so you know, this show has a good track record for success," the stunning producer added, drawing closer. She bent low and gave Macey a pat. The dog's expression turned blissful.

"Out of the fifty couples over the ten seasons so far, more than half of them are still together, and they have a total of forty-five children between them." She grinned again. "Not bad, hey?"

He nodded. "That's a reasonable success rate, for sure."

She rolled her eyes at his understatement and straightened. "Now, don't forget what we talked about. You can't show any lady preferential treatment. It's important to keep the viewers guessing about who your final pick will be. There'll be a farewell dinner this Sunday night. That's when you'll choose one lady to send home. The final two will stay on the farm until the next farewell dinner at the end of the second week. It's important you don't give too much away. We don't want to know which lady you're planning to choose until the very last moment, okay? Our audience loves the suspense."

He chuckled to hide another wave of nerves. "Okay. I hope when the time comes that *I* know which one I'm going to choose."

"Don't worry. You'll get plenty of time with all of them. Again, make sure you share your time with the ladies equally.

Although, if you're drawn to one over another, then that's okay. Sometimes the women can get a little put out if that happens, but a bit of drama is always good for the show and even better for the ratings."

He hid a grimace. He wasn't sure what Lily meant by "drama," but he was pretty sure it was the kind of thing he'd rather steer clear of. He'd never been any good at playing games, especially where relationships were concerned.

At twenty-seven, he'd had a few relationships, but none that had lasted longer than twelve months. The closest he'd come to falling in love was with Emily Dwyer back in high school. But witnessing the joy in his older brothers as they found the loves of their lives had filled him with a sense of yearning to have what they did. Now Raine's wife, Isabella, was soon to give birth to their first baby, and from what Brock had said to him only yesterday when they'd spoken on the phone, he and his new wife, Kelsey, were also trying hard to add to their family.

Being one of ten children, Cayd had always been surrounded by family. They centered him, gave him security, made him whole. He'd gotten to an age where having a family of his own had become important. If he could find a potential wife by taking part in a TV show, then why not? The publicity might even give his dream of opening the station to paying visitors a boost. As long as the drama Lily hinted at didn't get out of control. He shuddered at the thought of being caught up in a catfight.

"Looks like they're nearly here," Lily murmured.

Cayd stared in the direction of the front drive. A cloud of red dust billowed into the air. Macey stood and came to attention, her ears pricked. "Yep. I'd say they're about three minutes away." A fresh wave of nerves swarmed his belly, and he drew in a deep breath.

This is it... The moment I've been waiting for...

Beside him, Lily chuckled softly. "Relax, Cayd. They're your ladies. The ones you chose. They're not going to eat you up."

Easy for you to say...

He shot her a tight-lipped look and then forced himself to relax. "You're right. It's not like I haven't met them already. I'm sure we'll all get along fine."

Lily Calimeris glanced sideways at her latest farmer. He was the epitome of a tall, strapping cowboy. Black hair that was probably a little too long to be fashionable. Golden skin that was tanned from years spent in the sun. The denim-colored chambray shirt brought out the piercing blue of his eyes. Levis emphasized his narrow hips and hugged his muscular thighs. His feet were shod in battered, dusty boots that were definitely not for show. To top it off, he wore an Akubra a shade darker than his hair that was accompanied by a wide, white, sexy smile.

He was so different from her fiancé, Alexander Vasco. An accountant for a small, family-run accountancy firm in the Sydney suburbs, Alex drove a hybrid car, owned an electric scooter, and wore a suit and tie every day. He barely saw the sun. The only time he tanned was during the summer when she'd force him out on weekends to the beach. Still, he might not be a red-hot cattleman, but he was hers. And she loved him. That was all that mattered.

She glanced again toward the cowboy. There was no doubt he was a handsome devil. That would play well for the cameras and was most definitely good for ratings. But there was also an authenticity about him that was equally attractive. He wasn't playing at cattle farming. He was the real deal.

The cloud of red dust drew closer. Lily turned and walked over to the camera crew, who were lounging against the homestead fence in the shade. Two cameramen, a sound guy, a lighting technician, and a gopher who carried all the equipment and did everything else that was required.

"Are we ready to roll?" she asked.

Nigel, the cameraman who'd accompanied her on her five previous trips, saluted her. "Ready when you are, boss."

"Good. Let's get some footage of the vehicle arriving and then keep filming while the girls step out of the car. I want their initial reactions, including when they greet Cayd. Got it?"

Nigel grinned. "Got it."

The rest of the crew nodded and offered mumbled acknowledgments. They straightened from their positions and started to prepare for the upcoming segment.

Lily turned away, confident in their ability to do as she'd asked. Most of the crew had been together for a long time. With a cumulative ten seasons under their belt, they had this down to a fine art. In anticipation of the imminent arrival, she returned to Cayd's side. He still looked tense. No doubt the nerves were about to kick in tenfold. She'd witnessed many a nervous farmer at this point in the game and she knew just how to get them to relax.

She squeezed his bare forearm just below his elbow, where his shirt sleeve had been rolled up. She registered the warmth of his skin and the strength of his muscle beneath her fingers. Ignoring the pleasant sensations that tingled up her arm, she gave him a reassuring smile.

"Relax, Cayd. Smile. Ignore the cameras. Pretend they're not even there. In fact, the best thing to do is not to pay any attention to whether they're rolling or not. Think of them as a tree, or a fence post. Present, but unobtrusive." She chuckled wryly. "Well, as unobtrusive as a cameraman holding a camera can be."

The sound of the 4WD drew closer and then the vehicle appeared out of the dust. Lily gave Cayd's forearm another friendly squeeze.

"Here they are. Let's see you looking beyond excited to meet your ladies. Big smiles, Cayd."

Cayd's heart thumped. He wasn't sure if it was from the hot little producer's casual touch or the fact that the arrival of his women was imminent. A late-model white Toyota Land Cruiser swung into the driveway and came to a halt in front of them. No doubt the vehicle had been clean and shiny when it had left Brisbane. Now it was covered in red dust. The station had been in flood less than a year ago, but there was no evidence of that now. It had been more than two months since it had rained, and the grass was dying off.

He was certain the show's producers had chosen the 4WD on purpose. This was their tenth season. They had previous experience driving on outback roads. Lily had told him the show had been sponsored by Toyota. In Cayd's opinion, the 4WD Land Cruisers were the only vehicles tough enough to withstand the harsh conditions. Most of the time, the dirt roads in the outback left a lot to be desired.

Cayd glanced sideways at Lily. She held a clipboard and a pen in her hands. Macey was now perched at her feet. The camera crew had shifted into place. They'd already filmed a segment of him talking about how excited he was to welcome three beautiful ladies to his farm. He'd been pleased to be able to speak the truth. His initial motivation for signing up for the show might have been to breathe life into the bed and breakfast farm stay project he hoped to soon get off the ground, but he was almost as keen to spend time with the women. Finding an outback bride wouldn't be the worst thing that could happen.

Marissa was seated in the front, next to the driver. No surprises there. At twenty-five, she was the oldest of the three. She was also the most confident. In fact, she'd surprised him by challenging him to an arm wrestle the first day they'd met. He'd let her win and she'd crowed about it the rest of the day. It had been fun to hang out with her, and he looked forward to spending the next two weeks getting to know her better.

Surreptitiously, he wiped his now-sweaty palms along the sides of his jeans. The cameras kept rolling. Lily kept issuing instructions.

"We need a close-up of the vehicle with the dust coming off it," she said. "That gives it the authentic country look."

Cayd went to roll his eyes but stopped himself just in time. This was what the producers wanted. An authentic outback experience to be shown to their city viewers, who apparently found all things country romantic. Even the dust.

Marissa was the first to climb out. Dressed in designer jeans and boots that were so shiny they must be new, she looked the epitome of an urban cowgirl. The designer plaid blouse with the top three buttons undone gave him an ample view of her impressive cleavage and completed her sophisticated look.

Not waiting for any instructions from Lily or the camera crew, she came straight up to him and greeted him with a kiss on the lips. The look in her eyes left him in no doubt she was attracted to him, and he was fine with that. It was one of the reasons he'd chosen her. She was as tall as he was. They'd fit together well. He was curious to see what might develop between them.

"I'm sorry, Marissa. We didn't the start of that. Can you greet Cayd again?" Lily turned to the cameramen. "And get a close-up of both of them," Lily instructed. "I want shots of their faces."

Marissa winked at him. "How about a hug?"

He grinned. "Sounds good to me."

He stepped forward and drew her in his arms. "Welcome to Marlowe Downs."

"Can we get a smile, Cayd?" Lily asked.

He smiled at Marissa. She smiled back. He winked. She grinned. He could think of worse things than to be flirting with a beautiful woman.

"Okay, cut. I think we have enough," Lily said. She smiled distractedly at both Cayd and Marissa. "Thanks, guys. That was great."

The rear doors opened, and Lily turned her attention to the other two girls. "Okay, Olivia. Chelsea. Who's next?"

Olivia climbed out of the 4WD and stepped forward a little hesitantly. She'd told him she was twenty-four, but her lack of confidence and the smattering of freckles on her open, inno-cent face made her appear younger. Cayd met her halfway. Lily called "action," and the cameras started rolling again.

It had been a week since he'd first met the women. It was obvious both Olivia and Chelsea were feeling as awkward and nervous as he was.

Olivia approached him with a shy smile. "Hi. It's good to see you again."

"You too."

Her dark-red hair had been pulled back in a low bun that rested on the nape of her neck. She was of average height, with a tidy figure and a cute button nose. Her friendly smile put him at ease. He pecked her on the cheek and hugged her briefly. "Welcome to Marlowe Downs."

When Cayd dropped his arms and went to step out of the hug, Lily shook her head.

"Sorry, Cayd. Just give us a few more moments. We need a bit more footage of that hug."

Cayd swallowed a groan and complied. Greeting Olivia in such an orchestrated way felt unnatural, but he understood this was what was required. They were filming a TV show, after all. He drew the woman into his arms and held her close. The difference in their height made things a bit awkward, but short of lifting her off her feet, there wasn't much he could do. Unperturbed, Olivia sent him a flirty grin.

"You're taller than I remembered," she teased.

He chuckled and then looked at Lily for a signal that he could now release his hold. She nodded.

"And…cut. Thanks, Cayd. Thanks, Olivia." She turned to where Chelsea stood waiting patiently near the vehicle. "Last, but not least, Chelsea. I'll tell you when we're ready."

Cady pushed down a surge of impatience. This was only the opening scene of the girls' arrival on the station and it had already taken up far too much of his day. He understood that filming took time, and they didn't always get the shot they wanted first up, but this was a working station. He had chores that needed to be done.

As if sensing his irritation, Lily sidled up close and pulled him to one side.

"It's okay, Cayd. Relax. This is all so new, and you're not used to having every minute of your life put under the microscope. But you signed up to be part of a TV show. This is how it works."

He managed a tight smile. "I understand. I guess I wasn't expecting everything to take so long. I mean, I haven't even taken them to their lodgings or shown them around."

Lily's brown eyes filled with understanding. "Hey, I get it. It takes a little getting used to, having me and a camera crew following your every move, but like I said, try to forget we're here. Be as natural as possible. We'll do our best to remain invisible."

With that, she moved away and went to speak with Chelsea. A few moments later, Lily called "action" and Chelsea stepped forward and smiled at him.

"Hi, Cayd. It's so nice to see you again. Thank you for inviting me to your farm."

Cayd smiled and pecked her on the cheek. He followed that with a hug, keeping one eye on Lily, who nodded to let him know when it was fine to step back. At twenty-three, Chelsea was the youngest of his ladies. His gaze scanned over her from top to toe. Brown hair curled endearingly around her heart-shaped face. Faded blue jeans and a no-nonsense plaid shirt. Her well-worn work boots were testament to the fact this wasn't the first time she'd been in the bush.

She'd told him during their first meeting that though she'd been born and bred in the city, she'd grown up spending weekends on her grandparents' hobby farm a couple of hours south of Sydney. Though their fifty-five acres was only large enough to run a couple of cows, three sheep, a goat, some chickens, and a pet pig, she'd always loved spending time there and she was sure she'd love his cattle station just as much.

Cayd had a few doubts. There was a big difference between a hobby farm that ran a menagerie of livestock that were mostly regarded as pets, and a working cattle station that spanned more than two hundred thousand acres and supported Cayd's parents, brothers and sisters and a handful of employees. Still, he'd invited her there and he was eager to see where things went. She wasn't as drop-dead gorgeous as Marissa or as pretty as Olivia, but she had her own appeal and he was prepared to keep an open mind, like Lily had urged him to do.

Speaking of Lily...

Chapter Two

♥

C ayd looked around and found the producer in conversation with one of the cameramen a short distance away. Talking shop, technical terms he barely understood. As usual, his dog wasn't too far from her side. It seemed the kelpie had taken a liking to her. Cayd could understand why.

Like his guests, she wore a pair of Levi's and a blouse that was tucked in at the waist. Her leather belt emphasized her narrow hips. Her boots, while obviously not new, weren't quite as battered as Chelsea's. No doubt Lily had been on many a farm before. This was her sixth season as a producer on *Outback Bride*, after all.

She laughed at something one of the cameramen said, and Cayd's gut clenched involuntarily at the throaty sound of it. His initial attraction to her hadn't diminished. It was only the presence of the weighty engagement ring on her finger that kept it in check. She was off-limits. Too bad that message had yet to make its way to his cock.

Her long black hair was pulled back into a ponytail, making her appear as young as the women he'd invited back to the station. He had no idea how old she was, but he guessed she was close to thirty.

As if becoming aware of his scrutiny, she turned her head in his direction. Their gazes locked. For half a beat, he was mesmerized. She gave him a friendly wink and then turned away, once again focused on her conversation with the cameraman.

Cayd felt the impact of her wink all the way through him. He pressed a hand against his chest and dragged in a breath.

This is crazy... She's taken... Get a grip.

He'd invited three beautiful women back to his farm, one of whom he hoped might become his wife. After all, that was the idea of the show. It wasn't called *Outback Bride* for nothing. He was expected to find love.

Yeah, with one of my ladies... Not with the sexy producer who's already engaged to someone else... Hell...

He didn't realize he'd groaned aloud until he caught sight of the frown that marred Marissa's smooth features.

"Cayd? Is everything all right?"

"Yeah. Sorry. I'm fine. I was thinking about the cattle I should be mustering. This is taking a lot more time than I anticipated."

She nodded with understanding and grinned. "But it's more fun than mustering, right?"

He shrugged. "Yeah, I guess."

She pouted. "That doesn't sound very convincing! We've come a long way to spend time with you. We caught a plane from Sydney to Brisbane at some ungodly hour this morning and then drove for miles and miles and miles. You need to sound happier about us being here than that."

He flushed with embarrassment. "You're right. I didn't mean that the way it sounded. Of course, I'm thrilled to have all of you here. I can't wait to show you around."

She ambled closer, lowered her eyes, licked her lips, and then ran a painted fingernail down his chest. Her voice dropped to a husky drawl. "That's more like it."

His gut tightened reflexively. His cock stirred. Though he was a little surprised by her forwardness, he wasn't repulsed by it. Confident women who were prepared to go after what they wanted were incredibly attractive.

As if sensing one of her rivals was moving in on the prize, Chelsea linked her arm with his and turned him away from Marissa.

"I can't wait to see the cattle. How many do you run?"

"In a good season, we run about twenty thousand. During the drought and then the flood, we were forced to destock. We got down to five hundred of our prime breeding stock. That's all we could afford to feed. Fortunately, the seasons have been more favorable in recent times. We're in the process of restocking now. We're currently running about five thousand head. A long way to go before we get back to our earlier stocking rates, but it's a good start."

Olivia had come up behind them. Her eyes were wide with disbelief. "Did you say twenty thousand cattle? Where do you put them all?"

From the corner of his eye, Cayd caught Lily's chuckle. He smiled at Olivia. "This station covers two hundred thousand acres. That's a fair bit of land. Plenty enough to run that many cattle. Don't worry, they all have somewhere to sleep."

At that, Lily snorted. Once again, their gazes clashed before sliding away. Once again, Cayd experienced a visceral reaction to the beautiful producer.

This is madness... I have three beautiful women to choose from and she's not one of them.

He spread his arms wide to encompass Chelsea, Olivia, and Marissa and drew them away from Lily and her camera crew and toward the homestead. From behind him, he heard Lily instruct the crew to film them as they walked across the wide expanse of green lawn and neatly tended flower beds that bordered the wide front steps.

"I'll show you to your lodgings later," he told the women. "Right now, let's go and have some coffee and cake."

Lily watched after Cayd and his ladies while they walked up to the homestead. His kelpie nudged at her hand. Absently, she patted the dog and took in the surroundings. Marlowe Downs was nestled in a valley and was bordered by mountains on three sides. Only an hour's drive from the beautiful Carnarvon Ranges, the reds and golds and khaki greens of that landscape were reflected all around them. As far as farms went, it was one of the most spectacular Lily had seen.

Of course, Cayd had told her they were in the middle of a good season and that accounted for the lush greenery, the flourishing gardens, the thick ground cover that now grew in paddocks that not so long ago had been bare. The clear blue sky was dotted with fluffy white clouds, and the fresh country air carried a hint of honeysuckle, no doubt wafting across from the enormous, flower-laden Murraya tree that stood in one corner of the front yard. All of it contributed to the welcoming feel of the place.

And then there was Farmer Cayd. Tall, broad-shouldered, and sexy as hell. She could see what the women had gone for. It was no surprise that Cayd had received more applications from wannabe wives than any farmer in the history of the show. Given that this was their tenth season, that was no mean feat.

Over the years, Lily had seen her fair share of cute farmers, but there was something about Farmer Cayd that drew her. That wasn't good. He'd chosen three lovely ladies to spend the next two weeks with. It was hoped he'd fall in love with one of them, or at least be interested enough to invite the lady to stay on.

An unexpected twinge of jealousy took her by surprise. She was engaged to a lovely man who thought the world of her.

She had no cause to wish for anything more. That wasn't fair to Alex. He'd loved her since they were children. Besides, the name of the show was *Outback Bride*. It was her job to see that by the end of the series, a potential wedding was in the cards. That was her only priority. She wasn't getting paid to get distracted. She had a job to do. She needed to set aside any feelings she might have toward the sexy cattleman and focus solely on that.

Linking arms with Marissa and Olivia, Cayd strode toward the homestead. Chelsea followed a couple of steps behind. Though the TV executives had asked, for the sake of the show, that he pretend this was his station and he lived on it alone, it was very much a family-run operation and a family home. Both of his parents and most of his siblings still called the place home. His younger brothers, Justin, Aiden, and Lachlan all lived in the homestead and worked on the station. It was ludicrous to expect viewers to believe a two-hundred-thousand- acre cattle farm could be operated by just one person, but apparently that was what the TV executives were going with.

At Lily's request, his family had been kind enough to agree to stay out of sight of the cameras until such a time as the TV execs were ready to introduce them to their viewers. The show worked on the pretense that this was Cayd's home. The ladies were expected to help cook and clean and assist with other farm chores.

The reality was quite different. His mother would be responsible for most of the cooking and cleaning, as she usually was, but apparently, having Cayd and his ladies waited on by his mother didn't make for good TV. Nor was the fact that at twenty-seven, he still lived with his parents.

Cayd didn't give a toss about any of those things. He loved living with his family on the station. For his younger sisters, Marnie and Skyla, though both living in Brisbane, Marlowe Downs was their only home, and though his older sister, Maggie, managed the neighboring station, she dropped in regularly for visits, as did his younger sister, Emma, who worked for the Royal Flying Doctors and was rarely in one place long enough to put down roots.

They were a close-knit family and got on well most of the time. Cayd liked to bounce ideas off his father who'd lived on the station all his life, as had his parents before him. There was something about that history, handing a farm down through the years to later generations that appealed to Cayd. He hoped one day to raise his own family there.

But first, I need to find a wife...

The three girls he'd chosen were all very different. He'd never had a type. He'd dated blondes, brunettes, and every shade in between, though Olivia was his first redhead. Each of the ladies he'd chosen had their own appeal: Marissa—stunningly attractive and confident in her appeal. Olivia—sweet and disarming. Chelsea—cute and pragmatic. He looked forward to spending time with them and getting to know them better. He wasn't sure yet if one of them was wife material, but he was prepared to give it his best shot.

The smell of freshly baked apple and cinnamon cake wafted in the air as they entered the large and airy country-style kitchen. The room was his mother's domain, but in accordance with the contract he'd signed for the TV show, Ellen Fairfax had made herself scarce. But not before setting out a plate of delicious-smelling cake and a pot of fresh coffee. The women stood around the large island bench and *oohed* and *ahhed* over the spread.

"Someone's been busy in the kitchen," Marissa said and raised an eyebrow at him.

The sound of the front screen door slamming saved him from answering. Cayd looked up as Lily and the camera crew entered the room.

"Just keep on doing what you're doing," she instructed. "Ignore the cameras. We'll keep out of your way as much as possible."

Doing his best to follow her instructions, Cayd poured the coffee and then offered milk and sugar. He and his ladies chatted among each other, and Cayd did his best to act natural. Lily continued to give directions to each of them and the crew. The screen door slammed again and was followed by the heavy tread of boots on the polished floorboards that lined the hallway. A moment later, Cayd's younger brother, Justin, appeared in the open doorway that led to the kitchen. He took one look at the crowd and cursed under his breath.

"Shit. Sorry. I forgot this was happening today," he mumbled, and then beat a hasty retreat.

A part of Cayd wished he could join him. He wasn't used to being surrounded by young women all vying for his attention, and though he'd willingly put himself in that position, he hadn't really thought it through. His main goal had been to create publicity for his fledgling bed-and-breakfast project, and to have a little fun. But having his every movement, every conversation monitored and recorded was hard work and not exactly what he'd had in mind when he'd signed on. Still, it was too late for regrets now. The ladies were there and expecting big things. He'd best not let them down.

"Who wants a tour of the farm?" he asked.

He was met with a chorus of cheers. After finishing their coffee and rinsing the cups in the sink, he set his Akubra on his head and urged the ladies to follow him out the door.

Lily and her camera crew followed Cayd and his entourage out the front door and across to the machinery shed. Cayd disappeared inside for a moment and then came out pushing a quad bike. Lily signaled to the cameramen to start shooting.

"Does anyone know how to ride one of these?" Cayd asked, looking at his ladies.

Both Marissa and Olivia shook their heads. Chelsea put up her hand. "I do. I've ridden a quad before on my grandparents' farm."

"Great." Cayd disappeared again and then returned with a second quad. He parked it beside the first one. "We can double up on them. "I'll drive one. Chelsea, you can drive the other. Marissa and Olivia can ride shotgun."

Lily wasn't surprised when Marissa hastily volunteered to sit behind Cayd. Lily hid a smile as she watched the woman tuck herself up nice and close behind the farmer, her arms catching him around the waist. Then she leaned forward and pressed her breasts against his chest.

Irritation replaced Lily's amusement, and she was forced to tamp down on another surge of jealousy. This wasn't good. She wasn't one of the ladies vying for his affections. She needed to remember that.

She twisted the engagement ring on her finger and conjured an image of Alex's smiling face. His Greek heritage was as obvious as hers in their dark hair, dark eyes, and olive skin. Their families had been friends forever. She'd known Alex all her life. Three years older than her, it had long been understood by both their families that the two of them would one day marry. That day had now arrived.

Though they hadn't yet set a date, they'd been engaged for three years already. Their families were growing impatient. She didn't know why she kept dragging her feet. She told her parents she was too busy to plan a wedding. And she was. But she knew that if it were Cayd Fairfax waiting for her to make things legal, she'd have walked down that aisle in a flash.

Stop this nonsense. We can't all marry men who look like movie stars. Alex is a perfectly lovely man. And he loves me to bits. He always has. And I love him.

She watched as Cayd climbed off the bike and handed out helmets and then waited until the women had put them on. Marissa predictably pretended to have trouble with her chin-strap and then smiled brilliantly up at Cayd when he offered to help. Lily only just managed to stop herself from rolling her eyes. Olivia glared at Marissa.

Lily hid a grin, pleased that at least one of the girls was aware of the potential threat Marissa posed to their chances of winning Cayd's heart. Lily made a mental note to have a quiet word with Chelsea, who so far appeared oblivious to Marissa's machinations. The viewers wanted drama. It was Lily's job to provide it. If that meant pitting the ladies against each other, then so be it. There was nothing like a catfight to send the ratings soaring. She might even get a raise. Now *that* would be something.

As the bikes roared to life and started forward, the camera crew filmed their departure. When they had the footage they needed, Lily and her crew climbed into their 4WD and followed along behind.

Cayd had offered to take the ladies for a quick tour around the station in the hope that the cameras would capture some of the station's natural beauty and perhaps encourage city viewers to take a road trip. Though it had been some time since the last fall of rain, the floods that had ravaged the land nearly a year ago had brought wonders. Thick pasture, overflowing dams, trees and shrubs that had been given a new lease on life. Then there was the multitude of birdlife that filled the clear blue skies. Surrounded by the red and gold and khaki landscape of the Carnarvon Ranges, it was a glorious sight and far removed from the steel-and-glass landscape of the city.

Marissa was pressed tightly against him, clinging to his waist. He enjoyed the feel of her breasts molded against his back. He glanced across at the other bike. Chelsea appeared more than capable of handling it, although Olivia looked a little scared. Cayd gave them a thumbs-up. Chelsea grinned and returned the gesture. Olivia managed a nervous smile.

They pulled up next to a paddock that housed some of the cattle. No doubt the ladies had never been up close and personal to such huge beasts. As they climbed off the bikes and pulled off their helmets, he explained a bit about the breed.

"These are Droughtmaster cattle. It's an Australian breed of beef cattle. They were developed from around 1915. They crossed Zebuine, primarily Brahman cattle from the US, with British origin Beef Shorthorn and came up with the Droughtmaster. They're specially bred for the tough conditions experienced in North and Central Queensland and are resistant to ticks, heat, eye cancer, and drought."

"They're enormous!" Marissa exclaimed, clinging to Cayd's side.

He nodded. "Yes, although not as large as some of the other breeds."

"Do they come in different colors?" Olivia asked, inching closer.

"They're mainly red, like these ones, but there are variations from a golden honey color to a much darker red."

While Marissa and Olivia remained plastered to Cayd's side, he was interested to see that Chelsea felt confident enough to walk up to one of the beasts and attempt to pat it. The cow shifted slightly away but was mostly unperturbed by the attention.

Marissa reached for his arm and clung to him. Olivia pressed close to his side. Amused, Cayd hurried to reassure them.

"It's all right, ladies. There's no need to be scared. They might be big, but these beasts are some of the most docile cows you can find. Go ahead, give them a pat. They won't bite."

Marissa shot him a doubtful look. "Will you come with me?"

Cayd chuckled. He wasn't sure if she was truly that frightened of the cattle, or if this was just another ploy to keep him close. Either way, he complied. Taking her hand, he led Marissa over to one of the beasts and stood next to her while she gingerly reached out to pat the sleek red hide.

"She's so soft!" Marissa exclaimed. "As soft as my own hair! I didn't expect that. And so clean. How come she's not covered in dust?"

"Oh, there's plenty of dust in her coat, don't worry. You can't live in this part of the world and not get covered in dust. It's just that it's red, like her. It blends in with her coat."

Marissa looked at him with wide eyes filled with wonder and batted her eyelashes at him. "You're so knowledgeable about your cows. That's such a big turn-on."

Cayd's eyebrows rose at the frank interest in her baby blues. There was an answering stirring in his loins. The next couple of weeks with a woman like Marissa in the picture was going to keep things interesting. Very interesting indeed.

Chapter Three

♥

Lily found it increasingly difficult to remain unaffected by Marissa's constant touching of Cayd. It was obvious the woman wasn't going to waste any time staking a claim, but she barely knew him. How Cayd didn't get irritated with her constant pawing, Lily didn't know, although when the woman in question looked like a real live Barbie doll, no doubt they got away with things ordinary women didn't. The other two girls had better watch out or they'd be left behind in the dust.

It was up to Lily to even the playing field, or at least do what she could to ensure the other girls remained in the race. With that thought in mind, she drew Olivia aside.

"How about you ask Cayd if you can swap with Marissa and ride behind him to the next stop?"

Olivia's eyes widened with sudden comprehension. "Great idea."

She gave Lily a grateful look and then walked back to where Cayd and Marissa chatted quietly together. Lily signaled to the cameramen and instructed them to keep their focus on the two women. Her crew got into position and started rolling. Lily stood off to one side with her arms loosely folded over her chest and listened in while Olivia made her request.

"Of course," Cayd agreed affably. Olivia shot him a winning smile.

He threw an arm around her shoulder and gave her a friendly hug. He didn't appear to have a favorite among the girls yet, but time would tell. At the end of the week, he had to send one girl home. Right now, Lily wasn't sure which one of them that would be.

Marissa glared at Olivia and stomped off to climb on behind Chelsea. Lily stifled a giggle and silently congratulated Olivia for pulling off that move, no matter that it probably wouldn't have occurred to her if Lily hadn't put the thought in her head.

Lily refused to feel guilty. It was her job to create drama, to ensure each girl got a fair deal. It wouldn't do anyone any good if Cayd had an obvious favorite from the beginning. She'd warned him against giving any of the girls special treatment, but that didn't mean subconsciously he wasn't ordering them into a list of front-runner to last. Besides, Marissa wouldn't have hesitated to do the same to the other girls if their positions had been reversed. Of that, Lily was certain.

Cayd's gaze trailed after Marissa. It was obvious she was put out, but there was nothing he could do about that. Lily had been clear that it was important not to play favorites, at least not in the early days. All three women deserved equal amounts of his time to ensure he got to know all of them. According to Lily, their TV viewers always chose a lady to root for and it wasn't possible to know who'd gain their favor ahead of time. It would be months after filming finished that the show would go to air. Only then would they know who was popular among the viewers and who wasn't.

He admired Olivia for coming forward and asking to ride with him. Of average height and average build, her red hair had escaped its bun and was now windblown and hung around her face in a tangled mess beneath her helmet, but her grin lit up her blue eyes with good humor and warmth. As he started the ignition, he glanced back at her.

"Put your arms around my waist. It's going to be a little rough where we're going next."

She blushed, but her arms snuck out and loosely encircled his waist. She certainly wasn't as bold as Marissa, but that was okay. Confidence was appealing, but there was always room for someone a little less forthright. That could be just as attractive.

Cayd waited while Lily and her crew returned to their vehicle and stacked their camera gear into the back. Putting his bike into gear, he indicated with his hand for them to follow him before he set off toward the billabong. The natural spring was fed from underground and was now full of sweet, clear water. Surrounded by tall reeds and shady gum trees, one side of it was bordered by a sandy shore.

As they drew up to it and switched off the bikes, the girls exclaimed in delight and surprise.

"Oh, this is amazing!" Marissa cried.

"An oasis in the middle of the desert. Who'd have thought?" Chelsea murmured.

"Is it safe to swim?" Olivia asked.

Cayd grinned. "Absolutely. Why do you think I brought you here?"

The November day was hot enough that a cool swim sounded sublime. The girls didn't need any more encouragement to kick off their shoes, roll up their jeans, and paddle into the water until it was up to their knees. Cayd stood back with Lily while the cameramen captured the scene.

"I think you should join them," she said, shooting him a sideways glance. "Feel free to take off your shirt."

He looked at her in surprise. "Take off my shirt? Don't you mean a bit of skin would go down well with your viewers? Isn't that what this is really about?"

She flushed. "Okay. You're right. At the risk of sounding sexist, our audience tends to be mostly female, and they swoon over half-naked men. But if you're not comfortable taking your shirt off, then I'm perfectly fine with that. This is your decision. No pressure from me."

He thought about it for a few seconds. He'd never been shy about his body, not even when he'd been a kid. Growing up with so many siblings and sharing bathrooms all his life had taken care of any potential attacks of modesty.

He glanced back at his ladies. They were splashing and squealing and obviously having fun. It was hard not to want to be a part of it. Coming to a decision, he pulled off his boots and socks and set them to one side. Then he rolled up his Levi's to his knees. He looked across at Lily, who was staring at him. Slowly, he eased the buttons from his shirt and slipped it from his shoulders.

Her eyes slid boldly over him. When her gaze swept back to his, he was gratified to see a faint blush staining her cheeks. His gut clenched, and his pulse picked up its pace. He couldn't have said whether it was from the anticipation of joining the girls in the pool or from the avid interest in Lily's bright gaze.

Don't be ridiculous. She's not interested in me. I don't care what kind of look she's giving me. The rock on her finger tells a different story.

Deliberately turning his back on her, he strode toward the water. The ladies started cat-calling. Chelsea let out a wolf whistle. Grinning widely, he stepped into the water. It was cool and refreshing on his heated skin. He continued walking until he was knee deep. Marissa instantly appeared by his side. She raked her fingernails across his biceps.

"Oh, boy. I thought you looked good in clothes. I had no idea you looked this delicious without."

Her voice was a throaty drawl. Cayd's body reacted instinctively to the raw need in her eyes. He only hoped Lily wouldn't call them out of the water until he'd gotten his erection under control. Then Olivia sliced the water with her hand and sent a flood straight into his face. He sputtered in surprise, wiped the water out of his eyes, and then returned fire.

Before long, a full-blown water fight had erupted. Amid squeals of laughter, they all got roundly soaked. Beside him, both Marissa's and Olivia's damp blouses now clung to their chests, doing very little to conceal their generous breasts. Once again, Cayd's cock thickened. Then Chelsea charged toward him and tackled him, following him down into the water, chasing all thoughts of erections and bountiful breasts away.

They both stood up, drenched. Cayd swiped at the water on his face. Chelsea laughed and flicked her short curls, obviously pleased with herself. Cayd frowned. Not only were his jeans soaked through, his phone had been in his back pocket and had also been submerged. He pulled it out and tapped the screen, relieved when it illuminated. Still, there was no telling if the dunking had caused serious damage. The biggest pain was that it was a five-hour trip to Rockhampton to replace it.

Something in his demeanor must have telegraphed to Chelsea that he wasn't exactly pleased. She bumped her hip against his.

"Oh, I'm sorry, I didn't realize you had your phone. Now it's gone for a swim!" She appeared completely unrepentant.

"Yeah," he muttered, unimpressed.

"I left mine in my suitcase," Chelsea added. "No need for one out here, right? I mean, is there even phone service so far out here?"

"The service isn't great, that's true. But it works most of the time. Besides, this is a working farm. People need to be able to reach me. This"—he spread his arms wide—"is my office. Having fun with you and the others isn't how I usually spend my time."

Some of his displeasure must have finally penetrated. Chelsea flushed with embarrassment and averted her gaze. He cursed under his breath for coming down so hard on her. It had been an innocent bit of fun. She hadn't meant to submerge his phone. She hadn't even been aware it was in his pocket.

He made a deliberate effort to soften his tone. "Hey, I'm sorry." He tried on a reassuring grin. "Call me an asshole. Who cares about a stupid phone?"

Her relief was immediate. She smiled up at him and then punched him playfully in the arm. "You're a bit of a kidder, aren't you? For a moment there, I thought you were seriously upset."

With an effort, he suppressed another surge of irritation. The cameras were still rolling, adding to his discomfort. He glanced in Lily's direction and found her gaze on him. She was frowning. Embarrassment seared his cheeks. He was meant to be doing what he could to get to know his ladies, not antagonizing them.

"Hey, Chelsea. How about you ride behind me on the way back?" he suggested.

The woman's eyes lit up with excitement. At the same time, Marissa pouted. She pointed to herself and Olivia. "How are *we* supposed to get home?"

"I'm sure one of you can work out how to steer the bike. We'll take it slowly, okay?"

He shot his ladies what he hoped was a winning grin in an effort to placate them. He was met with grumbles and halfhearted smiles.

He sighed inwardly. Keeping three women entertained and happy was harder than he'd imagined. And this was only day one. There was a whole two weeks of this left.

Hell. What have I let myself in for? How am I going to survive?

This time, he couldn't suppress his groan.

After ensuring the cameramen had secured enough footage of Cayd and his ladies enjoying the evening meal, Lily took a seat around the firepit next to a member of her crew. Macey dropped to the ground a short distance away, panting, and regarded her through curious eyes.

She'd woken that morning to find the dog asleep on the veranda outside her cottage. Though she'd had nothing to offer the kelpie by way of food, she'd chatted to her and given her a good rub and a scratch between her ears. Macey had appeared pleased with the attention.

Ever since, whenever she was around the homestead, the dog was never far away. So much so that one of her crew had joked that she'd found a farm companion of her own. Lily didn't mind. She'd always been a dog lover. The only reason she didn't own one was because she lived in an apartment with zero green space.

Cayd was seated across from her, sandwiched between Marissa and Olivia. Chelsea had taken a seat farther away, whether by choice or not, Lily couldn't say. They'd all enjoyed a delicious dinner of smoky ribs, fresh salad and mashed potato cooked by Ellen Fairfax. Ellen had kept out of sight of the cameras during the meal, but Lily had made sure to go and thank Cayd's mother afterward for her hard work and efforts in the kitchen.

"That's okay," Ellen said. "I hope you enjoyed it. It feels a bit weird serving up a meal and then eating it in a different room."

Lily understood how awkward their rules could be sometimes. But the show was about Cayd and his ladies. The viewers weren't interested in anyone else. Lily was grateful Cayd's family appeared to understand the situation and so far had been gracious enough to accede to her wishes, even when that meant they were forced to eat somewhere else.

A peal of throaty laughter interrupted Lily's thoughts. She glanced across the flames in time to see Marissa tilt her head back, mouth open, white teeth exposed in a wide grin. At the same time, the woman clutched Cayd's arm and held it possessively to her chest. Cayd leaned toward her and said something in response, and Marissa laughed again. She scooted even closer, until her jean-clad thigh was pressed up against his.

Lily ignored a burst of irritation and then silently cheered when Olivia linked her arm with Cayd's and tugged, drawing his attention away from the other woman next to him.

You go, girl. All's fair in love and war. If you don't take Marissa head-on, she'll steal away with the prize.

Olivia had changed out of her plaid shirt and jeans and into a slip dress with a low V neck that emphasized her tidy figure and drew attention to her generous breasts. A cool breeze had started blowing and Olivia must have been feeling the chill, but what did that matter if she managed to snag Cayd's interest? Lily had caught Cayd's gaze straying in the direction of Olivia's cleavage more than once. He was obviously a boobs man.

Aside from that, Olivia was pretty and wholesome in that girl-next-door kind of way. Wide blue eyes, nice smile, pale, freckly skin. Some guys liked that. It was obvious Cayd did. He'd chosen to bring her back to the farm, hadn't he?

An unwelcome stab of jealousy coursed through her. Lily scowled. She was annoyed with herself for feeling even an instant of envy. She'd been doing this show for five years and had never felt an ounce of jealousy for the other ladies she'd met. What was so different about Cayd that she almost felt like a loser that he hadn't picked *her*? How ridiculous was that? She wasn't even in the running—and she didn't want to be.

Coming abruptly to her feet, she walked over to her senior cameraman. "Nigel? Can you get some more footage of Cayd and the ladies talking around the fire? And make sure you capture any sneaky good-night kisses. Okay?"

Nigel saluted her with a smile. "You got it, boss."

"Thanks. I think I'll call it a night. See you in the morning."

Tamping down a surge of restlessness, Lily gathered up her clipboard and the folder of notes she'd already compiled about possible scenes they could stage to ramp up the drama over the coming days. She bid everyone good night and headed toward the guest cottage. Though her path across the wide expanse of front lawn was still largely unfamiliar, the full moon high overhead illuminated her way. She was joined by Macey, who padded silently beside her.

A hundred yards away from the cottage were the newly renovated shearer's quarters. When Lily had made her first visit to the farm a couple of months earlier with a view to assessing the suitability of both Cayd and the station to participate in the show, he'd given her a tour of the facilities where his guests would be housed. Lily had been impressed with the size and comfort of the quarters. Though a long way from five-star accommodations, the rooms were clean and comfortable and came with their own ensuite.

When she'd asked Cayd why there were shearer's quarters on the station when they'd never run any sheep, he'd told her they'd sourced the quarters from another farm and had transported them to Marlowe Downs on the back of a semitrailer. Once the quarters had been secured to new foundations built by Justin and Aiden, their father had installed plumbing and electricity. Cayd and Lachlan had painted the internal and external walls. His mother had chosen the fittings and fixtures, along with the navy-blue, rich cream, and pale gray color scheme.

All in all, it had been a family effort. Cayd had beamed as he'd spoken about the project. It was clear he was proud of how his family had come together to make it happen.

"I'm a bit of a novice interior decorator myself," she surprised herself by saying. "I bought a run-down apartment a few years ago, and I've been renovating it room by room as money allows. It's almost finished, and I've discovered I've really enjoyed the process. I especially love choosing the paint colors."

It was then that he'd confided that he had a long-term desire to see the station earn extra income by opening itself up to farm stay accommodation. The shearer's quarters were the first step in that direction. In the meantime, it would serve as a comfortable place for the ladies to stay.

Lily agreed and was more than happy to report back to her boss that Marlowe Downs and its farmer would be a good addition to the show. She still felt that way, although it was unsettling to discover that she was attracted to the star. No wonder she was feeling restless and out of sorts.

Of course, her reaction to Cayd Fairfax was nothing more than what any young woman in control of her faculties would experience. He was an incredibly attractive man in search of a wife. There was no part of that scenario that most single women of marriageable age wouldn't find desirable. She just happened to be one of them.

That wasn't a deal-breaker. She was a professional. No matter her personal feelings, the show would go on and she'd make sure it was a ratings hit, like all the other series she'd been involved in. That's what professionals did. In the meantime, she'd do whatever she could to stay in regular contact with Alex and remind herself of how wonderful he was and how much she looked forward to being his wife.

She mounted the steps to the front veranda and opened the cottage door. Macey sat on her haunches and gave Lily a mournful look, but she'd noticed the Fairfax family didn't allow their dogs inside. Respecting that rule, she shook her head at Macey.

"Sorry, girl. You need to stay out here."

Pulling the screen door closed behind her, she reached for the light switch on the wall near the entryway. The cozy living room was immediately flooded with yellow light. The rich cream-colored walls gleamed under the glow, giving the room a welcoming feel. Along with the red brick fireplace with its mantel covered in various knickknacks and the rows of framed family portraits that hung on the walls, the place was warm and inviting. It didn't feel like a guest cottage. It felt like someone's home. No doubt Ellen Fairfax had woven her magic around here too.

Thoughts of Cayd's mother immediately brought to mind images of the sexy farmer. He was the hottest man she'd ever met. Such an admission wasn't meant to reflect negatively on her fiancé. It was pure and honest fact. The man had a smile that could curl any woman's toes and set her heart to pounding. Lily was irritated that she wasn't immune to his charm. Her unwanted attraction to him only made her job harder.

Keeping her distance from him would be next to impossible. She was the producer. She provided input into the show every step of the way. She was also responsible for guiding her crew, informing them of the scenes she wanted filmed, the spontaneous shots she knew instinctively would play well with their audience. This was what she did, and she was good at it. Not only that, but she also loved it. If only thoughts of Cayd would stop getting in the way and complicating things...

With a sigh, she dropped her clipboard and folder onto the antique cherrywood coffee table and wandered into the kitchen. An old-fashioned wood stove stood against one wall. Next to it was an electric hot plate, and on the shelf above that was a microwave. There was an open-shelved cupboard containing crockery and glassware and three drawers that held cutlery and cooking implements. Not that she'd had to do any cooking. So far, Ellen had seen to that.

Crossing over to the sink, she filled the kettle and set it to boil. A cup of chamomile tea was just what she needed to soothe away the turmoil of the day and help her get to sleep. The last thing she needed was thoughts of Cayd keeping her awake.

It was ridiculous how quickly the handsome farmer had come to dominate her thoughts. She barely knew the man. On the other hand, she'd known her fiancé forever. They'd grown up together. Their families did practically everything together. As her parents' only daughter, it was natural for her to be the one to officially join their families together through marriage. Everyone was thrilled with the arrangement, including her. It was only because her job often entailed time away from home that she kept prevaricating on setting a wedding date.

A wife's role was to be by her husband's side. At least, for most of the time. Her current job didn't allow for that. Hence why she kept putting off the time when she and Alex would finally make things legal.

Alex.

Intelligent, kind, loyal, dependable Alex. He'd never made her pulse beat faster like Cayd, but why did that matter? Not everyone needed white-hot passion, if such a thing even existed outside the walls of a TV studio or a sappy romance novel.

A slow burn was good enough for her. Good enough for most people. She couldn't imagine ever wanting to tear Alex's clothes off in a fit of passion, but so what? She was glad he'd asked her to wait until their wedding night to have sex. That decision took all the pressure off. As she poured boiling water over the teabag in her cup and wandered back into the living room, she refused to ponder why she was relieved about that.

Chapter Four

♥

The morning sun beat a warm tattoo on Cayd's shoulders as it beamed through the window where he stood leaning against the kitchen counter. Lily and her film crew were busy capturing the drama and laughter as Cayd's ladies attempted to make pancakes. At Lily's suggestion that the girls have a go at cooking breakfast, his mother had graciously agreed to let them have the run of her kitchen.

Cayd felt a bit guilty about having to push his family out of their own house. Though they'd been given prior warning, the reality of having the house taken over by strangers wasn't as easy as he'd anticipated. Not the least that his family were forced to live and eat separately from those taking part in the TV show.

His parents and brothers had breakfasted earlier. They'd cleaned up after themselves and disappeared just as Lily's crew were setting up for filming. He couldn't help but notice how beautiful the producer looked. Today, her long black hair was loose around her shoulders and looked shiny and clean. Citrusy shampoo wafted toward him on the gentle breeze that blew in through the window. He watched her while she instructed the girls about the breakfast scene they were about to shoot.

"Okay, so we're going to cook pancakes. Does anyone know how to do that?" Lily asked, looking around at each of the ladies.

Marissa shook her head. "I have zero cooking skills. Mostly, I eat out."

Cayd admired her honesty, though he was a little concerned that if she ended up being the woman he chose to stay on with him at the farm, the isolation might be too much for her. The nearest town was a good hour away, with nothing much in between. Eating out was only enjoyed on rare occasions in the outback. Mostly, folks cooked for themselves and ate at home.

"I'll do it," Chelsea said in a no-nonsense tone.

"I'll help," Olivia quickly added and flashed a smile in his direction.

He nodded his approval. The girls were well aware they were competing for his attention. This was a chance for them to impress him, and he was pleased at least two of them were going to take advantage of the opportunity.

Lily chuckled. "Thank you, ladies. If you'll step up to the stove. I have the batter already prepared. Here." She handed Chelsea and Olivia each a bowl. "Give it your best shot. After all, we all know the way to a man's heart is through his stomach, right?"

She grinned at the girls and then glanced in his direction and gave him a cheeky wink. His gut somersaulted with desire. He quickly looked away, silently cursing the flush that crept up his neck. As if sensing she'd lost his attention, Marissa sidled up next to him, standing close enough that their arms brushed.

"I hope this doesn't mean I've lost brownie points." She pouted.

He chuckled. Her hair looked like it could have been professionally blow-dried. Her makeup was flawless. Her full lips, covered in sparkly pink lipstick, begged to be kissed. Predictably, his cock stirred.

"Cooking is a much-admired skill," he said affably, "but there are plenty of other things I admire too. I bet there's something you're good at."

Marissa beamed. "Of course there is! I'm super at doing TikTok videos. Everyone just loves my style. I give out makeup and fashion tips. I have more than twenty thousand followers. I've started my own online fashion business."

Cayd's eyebrows rose, and he nodded. It was obvious he was meant to be impressed. And he was. At least, he would be if he knew what the hell she was talking about.

"TikTok?" he asked.

Marissa's eyes went wide. "Don't tell me you don't know about TikTok?"

He shrugged. "I'm afraid I don't have much time for anything but the station. Most of the time when I come in from work, I'm too tired to bother with much else."

"But you must have a social media presence. Facebook? Twitter? Instagram?"

"I have Instagram. That was a requirement under my contract for this show. I'm supposed to post about things we've been getting up to on the station."

"And have you?" Marissa asked.

"Not so much," Lily responded. "In fact, I need to talk to you about that."

Cayd turned to find Lily standing a few feet away. She looked even better up close. In stark contrast to Marissa's immaculate makeup, Lily had opted to go *au naturel*. No eyeshadow, no mascara, no eyeliner, no lipstick. Her clear olive skin didn't require foundation unless she wanted to cover up the smattering of faint freckles on her nose. Though no one could deny Marissa's stunning looks, he was just as drawn to Lily's natural countenance.

No, don't be stupid. Lily isn't in this race. Forget about her. I need to focus on the women I chose. That's what we're all here for.

"You agreed to post regularly on Instagram. It's important that your followers get to know you," Lily said in a brusque tone.

"I didn't realize I had any followers," he said dryly.

"You only have a handful now, but that'll change once the show goes to air. It's important to get into the habit of posting regularly, so you're not overwhelmed when your social media explodes."

He raised a single eyebrow as he looked at her. "You think it'll explode?"

"Have you looked in the mirror recently? Of course, it'll explode," she muttered.

The smell of burning pancakes reached them at the same time Lily turned away, a flush reddening her cheeks.

"Oh no! It's ruined!" Olivia wailed.

"You have the heat up too high," Chelsea said.

"I thought you said you could cook?" Marissa commented snidely.

Lily stepped closer to the stove where the cameramen were capturing every moment of the girls' attempt to cook breakfast.

"Clean out the pan and try again," she encouraged, smiling at Olivia. "We can always edit that bit out. No one need ever know you burned them."

Olivia's eyes lit up. "Would you do that?"

Lily shrugged. "The final editing decisions aren't up to me, but I can certainly put forward my suggestions."

Olivia smiled with relief. "Oh, thank you, Lily! I mean, who wants to go on national television and demonstrate to everyone they can't cook!"

Olivia's gaze slid to Marissa and rested on the woman for a few meaningful seconds. Marissa's eyes narrowed. If looks could kill, Olivia would have been out cold by now. Cayd looked at Lily in time to see her hide a grin. Then her gaze cut to the cameras. Her smile made it obvious she was pleased to see they'd captured the entire scene. No doubt it would make good TV.

Then Lily clapped her hands together. "Okay, girls. We need to finish breakfast and get this place cleaned up. We have a full day of filming ahead of us."

"What's on the agenda for today?" Chelsea asked.

Lily listed them off. "Mucking out the stables, feeding animals, horse riding. And that's just for starters. We don't have any time to waste."

Olivia exclaimed in alarm and went pale, staring down at her long fingernails. Marissa groaned aloud in protest. Cayd grinned and then almost laughed out loud when he caught Lily surreptitiously rolling her eyes. It wasn't good that he was so aware of her. Forming a connection with her would do neither of them any good.

Without conscious thought, his gaze was drawn to the sparkling diamond that decorated her finger. With a deliberate effort, he shifted his thoughts away from the beautiful producer and focused on the job at hand: choosing a wife from the ladies on offer, and that didn't include Lily Calimeris.

After finishing up her instructions to the women and checking in with the camera crew, Lily crossed the room and halted beside Cayd.

"I hope you're on board with the activities I've scheduled for today," she said.

He nodded. "Fine with me. I'm looking forward to seeing the girls get their hands dirty."

The lazy grin he sent her way did funny things to her insides. She forced the feelings aside.

"Is there any particular order you want things done?" she asked.

"Nope. But just so you remember, this is a working farm. I can't spend all day playing around for the cameras."

"I understand," she said. "Once we get the footage we need, you're free to do whatever you want."

"Thanks."

"Just make sure you do your best to spend equal amounts of time with each of your ladies," she reminded him. "We never know ahead of time who the public will root for. Sometimes they surprise us."

Cayd grimaced. "It all sounds so clinical. I thought it would be more romantic than this."

She chuckled. "You sound so naive. Don't forget what this is really about. We're making TV. If you fall in love along the way, that's a bonus. If you don't, then that's okay too, just as long as you make it appear that at least one of the ladies has the possibility of winning your heart."

Disquiet flashed in his eyes. "So, you're okay with me deceiving these girls for the sake of your TV show?"

Lily held his gaze. She deliberately kept her tone neutral. "You read your contract. This shouldn't come as a surprise."

Cayd stared at her. "Right. But when I signed that contract, I hadn't met any of them. They weren't real to me. Now that I have, I hate the thought of hurting anyone."

The fact Cayd cared about their feelings impressed Lily. He was obviously a decent guy. But she'd been a producer on this show for five years. She knew exactly the kind of footage the director wanted, and it would be her ass on the line if she didn't deliver.

"I'm not saying you have to go out of your way to hurt or deceive. The ladies are well aware this is first and foremost a TV show. No one went into this with their eyes closed. They signed contracts too. Be as upfront and honest as you like. I don't care how you do it, just as long as we get what we want."

"Which is?"

"High-stakes drama. Something that keeps our viewers on the edge of their seats and tuning in night after night to find out what happens. All the things set out in your contract, remember?" She gave him a friendly slap on the back. "Don't look so morose. It's not all bad. You have three beautiful women hanging off your every word and wanting to spend time with you. Go and have some fun."

Cayd shot her a baleful look and then announced to the women that they were heading to the stables. A buzz of excitement and apprehension went through the room. As Cayd opened the fridge and pulled out a handful of carrots, Lily signaled to the cameramen to start filming. Cayd and his ladies filed out.

"Just ignore the cameras. Pretend we're not here. Carry on as you normally would, and don't forget, we want some riveting television," Lily called after them.

Cayd glanced at her over his shoulder and rolled his eyes. Lily held his gaze and smiled sweetly. "Go for it, Cayd. You're the star of the show. I know you won't let me down."

Cayd scowled at the sight of Lily's teasing smile. She was so darned attractive, with her shiny hair, sparkling eyes and wide, white grin. There was no point in letting his thoughts go in that direction. The best thing he could do was to concentrate on the three women he'd invited there. With that thought in mind, he led the way out of the house, across the front yard, and through the gate. The women followed obediently behind him. They caught up to him as he strode across the dirt that led to the stables.

Marissa sidled up close to him. Her arm brushed against his. He glanced at her, unsure whether it had been deliberate or not. The knowing look she gave him left him in no doubt. Self-confidence had always been a turn-on for him, and it came as no surprise when his body instinctively reacted. As if aware of her effect on him, she shot him another knowing look.

"Ever mucked out a stable?" he asked.

She shook her head. "Never even been near a horse."

He chuckled. "Well, then. You're in for a treat. We breed our own right here at the station. One of our broodmares had a foal about six months ago. A little filly. She's pretty cute."

"A foal! How gorgeous! I can't wait to see her," Olivia said, catching up with them and flanking his other side.

Cayd glanced behind him. Chelsea brought up the rear. The gentle breeze lifted her curls and blew them around her face. Her shorter stride meant that she struggled to keep up with the rest of them. He deliberately slowed his steps until she drew alongside them. She gave him a grateful look.

"Thanks, Cayd. It must be nice to have such long legs."

He gave her a once-over. She might have been petite, but she was in proportion, and though she wasn't as stunning as Marissa, or even as pretty as Olivia, she had a down-to-earth attitude that made her easy to be around, notwithstanding his earlier irritation with her over his phone.

They continued into the stables, where Cayd blinked to adjust his eyes to the sudden dimness. He passed around the carrots. The smell of fresh hay and horse manure filled his nostrils. Built to hold up to ten horses, the stables currently housed six, including the new foal.

"It's fairly close to the homestead," Chelsea commented. "Aren't you concerned about flies?"

Cayd was quietly impressed with her question. It was obvious she had some experience with farm animals.

"That's why we situated it downwind of the residential buildings. That way, we minimize odors and flies. We've also oriented it to avoid the worst of the summer sun and take advantage of the breeze. Good ventilation's important. You'll note we left openings between the roof and the eaves. That allows extra air to flow through."

Cayd led them up to the young filly's stall and opened the door so the girls could enter.

"Oh, she's beautiful," Chelsea exclaimed, walking right up to the foal and patting her on the neck.

Olivia took a few tentative steps into the stall, holding out a carrot toward the foal. "Is she still being fed by her mother?"

"Yes. We won't wean her until she's nine months."

Marissa stood well back. The cameras alternated between being focused on her and her obvious reluctance to get up close and personal with the foal, and Chelsea and Olivia, who were now completely won over by the filly.

Cayd looked around for Lily and found her in the stall next door. The filly's mother was eating a carrot out of Lily's hand.

When she caught Cayd watching her, her face filled with embarrassment.

"Go right ahead," he urged. "Cassiah loves carrots."

"Cassiah. That's a lovely name," Lily murmured.

"My sister, Maggie, named her."

Lily patted the horse's nose. "She's a beauty, isn't she?"

Cayd stepped closer and rubbed Cassiah's shoulder. "Yep, she certainly is."

His gaze clashed with Lily's, and suddenly, the air between them became charged. Long seconds passed before Cayd managed to drag his gaze away. His heart thumped. He cursed under his breath and turned away.

"Okay, girls. Fun's over. Time to get to work."

With that, he walked over to the tack room and collected three shovels. He brought them back to the would-be brides and handed them one each. Then he retrieved a wheelbarrow and brought it to a halt outside the first stall.

"Give me a minute to lead the horses outside. Then you can get to work mucking out the stalls," he said.

Marissa stared at the shovel dubiously. "What exactly does that entail?"

"Scooping up manure and dropping it into the wheelbarrow." Cayd grinned. "Think you can handle that?"

From the way she screwed up her face, Cayd guessed Marissa wasn't on board with the whole thing, but cleaning out the stables was a regular job on the station. It needed to be done, and it was a good opportunity for him to observe his women getting their hands dirty. She'd know that as well as he, and she wasn't about to give her competition the upper hand.

Even so, as Marissa continued to regard the shovel with distaste, he couldn't resist a final teasing jibe. "Watch you don't drop any manure on your boots. Some of it's pretty fresh."

She pouted prettily and huffed out a breath, but reluctantly strode over to an empty stall and began shoveling up the waste. Olivia and Chelsea were already busy. As Cayd led one horse after another outside and released them into the holding yards, he caught a glimpse of Lily out of the corner of his eye. She stood with her crew, talking quietly to them, no doubt giving them instructions on the best shots, angles, and close-ups of the girls working. Anything to keep the viewers glued to their seats.

He grimaced. That wasn't fair. They were filming a TV show. Of course, she had to make it interesting enough for the audience to keep tuning in. If no one watched the show, it would be discontinued and then Lily would be out of a job. She was only doing what she'd been paid to do, and after all, he'd been well and truly apprised of what was expected of him in the lengthy contract he'd signed prior to filming. If he was disgruntled over the intrusion into his life, he had no one to blame but himself.

"Ouch!"

Olivia's sudden cry of alarm sent everyone running over to her side. Cayd closed the gate against the last of the horses and went to see what all the fuss was about.

"I've broken a nail!" Olivia wailed, holding up a finger to his gaze.

He tamped down his impatience and dug deep for some sympathy. He'd never broken a nail before, but judging from Olivia's pinched expression, it was painful. He reached out and took the shovel from her and leaned it up against a post.

"You could always kiss it better."

Chapter Five

♥

Cayd whirled around and stared at Lily, surprised by her suggestion. Then again, that's what the viewers wanted, right? To see something developing between him and his potential brides, so they could get behind one of them, show their support. What had Lily said? Root for them?

The illuminated red light on the cameras confirmed they were still rolling. Plastering a smile on his face, he winked at Olivia and then slowly brought her injured hand up to his mouth. Making a grand gesture out of it, he kissed her finger, lingering over her hand before releasing it. A becoming blush stained her cheeks.

Marissa glared at them, not even bothering to hide her displeasure. With another loud huff, she tossed her shovel to the ground and shook her head.

"I'm done. It's too hot. And smelly. Perhaps I could give the horses a rub?"

Cayd shrugged nonchalantly, once again hiding his irritation. "Why not?" With that, he retrieved a brush from the tack room and tossed it toward her. She caught it against her chest.

"Which one should I tend to?" Marissa asked.

"Take your pick. They all love a good rub."

She looked a little doubtful as she gazed at the horses now standing against the railings of the yard. "Will they bite me?"

Cayd laughed. "No, they're not going to bite you. Just stay away from that big black stallion. He's not as friendly toward strangers."

"He's a real beauty," Lily said, joining the conversation. "What's his name?"

"Calypso. He's mine."

His gaze clashed with hers. The moment stretched out between them. It took all of Cayd's willpower to drag his gaze away. He deliberately focused on Chelsea who was still busy mucking out the stables. Cayd admired her work ethic and her willingness to get in and do what had to be done.

Too bad she doesn't light my fire...

Still, it was early days yet. This was only the second day. They had a whole week to get to know each other. A whole week before he had to decide who he'd send home. Reaching for a shovel, he joined Chelsea and started shoveling manure. She shot him an appreciative look.

"Thanks for giving me a hand. This is hard work!"

He nodded. "Yep. And we do this every day, whenever we have horses stabled."

The morning sun already had a bite to it, and it wasn't long before sweat formed on Cayd's upper lip and forehead. Pausing in his labors, he used his shirt to swipe at the film of perspiration on his face. Chelsea grinned at him and used the back of her sleeve on her own face.

"Whew," she said, a little out of breath.

"You're doing great. This job's so much quicker when there's someone to help you."

She blushed and smiled shyly. "I don't mind. I love being back out on a farm. The cattle, the horses, the dust. It feels like home."

Cayd compressed his lips. It was obvious Chelsea liked him. A lot. He wished he felt the same. He needed to give things more time. Perhaps as he got to know her better, his feelings would change? He hoped so. He hated the thought of hurting her. Then again, if he didn't hurt her, it would be one of the others. By the end of the week, he'd be forced to send someone home. That's the way the game went.

No, not a game. Real people are involved here. Real feelings, including mine.

If only he'd given more thought to that before he'd signed up for the show.

Belatedly, he registered Lily's presence. She stood a few yards away, watching him and Chelsea work.

"It's hot work, isn't it?" she commented.

He swiped his forehead with the back of his hand. "Sure is. Want to help?"

She chuckled as if he'd told a joke and then spread her arms wide. "I'm already working."

He rolled his eyes. "You call that work?"

She chuckled again. He liked the sound of it. Full and throaty. It slid across his skin and left his nerve endings tingling.

"How about you take off your shirt."

Her suggestion interrupted his musings. He glanced up at her. "Take off my shirt?"

She eyed him steadily. "Well, you're looking all hot and bothered, and surely it would be cooler with your shirt off."

She said it flippantly, but he didn't fall for her act for an instant.

"Don't you mean you want to take another peek at my body?" he teased.

She flushed and averted her gaze. Taking pity on her, he tugged at the bottom of his shirt and pulled it up over his head. Pretending to be oblivious to the appreciative stares from his ladies, it was only when Chelsea let out a wolf whistle that he turned to them and grinned.

"Show us your muscles!" Olivia chortled.

Cayd obligingly flexed his biceps. The girls howled their approval. His gaze strayed to Lily. Her cheeks were flushed. She hastily averted her gaze and suddenly appeared engrossed with her clipboard. Cayd was inordinately pleased by her reaction, but his inward grin quickly faded.

Wake up to yourself, Fairfax. She's not in the running. In fact, she belongs to someone else. How many times do you need to be reminded?

Lily kept her face turned away from Cayd's and made a deliberate effort to focus on writing her notes. She wasn't sure she'd ever get the image of taut golden abs, sculptured pecs, and bulging biceps out of her mind, but she was determined to do her best to forget Cayd's display of toned and tanned manly flesh.

Despite her best efforts, her cheeks still burned at the memory and her heart continued to pound. She only had herself to blame. After all, it was her suggestion that he take off his shirt. The fact was, she shouldn't be reacting like that to another man. She was an engaged woman, pledged to someone else. *In love* with someone else.

She'd never seen Alex naked. Not even his naked chest. He was modest when it came to showing off his body. Had always been that way. Even when they'd gone swimming as kids, he'd always worn a rash shirt. She hoped when she finally got to see him without clothes that she'd react as strongly to him as she had to Cayd. She hated that she wasn't certain of that.

Pushing the troubling thought aside, she did what she always did when doubts about her future husband assailed her: She focused on her work.

"Make sure you get plenty of close-ups of Cayd. A toned and muscled, half-naked farmer working up a sweat is exactly the kind of TV viewing our audience craves. I don't need to remind you how good that kind of footage is for the ratings. And don't forget to pan across the ladies. Their reactions to Farmer Cayd are just as important."

Nigel saluted her. "Don't you worry, boss. We'll get you the money shot."

Lily didn't bother to hide her satisfied grin. "Good." And then, because she couldn't help herself, she stole another peek at Cayd.

He continued to muck out the stables, shoveling load after load into the wheelbarrow. The smell of fresh horse manure was rather pungent, but she realized she rather liked it. The smell was earthy and raw and natural, just like the man she couldn't drag her eyes from.

Sweat ran down his neck and across his muscled chest. A fine sprinkling of dark hair covered his pecs. A thinner dark line disappeared under the waistband of his jeans. She blushed at the thought of what lay beneath the denim.

Though she was the ripe old age of thirty-one, she was still a virgin. She'd never had a serious boyfriend, not even back in high school. It had always been in the back of her mind that one day, she'd marry Alex. Their families had certainly made it clear they'd approve of such a match, and Lily had never been given cause to doubt that Alex was in her future.

As they reached adulthood, they'd gradually moved out of the friendship zone and into a boyfriend/girlfriend relationship. They went out on dates to the movies, to dinner, and to picnics in the park. Though they'd shared chaste kisses, that's as far as things went. Lily wasn't exactly against sex before marriage, but she respected Alex's request and the issue had never come up again.

But as she took in the sizzling-hot sight of Cayd Fairfax, naked from the waist up, she couldn't help but wonder whether she'd be so willing to agree to keep her hands off all that perfect male flesh. Her fingers tingled from the need to touch him. It was all she could do to stop herself from reaching out and placing her palm flat against his chest. She wanted to feel the warmth of his skin, the tightening of his muscles as he continued to put his energies into his work.

As if aware of her scrutiny, he lifted his head and gave her a searching look. Embarrassed, she dipped her eyes and once again pretended to be immersed in her notes. These feelings for her farmer were totally unwarranted and completely uncalled for. She was there to film a TV show about him falling in love with one of the three ladies he'd chosen for that purpose.

She needed to rid herself of her fanciful thoughts and concentrate on the job at hand. The last thing she needed was for the director to be displeased with her efforts. Being out there with a TV crew cost the studio a lot of money. They were okay spending it if they were confident they were getting good value.

Each night, she uploaded the rushes taken during the day. If her boss wasn't happy with what they were producing, she'd soon know about it. The last thing she needed was to put her job on the line. Too many people were relying on her. With that somber thought in mind, she shifted away from the temptation that was Cayd Fairfax and strode to the far end of the stables.

From the corner of his eye, Cayd spied Lily moving away from him. He ignored the immediate feeling of disappointment that followed her departure. With a concerted effort, he dragged his gaze away from the producer and focused on his girls. All three stood idly by, watching him work.

A spurt of irritation brought a scowl to his face. While he didn't expect them to work like farmhands, it would be nice if they helped out. Apart from Chelsea, the other two had barely lifted a finger. They'd volunteered to be part of the show. They knew they'd be spending time on a farm with a farmer who worked there. Surely it couldn't have come as a surprise that they'd be expected to join in. Especially if they wanted to be his final choice. He'd hardly choose a woman who'd expressed little to no interest in his home and livelihood.

Right now, he should have been out in the paddock doing real farm work, instead of putting on a show for the cameras. Thank God his brothers weren't there. He'd never hear the end of it. Swallowing a sigh, Cayd finished shoveling the manure and then reached for a rake. It was time to get his would-be brides earning their keep. Plastering a smile on his face, he tossed the rake toward Marissa. She caught it with a surprised yelp.

"How about you put that to use," he suggested.

She gave the rake a dubious look. "What do you want me to do with it?"

"Rake out the old hay." He turned to Olivia and Chelsea. "You two can collect it up and drop it over there." He pointed to a pile of rotting hay outside the stables. "My mother uses that as compost in her garden. I'll ask her later if she needs any taken over there."

With that, he stood back to catch his breath and watch the women work. Lily and the camera crew stepped closer. The cameramen didn't even wait for a signal from Lily before they started filming. Olivia was still complaining about her broken fingernail. Very gingerly, she collected one or two pieces of hay and dropped them in the pile. Cayd stifled a groan. Lily wasn't quite so reticent.

"Olivia! This is a farm. You're expected to get your hands dirty. You don't want to be the girl the viewers love to hate."

Lily's words appeared to have the desired effect. Olivia widened her arms to encompass a decent pile of hay. Holding it away from herself, she cautiously deposited it in the pile and then went back for more. Marissa continued to rake the hay into piles, but with even less enthusiasm. It appeared she was relying on her good looks and charm to win over the viewers.

At least Chelsea was giving it her best shot. For every modest pile of hay collected by Olivia, Chelsea did two, and she did it without complaining. It was obvious out of the three of them, she was the most suited to farm work.

But is she the most suited to me? That's the million-dollar question...

Keeping a discreet distance away, Lily made sure the cameras captured the women as they slaved over the hay. She also ensured there were plenty of shots of the still-shirtless Cayd. She idly watched as his gaze scanned from one woman to the other. She was curious as to where his affections might lie and whether there was a front-runner already.

It was hard to tell. There was no doubt he was attracted to the beautiful Marissa, but was she cut out for life on the farm? Chelsea probably suited him better in that respect, and the woman definitely had her charm. Olivia was a bit of a wild card. Her fiery red hair and bright blue eyes were enough to turn heads, but so far, she was the one who'd appeared to take to the farm the least, no matter her obvious interest in the farmer.

It came as no surprise to Lily that she felt so at home on Marlowe Downs. Despite her city upbringing, she'd always felt an affinity for the country. That was one of the attractions of her job. She loved escaping the hustle and bustle of the city and losing herself in the tranquility of acres of wide open spaces, clear blue skies, and limitless views. The fact she could see herself living and working on an outback station was an added torment she sure as hell didn't need.

Almost against her will, Lily's gaze was once again drawn to Cayd. So far, he'd kept his cards close to his chest. Only time would tell who his favorite was. As she wrapped up the scene with her crew, she took another moment to admire once again the sleek, firm pectorals, the washboard stomach, the bulging biceps, the ready grin. Then, with a wistful sigh, she forced herself to turn away.

Cayd watched Lily's departing back and wished he could join her. Everything seemed brighter when she was around. But it was crazy to think like that and certainly wouldn't help when it came to making the decision about which lady he'd send home at the end of the week. As the girls finished mucking out the stables, he fetched fresh hay from the shed and helped them spread it out. Mindful of the cameras still rolling, they all pitched in without complaint.

"Where to now?" Chelsea asked brightly.

Cayd led the way out of the stables. "We're off to feed the animals," he said. "Horses, chickens, pigs."

"What about the cattle? Isn't this a cattle station?" Olivia asked, doing her best to keep pace beside him.

Cayd chuckled. "For once, we have plenty of fodder. At the moment, they can feed themselves."

Chelsea flanked his other side. Her face had a pinched look about it. "Did you say chickens?" she asked.

He nodded. "Yep. We run about fifty of them. Mostly Rhode Island Red and some Sussex. Do you like chickens?"

She vehemently shook her head. "I'm terrified of chickens."

He shot her a quick grin in an effort to ease her fears. "They don't bite."

"I know, but they still terrify me. They'll come running at me and peck at me." She shuddered. "I hate it."

"How many times have you fed chickens?" he asked, curious.

"Only once. When I was five. On my grandparents' farm. It was a terrible experience. I've never forgotten it. I don't even like going into the poultry section at the Royal Easter Show. Too scary."

Olivia burst out laughing. "But those chickens are all in cages! They can't get anywhere near you. How can you be scared of them?"

"I just am, okay?" Chelsea snapped back.

Up ahead, Lily stopped and turned to face them. She waited for them to catch up with her before she spoke.

"It's all right to be afraid of something, Chelsea. In fact, showing vulnerability is a good thing. It makes you human.

That appeals to the viewers. They like to have someone to cheer for. Now, I understand you've had a frightening experience with chickens in the past, but do you think you might be brave enough to give them another go? Like Cayd said, they don't bite, and you're way bigger than them. In fact, truth be known, they're probably terrified of *you*. Did you ever think of that?"

She softened her words with a smile. Cayd marveled at her ability to get the best out of people. Then again, this wasn't her first season. No doubt she'd had plenty of experience getting what she needed out of the participants who made up the show.

Chelsea stared at her for a moment and then shook her head. "I never thought of it like that. I guess when I was five, I was a lot closer to their size than I am now." She drew in a deep breath and straightened her shoulders. "You're right. I'm five foot five. What do I have to be afraid of?"

"You go, girl!" Lily gave her a smile of encouragement.

Cayd merely stood back and took it all in, marveling not for the first time at Lily's superior people skills. She had a way about her that was so appealing. People wanted to please her. It was a good skill to have, that's for sure. Even he wasn't immune. Best he remain on guard lest he succumb to her charm. That wouldn't help any of them.

Chapter Six

♥

Lily kept out of the way while the cameramen got busy recording the amusing scenes that greeted them in the chicken yard. To her credit, Chelsea braved the large enclosure, albeit reluctantly, but the very first moment a chicken came running toward her, she squealed in alarm and turned tail. It didn't help that she held the bowl of grain in her hands. In her panic to put as much distance between herself and the chickens as possible, she tossed the bowl aside. Mayhem ensued. Even more chickens came running, until she was surrounded by clucking, pecking birds all anxious to be fed.

"Help me!" she wailed.

Both Olivia and Marissa were bent double, laughing. A grin tugged at Cayd's lips, but to Lily's relief, he strode forward, scattering the chickens in his wake. He reached out to Chelsea and put his arm around her shoulders, drawing her away from the melee. She clung to him and held on tightly.

Lily glanced across at the cameras to make sure they were still rolling. This was the kind of footage their viewers loved. A lady in distress and the strong, brave farmer to the rescue, even if it was only being rescued from hungry chickens.

It took a few moments of quiet words of comfort from Cayd for Chelsea to finally calm down. Olivia and Marissa watched on. It was obvious from their expressions that they wished it was them being comforted by the hot farmer. Still, Lily had no doubt Chelsea's distress was real. She felt a pang of sympathy for the woman. Time for them to all get out of the chicken yard.

"Okay, enough of the chickens. Where to next?" she asked, directing her question to Cayd.

Cayd dropped his arm from around Chelsea's shoulders. "We still have the pigs to feed. Any takers for that?"

Chelsea cracked a smile. "I love pigs! Do you have any babies?"

"Only about fifty-five of them," Cayd replied.

Chelsea's eyes widened. "Fifty-five piglets?"

Cayd nodded. "Yep. At the moment, we have ten sows and a boar and all of their offspring."

"So, you breed them, do you?" Marissa asked, drawing closer.

"Yes. But only for our own use. You might have noticed we're a long way from town. We grow our own fruit and veg-etables. We kill our own meat. Beef, chicken, pork."

Olivia looked a little squeamish. Marissa nudged her with her elbow. "Where do you think the steak you buy in the supermarket comes from? It started out on a farm just like this one."

Olivia drew in a shaky breath, but offered a brave nod. "Of course. But the thought of killing it yourself…"

"It's okay, Olivia," Cayd said. "We won't be doing any slaughtering while you're here."

She looked visibly relieved. "Oh, thank goodness."

Lily only just managed to suppress an eye roll. They were at a cattle station. The sole purpose of the enterprise was to produce beef for human consumption, and people didn't eat live meat. If Olivia wanted to have any chance of being chosen by Cayd, she'd need to come to terms with that fact.

Still, there was nothing Lily could do about that. Her job was to get scintillating footage that would keep the viewers riveted. With that thought in mind, she clapped her hands together to get everyone's attention.

"Okay, we're going to check out the piggery. After that, we'll break for lunch."

Cayd led his ladies away from the chicken yard and to another enclosure about five hundred yards away from the homestead. The sound and smell of pigs hit Lily in the face.

"Pooh! What's that smell?" Marissa complained.

Cayd merely grinned. "That's the smell of Fairfax pork. The best in the outback."

Chelsea chuckled. "Really?"

Cayd winked. "Well, that's what we think. If you're lucky, you might even get to try some yourself while you're here. Then you can make up your own mind."

The moment Cayd opened the gate that led into the pigsty, they were surrounded by squealing pink piglets. Lily couldn't refrain from crying out in delight.

"How gorgeous! They're so cute!" she said, bending low to scratch one behind the ears before moving out of the way of the cameras.

"Oh, my goodness! They're everywhere!" Marissa shrieked, clinging to Cayd.

Lily couldn't tell if the woman was genuinely frightened or just using the barrage of piglets as an excuse to get close to Cayd. The other two ladies were less standoffish. Under Cayd's instruction, Olivia and Chelsea poured feed into the troughs. The pigs immediately hustled beside them, snorting and snuffling at the grain.

"Olivia, would you mind topping up the water trough?" Cayd asked, extricating himself from Marissa. "There's a hose over next to the shed."

Olivia did as he asked, picking her way carefully through the muddy pigsty. She was almost to the shed when she slid on a patch of wet ground and fell in a heap on her butt. Lily quickly checked to make sure the cameras were still rolling and then felt guilty that her first priority was to the TV show and not to Olivia.

Keen to make amends, she hurried over to the woman, whose clothes were now covered in thick, black mud.

"Help me! Please!" Olivia wailed and then promptly burst into tears.

After a quick but thorough assessment, it was obvious to Lily that the only thing that had been hurt was Olivia's pride. As the woman tried to get to her feet, she slipped again and ended up in the mud a second time. Not only was her butt and the back of her legs coated with the filth, now she'd fallen onto her hands and knees.

From the corner of her eye, Lily saw Cayd striding toward them. She could tell he was working hard not to laugh. Lily struggled with the same thing. Covered in mud, Olivia was a sight to be seen. As a horde of squealing pigs came over to investigate, it was all Lily could do to hide her amusement.

Cayd extended his hand toward Olivia. "Here, let me help you."

Tears welled in Olivia's eyes. She reached for Cayd's hand. He pulled her upright. "Are you okay?" he asked.

The tears spilled over. Cayd's expression filled with concern. "Hey, it's all right. Don't be upset. It's just a bit of mud. No one cares."

Ignoring Cayd's attempt to comfort her, on a wail of despair, Olivia turned and slipped and slid her way out of the pig yard. The cameramen swung around to follow her progress and then panned across to where Marissa and Chelsea stood leaning against the fence, chuckling.

"Are you all right Olivia?" Chelsea called after her.

Intent on escaping, Olivia didn't respond. With her head down and walking as fast as she could, she left the pig yard and headed straight for the homestead. Lily felt a stab of sympathy. Poor Olivia. No doubt the whole experience was humiliating. It didn't matter that no one cared and that most of them found it funny. After all, it could have happened to any of them.

Moving closer to the camera crew, Lily lowered her voice before asking, "Did you get all that?"

Nigel grinned and gave her a thumbs-up. "You bet."

Satisfaction flooded through her. Though she didn't wish ill on any of the ladies, footage like that was gold. That kind of entertainment sent the ratings soaring, and it sure as hell would get her boss off her back. At least for now.

Cayd strode over to her, a wry smile playing around his lips. Marissa and Chelsea joined them.

Cayd took off his hat and slapped it against his thigh. "Well, that was fun. Who wants to go riding?"

After a delicious lunch of cold cuts, salad, and fresh crusty bread straight from the oven, all compliments of Cayd's mother, Lily made her way over to where Cayd stood lounging against the wall of the kitchen talking to his brother, Lachlan. He was yet another good-looking, broad-shouldered cattleman, but unlike Cayd, Lachlan sported thick blond hair and had a pair of striking green eyes that reminded her of his older brother, Brock.

Lachlan was another sibling who lived and worked on the station and had agreed to steer clear of the cameras while they were filming. Lily had met him on her first visit to the farm and now greeted him with a friendly smile.

"Lachlan. It's good to see you again."

Lachlan tipped his hat toward her and grinned. "Likewise."

Though he had a nice smile and an open and engaging demeanor, he didn't set her pulse on fire. *Not like his brother.* She frowned and deliberately shifted her thoughts from venturing any further into that dangerous territory.

Clearing her throat, she caught Cayd's gaze. "Do you mind if I speak to you in private for a minute?"

Cayd shrugged. "Of course not."

Lachlan looked from one to the other and then took a couple of steps backward out of the kitchen. "I'll leave you to it," he mumbled and left them.

"Are you still intending on going horse riding after lunch?" she asked.

"Yep. Do you ride? I've asked one of the station hands to saddle up some horses."

She shook her head. "Thanks for the offer, but the camera crew and I will follow in a truck. We don't want to risk damage to the equipment."

He leaned in close and shot her a look that sent a shaft of desire surging through her.

"Don't tell me you're scared?"

His husky voice, filled with challenge, shivered over her skin. Her nipples went taut with need. Her body's instant reaction shocked her. She'd never been so physically drawn to a man. She wanted to spend time contemplating what the hell was going on with her, but from the look on Cayd's face, it was clear he expected an answer.

Squaring her shoulders, she lifted her head and stared back at him. "Of course not."

"Prove it."

Her breathing quickened. Excitement rushed through her veins. She opened her mouth to respond, but then closed it again. She wasn't one of his would-be brides. She didn't need to prove anything.

"I must stay with my crew, and they need to look after their equipment. If you can make a farm vehicle available for our use, I'd appreciate it."

The look he gave her told her he didn't fall for her excuse for a minute, but to her relief, he didn't press any further. Instead, he called out to his ladies and told them it was time for their next adventure. With the cameras rolling, they all strode over to the stables.

Marissa looked terrified. Lily also caught a flash of fear in Olivia's eyes. The girl had recovered from her incident in the pig yard and now wore a fresh pair of tight jeans and a colorful, short-sleeved blouse that she'd tied in a knot beneath her breasts, showing her flat stomach to its best advantage. Only Chelsea seemed to take the prospect of riding a horse in stride.

Three reddish-brown mares and Cayd's dangerous-looking black stallion were already saddled and tied up to the slip rail. Lily signaled her cameramen to ensure they started filming. Cayd untied the reins of the first horse and led it over to Chelsea.

"Have you ever ridden a horse?"

Chelsea nodded. "Yes. But it's been a while."

He chuckled. "Don't worry. It's like riding a bike. You never forget how." He patted the shoulder of the mare. "This is Star. Named after the white star shape on her forehead. She's a chestnut. Star's a good little mare and won't give you any trouble."

Chelsea nodded. Though she looked a little nervous, she bravely took the reins from Cayd.

"Do you need a hand to mount her?" he asked.

Chelsea shook her head and got the job done without any fuss. Lily made a mental note to remind Chelsea that the more opportunities she gave Cayd to get up close and personal with her the better. He was on a quest to find a wife and she was in the running. The field had been narrowed to just three. Chelsea needed to do whatever she could to claim Cayd's attention. If Lily had been in Chelsea's boots, she'd have most definitely elicited the sexy cattleman's help, even if she didn't need it.

Oblivious to her thoughts, Cayd drew the next horse up beside Olivia. "This is Ronnie. Short for Veronica. She's a little bay mare and will get you anywhere you want to go without trouble."

Olivia regarded the horse with suspicion. "What if she bucks me off?"

Cayd smiled. "She's not going to buck you off."

Olivia continued to look unconvinced. "How do you know?"

Cayd eyed her steadily. "Because I've raised this little girl from a foal. I know her inside and out. She doesn't have a mean bone in her body."

Some of the tension in Olivia's shoulders relaxed. She breathed out on a sigh. "Are you sure?"

"I'm sure." He paused and then added, "Would you like to climb on her back?"

Olivia's face became pinched, but she bravely nodded and stepped closer to the horse. "How do I get on her?"

"Here. Let me help," Cayd offered.

While the cameras rolled, Cayd held the reins. At the same time, he guided Olivia until she was seated on the horse. Looking equal parts scared and triumphant, she shot him a brilliant smile.

"It's so high up here!" she exclaimed.

Cayd chuckled. "Not a bad view, is it? Here. Take the reins."

Olivia's confidence immediately collapsed. "No, no! I can't."

"Of course you can," Cayd replied in a soothing voice. "Here. Don't be frightened. Ronnie isn't going anywhere."

With great reluctance, Olivia reached for the reins. Gingerly, she held them in her hands. The fearful look had returned to her face.

"You're doing great, Olivia," Cayd encouraged. "You'll be fine."

With that, he directed his attention to Marissa, who remained tense and wide-eyed near the slip rail, as far from the horses as she could get. Cayd strode up to her.

"What are you afraid of?" he asked softly.

Lily signaled to the cameramen to move closer. She didn't want to miss a second of this scene. Cayd was being so gentle and tender with his women. It was the kind of thing that made their mostly female viewers swoon.

"I don't know," Marissa admitted, staring at her feet. "They're so huge and scary. I've never been on a horse. What if it bolts?"

Cayd smiled. "Wait here." With that, he turned toward the final mare and untied her reins. He led her up to where Marissa remained standing near the rail.

"Marissa, meet Shiloh. She's as sweet and gentle as can be. She won't buck. She won't bolt. In fact, she won't do anything you don't want her to do."

"How can you be so certain?" Marissa asked, her eyes still wide with fear.

"She was born right here on the station ten years ago. I broke her in myself."

Marissa looked at Cayd and then peeked at the horse and then returned her gaze back to Cayd. Her eyes were still wide with uncertainty.

"Do you trust me?" he asked.

Though Marissa barely knew him, Lily wasn't surprised when the woman slowly nodded. There was something about Cayd that inspired trust. These past few moments, Lily had been just as caught up in his magnetism as Marissa was. No wonder the woman responded to his question in the affirmative.

"I wouldn't put you on a horse that might cause you harm," he added. "Here. Come closer. Give her a pat. She loves a good pat."

He rubbed his hand down the horse's shoulder. She turned her head and nudged him with her nose. Finding her courage, Marissa took a step forward and tentatively reached out toward the little mare. Her fingers brushed the horse's nose, and her eyes widened in surprise.

"It's as soft as velvet," she exclaimed. "Just as soft as my skin."

Cayd grinned. "There you go. See, she's not as scary as you think. Come on, let me help you mount. We'll take it slowly, okay?"

With his gentle encouragement, Marissa hauled herself into the saddle, and though she sat as stiff as a board and continued to look fearful, at least she was up there. Lily checked with Nigel that he'd captured it all.

"Sure did. Is there anything else you want me to film?"

Just then, Lily's attention was captured by the sight of Cayd mounted on Calypso. The huge black stallion pranced around, flinging his head up and down and swishing his tail in his impatience to get going. Cayd was sexy enough on two legs. On the back of his magnificent horse, he stole her breath.

"Earth to Lily."

Nigel's words finally penetrated the fog that had momentarily surrounded her brain. She blinked. Nigel shot her a curious look. Heat exploded across her face. Ducking her head, she mumbled instructions, then tucked her clipboard under her arm and escaped toward the 4WD vehicle Cayd had provided for their use.

Chapter Seven

♥

Cayd stayed close to the three women as they bounced and jostled their way forward on the horses. Though he wasn't at all worried that any of the mares would take off without warning or try to buck their riders off, he was a bit concerned that Marissa might fall off of her own accord. Though Shiloh only plodded forward, as slow and sedate as he'd expected, Marissa slid and slipped in her seat, bouncing everywhere.

Clicking up his horse with his tongue, Cayd sidled up next to her. "Hey, how're you doing?"

She grimaced. "How does it look like I'm doing," she muttered through gritted teeth.

He shot her an encouraging smile. "Grip her sides with your thighs. It will help you stay in the saddle. And tighten your hold on the reins. You want them firm, not loose. Let her know you're in charge."

Marissa managed a wry smile. "You're kidding, right? There's nothing I can do to make her believe I'm in charge. She's completely in control. I'm merely along for the ride. Pardon the pun."

Cayd chuckled, pleased Marissa had regained her sense of humor. "You're doing great. I'm proud of you."

She flushed, obviously pleased with his comment. "Thank you."

"I mean it." And he did.

There was a lot to like about Marissa. *But is she cut out for life on a farm?* Right now, he didn't know.

He nudged his horse over to where Olivia sat on Ronnie's back looking only slightly less apprehensive than she had at the beginning.

"Hey, relax and try to enjoy it," he encouraged. "I promise she won't take off on you."

Olivia managed to smile, reminding him of how attractive she was. Her red hair was tucked up beneath her riding hat. Her blue eyes shone. He was glad she seemed to have recovered from the piggery incident. The muddy clothes had been replaced with fresh ones. He gave her a slow once-over. He couldn't help but notice how good her breasts looked pushed up under her shirt. Or the tantalizing glimpse of firm, pale flesh when her shirt rode up to expose the bare skin beneath the knot she'd tied in her shirt. There was a lot to like about Olivia too. She was definitely still in the race.

His gaze drifted to Chelsea, who trotted slowly beside them. It was obvious from her relaxed posture that she was the most comfortable of all three of the ladies on the back of a horse. Cayd liked her no-nonsense attitude. There was no pretense. No fuss. But so far, there was no burning attraction to her either.

He sighed and glanced over his shoulder. Lily was behind the wheel of the 4WD vehicle with her camera crew in tow. Three men stood on the back of the truck. One leaned out of the window. Both cameramen had their cameras on their shoulders, presumably filming. He ignored a spurt of irritation. This was what he'd signed up for: for his every waking moment to be captured on camera for the viewing pleasure of *Outback Bride*'s audience. Too bad he hadn't realized how intrusive it would be, or how quickly he'd tire of the attention. If it weren't for the publicity the show would bring his farm stay project, he'd have called a halt to the whole thing already.

Then again, without the show, he'd have no excuse to spend time around Lily. He couldn't deny it was her presence on the station that made the days more interesting. He looked forward to seeing her each morning and spending time with her in conversation. In fact, if he were honest, he preferred being with her more than he did with any of his chosen ladies.

And that's most definitely a problem...

With a conscious effort, he pushed those thoughts aside and concentrated on the beautiful afternoon. The clear, blue sky stretched overhead as far as the eye could see. A gentle breeze made the warm sunshine bearable. It wouldn't be long before the heat became stifling, and any outside work would be confined to the morning or late in the afternoon. But right now, they were experiencing perfect spring weather.

Of course, they could always do with some rain. It had been at least a couple of months since they'd had a decent fall and though the pasture was still plentiful, it had begun to dry off. It was ironic to think about needing rain when not so long ago they'd suffered such devastating floods.

But that's how the weather was in Australia. It was a land of extremes. Always had been. All he had to do was recall the famous Dorothea Mackellar poem he'd learned in school where she'd written about the droughts and flooding rains. The poem was first published early in the twentieth century. Nothing much had changed.

Conscious that the girls weren't used to riding and no doubt would be sore if they stayed out too long, Cayd told them to pull up on their reins and wait while he had a word with the producer. Wheeling around, he cantered back to Lily's vehicle. As he approached, she brought the 4WD to a halt.

Her hair had come loose from the ponytail, and tendrils now curled around her face. She had a smudge of dirt on her cheek, probably from when she'd crouched low to play with the piglets. She was a long way from the immaculately groomed and sophisticated TV producer he'd first met, but he liked this Lily better.

Her peach-colored blouse brought out the color in her cheeks and highlighted her olive skin tones. The shirt had been rolled up to the elbows, exposing slim, tanned forearms. The smile she gave him as he drew closer was natural and unforced. At the sight of it, his heart skipped a beat and then started racing.

Shit. I'm in big trouble...

It was the last thought he had before she spoke.

Lily's heart took off like a rocket as Cayd pulled up beside her. He looked so sexy, so masculine on the back of his horse.

"What's going on?" she asked.

Cayd pushed his Akubra to the back of his head. "Have you got enough footage yet? I don't want to overdo it. The ladies will feel it in the morning if we ride for too long."

"Fair enough," she replied, once again impressed by his caring and concern for women who were almost strangers. "Let me just check with the crew."

When both cameramen assured her they were good, she turned back to Cayd. His horse had stepped even closer and now nudged her arm through the open window with his nose. Chuckling, Lily patted the big brute.

"How are you doing, Calypso?" she murmured. "Are you enjoying this as much as the rest of us?"

She sent a wry smile in Cayd's direction. Her stomach clenched when his eyes crinkled with good humor and a grin widened his lips.

"What's not to like about following a bunch of women and a cattle farmer around, capturing their every moment—good, bad, and downright ugly—on film for the consumption of thousands of avid TV viewers?"

"Hey! You knew exactly what you were getting yourself into."

He rolled his eyes. "You're not talking about that contract again, are you?"

"You read it from cover to cover. I watched you. You're the first farmer I've come across to actually do that. I thought that was…interesting."

The truth was, she'd been surprised and intrigued by him. In all five of her previous seasons, not a single farmer had taken the time to give the fifteen-page contract more than a cursory glance before signing it. Cayd had been different. He'd not only read every word, he'd also asked quite a few questions. It was obvious he'd given the matter a lot of thought and wanted to go into it as informed as he could be.

That told her there was more to him than a pretty face, though pretty he definitely was. There was an intelligence in his blue eyes that appealed to her even more than his physical attractiveness. Along with his easy-going attitude and sense of humor, he was a tempting package.

She had no right to think of him like that. She had a fiancé she adored. A man she'd loved for most of her life. Soon they'd be married. Just as soon as she came up with a date.

She swallowed a sigh. So far, Alex had been patient. Though he was keen to get married, he hadn't pressured her into making a decision. He accepted that she was busy with work and that often took her away from home. It was impossible to plan a wedding while she was trying to put together a TV show.

But Alex wouldn't remain patient forever. He'd already asked her if she intended to sign on for another season when this one came to an end. She'd avoided giving him an answer, but she already knew she wanted to re-sign. Most of the time, she loved her job. Being busy and traveling away from home also gave her an excuse to delay their wedding.

Why do I need an excuse?

Her mind shied away from contemplating that. Instead, she focused on Cayd. The man was way too unsettling to her equilibrium. She needed to put some distance between them, figuratively and literally. What better way to do that than to push him into the arms of one of his ladies? After all, that's what they were all there for.

"Why don't you take one of the women for some one-on-one time this afternoon? Get to know her better. Let her get to know you. By the end of the week, you're going to have to send one of them home. There's nothing like a bit of individual attention to help you make that decision. Agreed?"

His smile faded. A look of somber concentration replaced the earlier good humor. He nodded. "Agreed. Which one should I choose? The one I like the least, or the best?"

She tamped down a stab of jealousy that he already had a favorite and offered up a bright smile. "That's entirely up to you. Whatever will help you make up your mind. Don't forget, you'll get the opportunity to have one-on-one time with all three before the week's up. We must play fair, remember?"

"Ah, there you go quoting that contract again," he teased.

Nerves fluttered in her stomach from the way he looked at her and the easy way his good humor was restored. No pouting, no sulking, no arguments. Just an acknowledgment of their agreement and an acceptance of doing what he had to in order to get the job done.

She cleared her throat and looked away. "Best get back to your ladies and give them the good news. I'm sure they'll be glad to get off the horses. We'll meet you back at the house."

With that, she put the vehicle in Drive, and, with a quick word to the crew on the back of the ute, they left.

Joining the ladies, Lily, and her crew on the back veranda for afternoon drinks and nibbles, Cayd found himself in a contemplative mood. Lily's reminder that by the end of the week he'd have to choose who to send home brought back to him that this wasn't a game. There were real people with real feelings involved. No matter who he chose, someone was bound to get hurt. He hated that he was going to be responsible for that.

When he'd quizzed Lily over the contract, it had been more from a practical point of view. How much time would he have to give to the women? What if he didn't like any of them enough to want to become involved with them? What if someone was injured? Was that on the station's insurance, or theirs? How many hours would he be required to make himself available for filming? This was a working cattle station, and he was one of the leading hands. He couldn't afford to be absent from the job of running the place for too long.

He hadn't given any thought to the actual machinations of having three women all vying for his attention and having to spread himself evenly among them with the goal of choosing one of them as his final mate. Though Lily had assured him no one expected a marriage proposal, a happy-for-now was something their audience demanded. This was explicitly stated in his contract. After all, no one wanted to let the viewers down.

He hadn't worried too much about that clause at the time because he'd assumed it wouldn't be that difficult to choose one of the women and ask her if she were willing to stick around. After all, he had three to choose from. Surely, it couldn't be that hard.

But he hadn't counted on the fact that though all three women were lovely and each had something unique that appealed to him, none of them ticked all the boxes or had him in such a state that they consumed his every waking moment. That was the kind of reaction he needed. He was concerned that he might not want to choose any of them as his final mate.

With a sigh, he shifted his thoughts to who he'd pick for the one-on-one time. Having some alone time with each of them might help to clarify his feelings. He was most attracted to Marissa, but it might be best to see if there was anything worth pursuing between him and Chelsea. She was the one he had the least attraction to. Some alone time with her might be enough for him to come to a decision.

Bringing his beer up to his mouth, he swallowed a few mouthfuls. The girls were draped across cane rocking chairs and chaise lounges, sipping cold drinks and snacking on crackers and dips and pieces of fruit on platters that his mother had thoughtfully prepared earlier. Lily's crew stood off to one side, chatting among one another. They'd been busy filming all day. No doubt they were also enjoying the break.

His gaze strayed to where Lily stood leaning against the veranda railing. She had her back to him and was engaged in conversation with her cameramen. Every now and then, she sipped her beer. While he watched, one of the men said something funny and Lily tilted her head back and laughed. The sound of her deep-throated enjoyment sent ripples of desire along his skin.

Too bad I can't have some one-on-one time with the sexy producer. Now that would be something I'd look forward to...

He forced the thoughts aside. On a surge of determination, he strode across the veranda and came to a halt beside Chelsea. She looked up at him from her spot on a lounger.

"Cayd!"

She sounded breathless. Before he could change his mind, he reached for her hand and gently tugged her to her feet.

"Chelsea, would you like to spend some time alone with me?"

Her answering smile was blinding. "I'd *love* to."

Swallowing a groan, he summoned a smile and responded. "Great."

Lily was too far away to hear their conversation, but from the look of joy on Chelsea's face, she guessed Cayd had just asked the woman for some alone time. Lily was curious about his decision. She'd been almost certain he'd go for Marissa. She was the most obvious choice. There appeared to be real chemistry between them.

Then again, maybe he was using this time to potentially eliminate Chelsea. After all, the decision to send one of his ladies home was drawing closer. Whichever way it went, Lily and the camera crew would be there to capture every moment. In the past, these opportunities often elicited personal confessions from the participants, and that was the kind of sensational stuff her viewers craved. To say nothing of her boss.

Pushing away from the railing, she approached the couple. "So, guys, where are you off to?"

Chelsea shot a questioning look at Cayd.

Cayd looked at Lily. "To the rose garden."

Lily forced back a twinge of jealousy. She'd scouted out the rose garden earlier as a possible shoot location. It was gorgeous, with a wide variety of beautiful, fragrant roses all in bloom. An ornamental pond surrounded by lush green grass and an antique wooden bench seat added to the romance of the place.

She forced a quick smile. "Sounds great. Just give us a few minutes to set up. We'll meet you there."

Cayd sat on the wooden bench seat that had stood in his mother's rose garden for as long as he could remember. Chelsea sat beside him. They were close enough that every now and then, her thigh would brush up against his. Each time it happened, color stole into her cheeks. He wished he were equally affected.

The truth was, he was struggling to maintain the conversation. It was hard enough to concentrate with two cameras pointed directly at them, but it was Lily's presence that kept distracting him. She hovered in the background, giving both him and Chelsea and her cameramen directions. She was just doing her job, but with every flick of her ponytail, he caught a whiff of her exotic shampoo, and it kept doing crazy things to his insides.

With an effort, he blocked out everyone but Chelsea. Determined to make the most of this time alone with her, he reached for her hand and threaded his fingers through hers. He caught her sharp intake of breath and took a moment to analyze his own reaction. Unfortunately, his body remained annoyingly unmoved.

"Tell me about your life back in Sydney," he encouraged.

She looked down self-consciously and then shrugged. "What do you want to know?"

"Whatever you'd like to share. I want to know what makes Chelsea tick."

She smiled. "I'm afraid I'm not that complicated. What you see is what you get. I work as a receptionist in a busy medical center in Burwood. Some days, it feels like the phones never stop."

She gave him a self-deprecating look. "I'm not complaining," she added hurriedly. "It's a great job and the pay's pretty good. No shiftwork. Weekends off. And it's close to my family."

"Tell me about them," Cayd urged.

During the speed dates he'd enjoyed with the ten ladies he'd initially chosen out of the hundreds of applicants, he hadn't been given enough time to ask more than perfunctory questions. He realized he was keen to know more about

Chelsea and why he'd been interested enough in her to choose her as one of the three he eventually invited to the station.

"Well, there's only me and my brother, Jackson. He's seventeen. He's an apprentice plumber and still lives at home with my parents."

"And where do you live?"

"I rent a studio in Strathfield. It's about as big as a shoebox and has about as much appeal, but it's cheap and convenient to work. Besides, I spend a lot of time at home. My mother cooks a decent lamb roast."

Cayd reared back in mock horror. "Sacrilege! Fancy talking about lamb on a cattle station."

She giggled, and the sound of it pleased him. His gaze swept over her short brown hair that hung in soft curls around her face. She stared at him. Seconds passed. Cayd leaned in. She met him halfway. Their lips met in a kiss.

It went on longer than Cayd cared for, but he didn't want to insult her by ending the kiss too quickly. But it was as he'd suspected. There was no spark, not even a flicker of desire. She was sweet and pretty and capable, but his heart wasn't interested. Neither was his body, it seemed.

Slowly, he pulled away. She stared up at him with eyes that were wide with wonder.

Shit.

Unwilling to dash her hopes or inflict hurt on her unnecessarily, especially in front of the cameras, he plastered a smile on his face, put his arm around her shoulders, and drew her close. She reached for his free hand and snuggled in beside him.

"And...cut," Lily said.

Cayd swallowed a sigh.

What the hell have I gotten myself into?

Chapter Eight

♥

Lily busied herself with helping her crew pack up their gear and ignored a spurt of irritation. Of course Cayd was going to kiss the women. That was all part of the show. It had been written in his contract that physical intimacy for the cameras was a requirement. That was one of the clauses Cayd had questioned.

"How do you define physical intimacy?" he asked.

"In the normal way," she responded. "Kissing, cuddling, holding hands."

He quirked an eyebrow. "So, no sex?"

She fought hard to hold back a blush. "Not necessarily, but we won't film that."

"Gee, thanks. Good to know there are some limits to where the cameras will go."

Now she couldn't help but wonder if Cayd had enjoyed kissing Chelsea. Though it had remained chaste, it had definitely been more than a peck. At least ten seconds' worth, maybe more.

Stop it! Just...stop it! I'm being ridiculous. What do I care if he likes kissing Chelsea? It's none of my business. Besides, it's good for ratings. I should be encouraging more of it.

What she should do was to call Alex again. She needed to hear his voice. Reassure herself that he was her man and that no cattle farmer, not even a sexy one who set her pulse racing, could make her change her mind on that.

Cayd came out of his bedroom the next morning to find the kitchen a hive of activity. Lily and her camera crew were already there with cameras rolling. Cayd's ladies were busy slaving over the stove. A pile of cooked bacon sat on the counter, next to a plate of buttered toast. Chelsea was finishing off a pan of scrambled eggs.

"Wow. What's all this?" he asked, snagging a piece of bacon, and popping it into his mouth.

Chelsea turned to him and grinned. "A cooked breakfast. What else?"

"Boy, you've all been busy," he remarked, looking around at the spread.

"Chelsea did most of the cooking," Olivia admitted. "Marissa and I buttered the toast."

Cayd smiled at Chelsea. "Thanks, Chelsea. You've done a marvelous job."

She immediately blushed in response. Hope flared in her eyes.

Shit.

He hated that she'd taken his casual expression of gratitude as something more. He had nothing against her. She was a strong and capable woman and fun to be around, but the kiss he'd shared with her had confirmed his suspicions. There was zero attraction. She was a perfectly pleasant companion, but she wasn't for him. At least he knew who he was going to send home.

With a plateful of food, he took a seat at the table. Marissa was quick to sit next to him. Chelsea wedged herself on his other side. Pouting slightly, Olivia pulled out a chair opposite and plonked herself down.

Conversation ceased while everyone got busy eating. The eggs were fluffy, the bacon crisp. Cayd opened his mouth to thank Chelsea once again for her efforts, but then decided against it. He was going to send her home. He didn't want to get her hopes up unnecessarily by giving her any extra attention that might be misconstrued.

After breakfast, Lily drew him aside. "So, how are things going?"

"You mean with Chelsea?"

"Yes, with Chelsea, and life in general. Are you doing okay?"

"I'm fine. You'd do better to ask my brothers. They've had to pick up the slack while I've been otherwise occupied. Mustering cattle one hand down is no fun for anyone."

"If it's any consolation, we're only planning on one filming session today. You'll have the afternoon free. That should give you some time to catch up on other jobs you've had to neglect."

Cayd nodded. "My brothers will certainly be relieved to hear that."

"So, tell me about Chelsea."

Cayd grimaced. "What do you want to know?"

"The two of you kissed... Did anything develop after that?"

"No. In fact, I've decided she's going to be the one I send home."

Lily's eyes widened in surprise. "Are you sure? This is only the third day."

Cayd didn't hesitate. "Yes. I'm sure."

"Okay. Well, I guess that takes the pressure off you as far as the decision goes, but I do want to caution you against making the decision so far ahead of time. In my experience, more time spent with a lady can sometimes change your mind."

Cayd's gaze remained steady on hers. "I'm not going to change my mind."

"Okay, well. Let's just see how it goes. You still have four days before you need to make your decision public. Let's just keep it to ourselves for now. No point in tipping the viewers off so early in the game. There's no incentive for them to keep tuning in for the rest of the week if they already know who's leaving and as you know, it's all about the ratings."

Cayd grimaced. "As if I could forget about the ratings."

Now that he'd come to a decision, he was reluctant to keep quiet about it, but he accepted Lily's reasoning, and no doubt there was something in the fine print of his contract that required him to keep things under wraps for as long as the producer demanded. It would be a challenge to keep treating Chelsea like she had a chance at winning his heart and he didn't know if he was up for the subterfuge, but he guessed he had no choice but to give it a shot.

Swallowing a sigh, he turned away and walked up to where the girls were finishing the washing up.

"What are we doing this morning?" Olivia asked, hanging up her tea towel.

Cayd rubbed his hands together. "We're going out on the quad bikes to do some fencing. Doesn't that sound like fun?"

As one, the girls groaned.

Lily held back with her crew while Cayd wheeled out the quad bikes. Without needing to ask, the cameramen brought their cameras up to their shoulders and started rolling. Quick as a fox, Chelsea climbed on behind Cayd before either of the other girls could. It was obvious she'd grown in confidence after their kiss. Knowing what she did, Lily felt sorry for the woman, but then she set the feelings aside.

The girls were well aware before they'd signed up for the show that some of them might get their heart broken. After all, only one of them would be chosen at the end. Their hurt feelings or otherwise weren't Lily's problem. Her job was to create entertaining TV that resulted in good ratings. That was her only goal. And entertaining TV required drama.

With that thought in mind, she went over to Marissa and Olivia. This time, Olivia was in the driver's seat. Briefly, Lily wondered if that was a wise decision, but then decided that having footage of Olivia bunny-hopping a quad bike was exactly the kind of entertainment her boss demanded. She also needed to offer them both some encouragement, particularly Olivia, who was less confident than Marissa.

"This is still a three-horse race, ladies. It's only day three. Chelsea might be riding with Cayd, but that doesn't mean you shouldn't do everything possible to get close to him. You have to make your own luck. Take opportunities when they present themselves and be brave. Don't lose heart because Chelsea had the one-on-one. There's no rule against having to wait for him to approach you. Why not ask him yourself for some alone time?"

With that, she winked at them and walked away. The seed had been planted. Now it was time to see who wanted Cayd badly enough to take her up on her suggestion. Lily's money was on Marissa, but she'd been around enough of these shows to know that sometimes it was the quieter ones who surprised her.

Not that it mattered. As long as there was conflict, her boss would be happy. That was all Lily cared about. That might have made her sound callous and unfeeling, but feelings didn't count as far as her job was concerned. Her parents relied on her income. She couldn't afford to lose it.

Cayd did his best to ignore the feeling of Chelsea seated behind him on the quad bike. It wasn't easy with her plastered so tightly against him and her arms snug around his waist. It still didn't sit well with him to let her go on thinking that something might develop between them. He wished he could set her straight, but he'd agreed to keep quiet and that was that. Until Sunday, he'd be forced to go through the motions and pretend she was still in there with a chance because that's what Lily wanted. Apparently, that's what the viewers wanted too. And there was no escaping the cameras. They captured everything.

At least he had something to distract him this morning. Earlier in the year, floods had ravaged the station. Though it had left their dams full and had provided much-needed moisture for crops, it had also left a deluge of damage in its wake. Some of the farm buildings had been torn from their footings and had floated away.

A good deal of their fencing had also been destroyed. As time and money allowed, they'd been making repairs. Today, he'd decided to get his ladies involved. Though they didn't know the first thing about fencing, he was sure he could teach them the basics and any additional hands were always welcome. His brothers certainly felt that way.

Lachlan, Aiden, and Justin all lived and worked on the station. In addition to the usual tasks that demanded their time, they'd been forced to add fence repairs to the list. With so many other things to attend to, they were making slow progress on the repairs. When Cayd had mentioned to them the previous evening about bringing the girls along to help, they were in full agreement.

"Don't forget to stay out of sight of the cameras," Cayd reminded them. "The producer wants everyone to think this is a one-man show. Apparently, in the city, they think that's how a cattle station's run."

Standing beside him, Lachlan nudged him in the ribs. "More likely she doesn't want her viewers to take a liking to me over you. That wouldn't be good at all. And I mean, how could they not?" He flexed his impressive muscles and grinned. "What's not to like about this?"

Cayd scoffed. "Get over yourself, Lachie. We all know I'm the best-looking Fairfax male in this family. As if any woman would prefer you over me."

Lachlan merely shrugged. "Need I remind you which one of us has actually had a girlfriend? Certainly not you."

Cayd was immediately on the defensive. "Hey! I've had a girlfriend! What about Emily?"

Lachlan laughed and shook his head. "Surely you're not counting your one and only love interest in high school? That was nearly a decade ago."

"So? That still counts. Besides, I've had my fair share of women. I've dated plenty since then. The last time I visited with Brock in Brisbane, we went out to a few bars. I couldn't keep the girls off me. I could have gone home with any number of them that night."

"And did you?" Justin's eyes gleamed with mischief.

Cayd waggled his eyebrows. "A Fairfax man never kisses and tells."

The four of them laughed. The camaraderie among his brothers was something Cayd treasured. The six of them were close in age, with only a year or two and a couple of sisters separating them. They'd grown up together, gone away to school together, and were now back home living and working on the family farm. Time spent with them like this, drinking beer, swapping stories, ribbing each other, was time he cherished. One day, there would be women in their mix—wives and girlfriends. Already, two of his brothers were married. And though Cayd was looking forward to joining them in that state and having a family of his own, he wouldn't give up the special relationship he had with his brothers for anything.

In the distance, he spied them working together on a fence. Lachlan, Justin, and Aiden, along with three young Aboriginal women who sometimes worked on the station, were busy running fencing wire through iron posts and tying it off. Cayd brought the quad bike to a halt and signaled to Olivia to do the same. She jerked to a sudden stop in a cloud of dust.

Behind them in the 4WD truck, Lily and her camera crew also came to a halt and got out. Within moments, the cameras were rolling. No doubt they'd edit his brothers and their helpers out of the final cut. Cayd climbed off the bike and made the introductions.

"Marissa, Chelsea, Olivia. Meet some of my brothers." He pointed to each one of them as he named them. The boys murmured greetings and tipped their hats.

"And this is Khloe, Zana, and Breeanna," Cayd added, introducing the Aboriginal girls.

Lily approached the girls, her face alight with curiosity. "Do you live here on the station?"

Khloe answered. "No. We're from Rockhampton. We come out here a few times a year for a week at a time to learn about working on a station."

"They're part of a government program," Cayd explained. "Local station owners provide opportunities for them to learn new skills. It's hoped that will ultimately increase their employment prospects."

"What kind of work do you do?" Lily asked, directing her question to the girls.

Once again, it was Khloe who answered. At nineteen, she was the oldest of the three and the most confident. "All sorts of things. Horse riding and grooming, feeding the animals. Sometimes we get to help muster and brand the cattle." She held up the pair of pliers in her hand. "Today, we're out fencing."

"Do you enjoy it?" Olivia asked, looking skeptical.

Khloe responded with a big smile that showed a row of straight white teeth. "Yeah. Of course. It's fun. We wouldn't keep coming back if we didn't enjoy it. Plus, it's going to help us get a job. My cousin was involved in the program last year. Now she's working as a jillaroo on a big place up north. She loves it."

Cayd grinned. "See? There you go, ladies. You never know where your fencing skills might take you. Now, who's ready to give it a go?"

For a moment, he thought Lily was going to volunteer. Then, as if remembering herself, she stepped back and folded her arms across her chest. Cayd went to the back of his bike and fetched the fencing gear he'd stowed there. Upon his return, his gaze was drawn to the producer. She stood where he'd left her, a naked look of yearning filling her face.

He blinked in surprise, confused about what had put it there. Then she gave her head a quick shake and the look disappeared and he was left to wonder if he'd imagined it.

As if sensing his scrutiny, she glanced in his direction and frowned. A moment later, she averted her gaze and looked around her distractedly. He wished he knew what she was thinking.

He swallowed a sigh and moved toward his women. It didn't surprise him that Chelsea was the first to step up and volunteer. She took a set of pliers off him and snapped them open and closed.

"Okay, what do I do with these?" she asked.

"Why don't you let Khloe show you?" Cayd suggested.

The Aboriginal girl grinned. She looked at Chelsea. "Follow me."

The two of them set off together a little farther up the fence line. Cayd turned his attention to Marissa and Olivia. Both girls looked less than impressed at the idea of manual labor. Given the length of their fingernails, Cayd could well understand why.

"Marissa, how about you run the wire with Aiden?"

Marissa frowned. "Run the wire? What does that mean?"

"It means you stand on either side of the fence and hold that pole." He pointed to a steel pole with spool of wire in the middle of it. "Then you both walk forward, and the wire unravels as you go. Olivia and I will come behind you and tie it off."

Marissa pouted. "Why can't *I* tie it off?"

Cayd had no doubt Marissa didn't care for either job, but she wouldn't overlook an opportunity to spend time with him. Since the one-on-one time he'd spent with Chelsea, Marissa had been even more determined to stick close.

"No. Cayd asked *me* to tie the wire off with him," Olivia said, her chin set at a stubborn angle.

Cayd couldn't care less which of the ladies he worked with, but he'd chosen Olivia, and from the look of determination on her face, she wasn't prepared to give up her opportunity. He liked her sudden show of spunk.

"Okay. That's settled. Let's get going."

The cameramen followed a short distance behind them. No doubt they were getting all the close-ups and wide angles they needed. He hoped they were at least capturing some good footage of the station. Scenery that might inspire travelers to come out and take a look at what the outback had to offer, particularly if he managed to get his farm stay project off the ground. After all, that was the main reason he'd signed up for this frivolity.

With that thought in mind, he glanced over to where Lily stood a short distance away.

"Keep doing what you're doing," he said to Olivia. "I'll be back in a minute."

With that, he tucked the pliers into the back pocket of his jeans and sidled up to the producer.

"There's a good view of the Carnarvon Range from here," he said.

She nodded. "Yes. I didn't expect the place to be so beautiful. When I think of the outback, I think of hot, dry, red dust with hardly a blade of vegetation to be seen, but this place is like an oasis. It's so much greener than I expected."

"It's not always like this. We had a flood earlier this year. Before that, we were in drought. This ground was as bare as the Chinese elms in my mother's garden in wintertime."

She looked around her. "That's so hard to imagine now. It's amazing what a good flood will do."

He grimaced. "Yes. It has its benefits. Then again, we wouldn't have suffered all this damage to our fences if the floodwaters hadn't rushed through here like they did."

She stared at him. "It's a tough life out here, isn't it? Droughts, floods, isolation. How do people live out here?"

Chapter Nine

♥

ayd laughed. The deep, rich sound of it did strange things to Lily's insides. She resolutely ignored the feelings. It was bad enough that a short time earlier she'd had a moment of madness and wished she was one of Cayd's women. Thank God she'd managed to quell that ridiculous feeling almost as quickly as it had taken hold.

"Spoken like a true city slicker," Cayd replied. "Let me guess. You were born and bred in Sydney, and the only time you've ventured outside the city limits is for work. Am I right?"

She grinned reluctantly. "You're right. I've traveled to various farms during my five seasons on the show, but I've never been as far west as this. The other farms I visited were all much smaller and within an hour or so of a major city."

"I figured as much."

"You didn't answer my question."

Cayd tilted his head. "You mean the one about how people live out here?"

"Yes."

"You're right. It isn't easy. And yes, we get our fair share of droughts and floods, but they don't happen that often. As far as the isolation… I guess I'm used to it. I was born out here. I don't think of this place as being isolated. There are still a fair number of Fairfaxes living here, and we have plenty of neighbors we catch up with whenever we need outside company. Besides, Roma's only an hour away."

"Is that the thriving metropolis we flew into?" Her tone was as dry as sandpaper.

"Hey! There's at least five thousand people who live in and around that town!"

She chuckled. It was impossible not to. She didn't want to enjoy this man's company. She didn't want to notice how good-looking he was. She didn't want to notice how easy he was to get on with.

Despite the intrusion into his and his family's lives, he'd accepted their presence with equanimity and good manners. It wasn't easy having every moment of his life recorded and viewed by a national television audience, and even though he'd been very aware of what he'd signed up for, that didn't necessarily mean he'd fully understood or appreciated the impact it would have on his life.

In Lily's experience, the farmers grasped in theory the idea of being followed around by cameras all day, but for most of them, the reality of it came as rather an unpleasant surprise. She was sure Cayd was no different. Though he hid his irritation better than most, every now and then she caught flashes of annoyance on his face. She suspected that had more to do with the time that it took to shoot the scenes. Time that was taken from doing more productive tasks on the station. It was possible he was already regretting his decision to be part of the show.

One of her responsibilities as a producer was to keep the farmer happy. With that thought in mind, she recalled how he'd told her about his dream of setting up the station as a farm stay.

"Tell me more about your plans for bringing tourists out here," she encouraged.

He smiled briefly. "I'm trying to diversify our income. After suffering through three years of drought and then a flood and having our herd decimated, it became obvious we need another stream of income—one that isn't so susceptible to the weather. Knowing how special this place is, filled with so much natural beauty, I thought it might be somewhere we could encourage tourists to stop for a night or two and take a look."

"You're right. It's beautiful."

The station was set in a wide valley surrounded by rugged mountains. With the recent floods, the ground was carpeted with lush grasses, and spring had brought forth a flourish of colorful wildflowers, spread throughout the paddocks for as far as the eye could see. It certainly was a picture, and so different to the city landscape many a traveler would be used to.

"It has a vastness and wildness about it that would appeal to people unused to living so far from the city lights. As a city slicker, I can assure you, this place is worth visiting. How are you intending to get the word out about it? Through social media?"

"Actually, that's where you come in, remember?" Cayd grinned. "Or, at least, the TV show. I'm hoping after they see it, some of your viewers might be inspired to come out and take a peek."

She nodded. "That's right. You mentioned that when we were looking over the newly renovated shearers' quarters. You'll be pleased to know that over the past ten seasons, we've managed to raise the profile of every one of our farmers. Some of them have gone on to launch successful businesses. How many social media followers do you currently have?"

He looked abashed. "I don't know. Twenty or so. Most of them are family. I don't get a lot of time to spend on social media."

"That's got to change if you want to get the word out about your station. Besides, don't forget it's a term of your contract that you regularly engage with your followers on social media while the show's airing on TV."

He gave a self-conscious laugh. "All twenty of them."

"Trust me, that'll change as soon as the first show goes to air," she said confidently. "You won't be able to keep up with the engagement you're going to get, especially from all the young and not-so-young single women."

He blushed and looked away. His humility was endearing. She found herself smiling at him and then checked herself. He was just another farmer she'd been put in charge of. There was no need to build a rapport with him that went beyond what was required for her to deliver on the show. Feeling anything for him other than professional and polite interest was dangerous, and she needed to put a stop to such reactions.

"I'm hoping to add a few self-contained cabins that are large enough to accommodate families, along with the shearer's quarters," he said, seemingly oblivious to the turmoil going on inside her. "I also plan on clearing some ground near the billabong to be used as camping grounds."

He turned to look at her, his striking blue eyes shining with excitement. "There are so many possibilities."

She smiled. "I understand your enthusiasm. I feel the same way about my apartment. Every time I finish a room, I'm eager to start on the next. Choosing paint colors, soft furnishings, floor coverings... And then seeing the finished product. It all gives me such a rush."

"Have you ever thought about a career in interior decorating?"

She laughed. "All the time! But I love my job working on *Outback Bride*, and right now, I can't afford to give up secure employment and take a risk on my own."

"Life's all about taking risks. Nothing ventured, nothing gained. Right?"

"I guess."

"Taking on this farm stay project isn't risk-free. There's a chance I'll pour all this money into getting the station ready for paying guests and no one will come. But I have to try. The truth is, I'm impatient to make it happen. It would also be nice if I had someone to help me run it." He shot her a wry grin. "Who knows? Maybe my future bride will be interested. Can you see either Marissa or Olivia cleaning cabins and checking in guests?"

Lily's stomach twisted with jealousy. She forced a smile and shrugged. "Maybe. As long as it doesn't involve typing," she said lightly. "Those long fingernails might be an occupational hazard."

Cayd nodded. "True. Still, it's food for thought. Having someone by my side through all this would be great. Someone to share my hopes and dreams, my wins, my disappointments. That's what life's about, isn't it?"

"I guess." Her voice sounded strangled. She wasn't sure how much longer she could stand there and be part of the conversation. All she could think about was that she wanted to be the woman beside him, supporting him through the ups and downs. And that was plain crazy thinking.

She cleared her throat. "We're taking a break from filming this afternoon, remember? You're free to tend to whatever you need to do. We'll reconvene before the evening meal. Is that all right?"

His answering smile was enough to turn her insides to mush. She forced herself to look away, all the time admonishing herself for reacting to him that way. Too bad she couldn't duck away for a few hours and call her fiancé. It seemed the more time she spent with the gorgeous farmer, the less she thought about Alex, and that wasn't a good thing. Not a good thing at all.

The sun hung low in the sky when the roar of a motorbike in the distance brought Lily out of the guest cottage. She scanned the wide expanse of open land and saw Cayd astride a motorbike heading toward her, dust billowing behind him.

She'd spent the afternoon going over the rushes they'd already taken. Cayd was so photogenic. Those rugged good looks, the sexy smile. There was no doubt her viewers would fall in love with him. No wonder he dominated so many of her thoughts. Any woman with a heartbeat would be stirred at the sight of him.

It was a good thing she'd managed to put in a call to her fiancé. She desperately needed to reconnect. Unfortunately, Alex had been too busy with clients to take her call and she'd been forced to be satisfied with leaving a message. She was still waiting for him to call her back.

Cayd had disappeared on the motorbike after lunch, no doubt taking advantage of her earlier offer to release him from official filming duties. Now he was on his way back. From her vantage point near the front fence, she watched him ride in and took a moment to admire from a distance the fine form he cut.

Tall and straight in the seat, he swung the bike in a wide and graceful arc and brought it to a halt outside the shed. He cut the engine and kicked down the stand before pulling off his helmet and slinging it over the handlebars. Then he swung his long leg over the side and dismounted.

Unaware of her perusal, he unselfconsciously ran a hand through his sweaty hair and brushed the dust from his jeans. His sleeves were rolled up, exposing strong, tanned forearms. She wasn't sure how he'd spent his time away from them, but no doubt it had involved some kind of physical work.

She never thought she'd be attracted to an outdoors man who worked with his hands. Her whole life, she'd been surrounded by men who worked behind a desk, or at least indoors. Her parents had owned a café from the day she was born until they retired. Many of her earliest memories were of sitting in a playpen at the back of the shop.

None of her four younger brothers had expressed interest in doing anything that could be remotely described as outdoor work. And yet, seeing Cayd, so raw and earthy and in his element in the outback, did strange things to her insides. When he turned and began striding toward her, nerves rushed through her veins. She still hadn't fully recovered her equilibrium when he stepped up onto the veranda of the cottage.

"Well, hello." His greeting was followed by a slow and sexy smile.

A little lurch of awareness clutched at her belly. "How was your afternoon?" she squeaked.

His smile widened. "Busy, but good. I helped my brothers to vaccinate about a thousand head of cattle. Hot and dusty and mindless work, but not a single camera lens in sight. It doesn't get better than that."

He chuckled as if to let her know that his jibe about the cameras wasn't intended to offend.

She smiled back. "Sounds invigorating." She paused. "I thought you and your ladies might like to spend some time in the vegetable garden. We could get some footage of you all walking through the garden, gathering fresh produce for dinner. I'm sure our audience would love to see how self-sustainable you are out here, and it will give the women a chance to spend some more time with you. How does that sound?"

"Okay, I guess. Showcasing my mother's garden to your national TV audience can only be a good thing for my farm stay project."

"Don't forget, we need to keep any mention of your family out of the show for now," she reminded him. "Our viewers are falling in love with the idea of you living out here all alone. That's why you so desperately need a wife, right?"

She offered him another smile to let him know she was teasing. The look he gave her in return sent her pulse racing.

"Right," he responded in a sexy drawl. "I'm nothing but a lonely cattleman on a desperate quest to find a bride. Someone to share this paradise with. Someone to fill my empty nights."

His gaze intensified on hers. The air between them was suddenly electric. Her heart pounded. Heat spread over her cheeks. But for the life of her, she couldn't look away.

The moment was broken when Chelsea appeared from nowhere and flung herself at Cayd. He stumbled backward as she threw her arms around him.

"There you are! I've been looking everywhere for you!" She lowered her arms and pouted. "You've been neglecting me."

"I'm sorry," Cayd replied a little testily. "I had to do some farm work."

Still flustered from her unexpected and unwelcome reaction to him, Lily took the opportunity to escape. Turning her back on the two of them, she put some distance between them and surreptitiously did what she could to slow down her breathing. It was ridiculous how a single look could put her in such a spin. She was a mature woman of thirty-one, not some giddy teenager.

To her consternation, Cayd began walking toward her. Chelsea remained close, clinging to his side and chattering incessantly. Lily glanced over her shoulder. She could tell from the bored look on Cayd's face that he was hardly listening.

When Marissa and Olivia emerged from the homestead and joined them beneath the shade of the gum tree that grew near the front gate, his face flooded with relief.

"Where have you been, Cayd?" Olivia asked, pushing her red hair out of her eyes.

"You were gone so long. We missed you," Marissa added, pressing herself against him and stroking his bare forearm with her fingers. Cayd looked down at Marissa and smiled indulgently. "I wasn't gone that long."

Lily tamped down the surge of jealousy and forced herself to look away. Her reaction to the way Cayd treated his ladies was becoming downright annoying.

"What have you been up to?" Marissa asked as she linked her arm through his.

"Cattle work," Cayd supplied. "I might be on a quest to find a bride, but I'm a cattleman first and foremost. I hope my future wife realizes that."

Though he encompassed all three women with his gaze, it finally settled on Marissa. As if sensing he'd bestowed special importance on her, she gave him a brilliant smile and drew him away from the others. Not to be outdone, Olivia followed beside them. With a look of irritation, Chelsea hurried to keep up.

As Cayd led the girls away toward the vegetable garden, Lily filled her lungs to capacity and then eased out her breath. Her pulse rate had almost returned to normal. Something soft and warm nudged at her leg, and she looked down to discover Macey at her side.

Lily paused a moment and bent down to give the dog a pat. "How are you, girl?"

Macey wagged her tail. With her tongue hanging out of her mouth, it almost looked like she was smiling. As Lily followed the progress of Cayd and his ladies, she was pleased to see Marissa and Olivia taking a more proactive role in seeking his attention and interjecting themselves into the conversation every chance they got. It looked like her words of encouragement had rubbed off, and that was a good thing.

There was nothing suspenseful about knowing who the farmer was going to choose before the final scene had played out. Predictably, ratings took a nosedive when that had happened in the past. The last thing she needed was to be on the receiving end of a dressing-down from her boss and potentially put her job at risk.

With that grim thought in mind, she rustled up her crew. They caught up with Cayd and the women in the garden. When the cameras were in position, Lily gave the go-ahead for the filming to begin.

"Why don't you go over there and pick some of those green peas?" she suggested to the group.

Cayd and the women did as she asked. Olivia planted herself beside Cayd and peppered him with questions about how he'd spent his afternoon. She appeared fascinated as he described the process of vaccinating a large herd of cattle.

Whether she was truly interested in the farmwork or just interested in Cayd, Lily couldn't tell, but the woman's gaze didn't once leave his face.

As if in an effort to break the connection between Cayd and Olivia, Marissa grabbed a garden hose and started spraying water at the two of them. Olivia shrieked in outrage. Cayd merely laughed. Lily made sure the cameras were capturing the frivolity. Then Cayd snatched the hose out of Marissa's hands and turned it on her.

"Not fair!" she gasped as the water rained down upon her.

Cayd laughed again. "Hey, what's good for the gander is good for the goose."

"But you're *soaking* me!" Marissa sputtered with mock outrage.

It was true. Marissa's blouse was saturated and clung to her generous breasts, drawing everyone's gaze. Including Cayd's. Out of nowhere, Lily was struck with another spurt of jealousy. She scowled. She'd never been jealous of attention women had paid to Alex. No doubt it was because she trusted him implicitly. They'd known each other forever. There was no way he'd cheat.

Her frown deepened. *Is that the only reason?*

It troubled her that she didn't feel possessive toward her fiancé, like she'd claw out the eyes of any woman who flirted with him, or even attempted to. That's the way she felt about Cayd, and it was disturbing. She was jealous of the time the other girls got to spend with him. Jealous of the attention he paid to them. *Jealous, jealous, jealous.*

She swallowed a groan of irritation and forced the thoughts aside. It wasn't healthy for a woman engaged to someone else to be thinking about another man like that. She wouldn't contemplate any of it a moment longer. Besides, she was sure it was only because Cayd was so fun and sexy and good-humored. And lived on an amazing outback station in a gorgeous part of the world. And had farm animals like horses and dogs and chickens and pigs. And he was nice to be around.

It had been so long since she'd seen Alex or had fun with him. She needed to rearrange her schedule so that she could return to Sydney for a couple of days and catch up with him. Maybe she could plan a romantic getaway, just the two of them, so they could reignite their love and she could erase these stupid, traitorous feelings toward Cayd once and for all.

Chapter Ten

♥

Cayd woke to the sound of rain on the homestead's iron roof. Relaxing against the mattress, he sighed quietly in relief. Not only would the rain give the grass in the paddocks a new lease on life, but its presence meant he wouldn't be forced to spend all day with the women. A wet day on the station usually meant time spent in the office catching up on bookwork.

It had been nearly a month since he'd given attention to the reams of invoices and other paperwork that were a constant presence on his desk. He did his best to stay on top of it, but the past few days entertaining his guests and even before then, doing the prep work in anticipation of their arrival, meant that his office duties had been sorely neglected.

His mind sheared away from thinking about the extra paperwork involved if his farm stay project got off the ground. He could hire a bookkeeper, but that wasn't as easy as it sounded. They weren't exactly overrun with professionals in the outback. Even more reason to find a wife who not only set his world his fire, but who shared his dream for the future and was willing to help him.

"Let's hope I've already met her," he mumbled.

A crack of thunder jolted him from his thoughts. Blowing out his breath on another sigh, he fluffed up his pillow and then stacked his hands behind his head. The whole situation wouldn't be so challenging if he didn't have the hots for the producer. That had certainly complicated things. He wanted to form a genuine connection with at least one of the other girls, but thoughts of Lily kept interfering and putting him off his game. He wanted *her* to be the one hanging off his every word, wanting to spend time with him. He wanted *her* to be the one he got to have fun with, telling her stories about his day. And that just wasn't ever going to happen.

He couldn't help but wonder how solid she and her fiancé were. He hadn't noticed her on the phone every five minutes, but that didn't mean she didn't speak to the man for hours every night when she excused herself after dinner and escaped to the cottage. There was every chance she was counting down the days before she could return to Sydney and be by his side.

Lucky bastard.

Then again, she gave every appearance of enjoying her time in the outback. She'd been close by the whole time the women had been there. Okay, so it was her job to make sure every moment was captured, but she'd appeared to genuinely appreciate the vastness of the land, the sheer beauty of the landscape, and had shown real interest in various aspects of station life, including the pigs. Then there was that look of yearning he'd caught briefly on her face.

What's that about?

He wished he knew.

Why are women so complicated? Since when did the thought of entering into a relationship become such a daunting task?

It wasn't that he didn't believe in love. He'd been in love before. Okay, so he'd been a teenager, but so what? The feelings had been strong and real at the time. Besides, he'd watched his older brothers find their soul mates. His oldest brother, Raine, was so in love with his wife, Isabella, it was nauseating. They now eagerly awaited their first child. Cayd was almost as excited as they were at the thought of becoming an uncle. It had taken Raine's impending fatherhood for Cayd to realize he wanted kids of his own. All he had to do was find their mother.

More recently, his brother, Brock, had found the love of his life and had tied the knot with Kelsey in a romantic ceremony held in the bride's hometown of Tampa, Florida. After spending several months in the US, the two of them had recently made the decision to return to Brisbane and set up their lives there. Word had it that Kelsey's mother was also along for the ride.

Apart from that, Cayd didn't have to look any further than his parents to acknowledge that true love existed. Bob and

Ellen had been married for more than thirty years and were still very much in love. No, it wasn't because he didn't believe in love that he was feeling so pessimistic about the next week and a half. It was more that he didn't think any of his ladies stirred in him the kind of emotion that was required for that to happen.

While each of them possessed qualities he found attractive, it seemed none of them were "the one." Still, the show wasn't called *Outback Bride* for nothing. There was an expectation that he would continue to do whatever it took to form a lasting connection with at least one of them. One thing was certain, his contract made clear that choosing none of them wasn't an option.

Lily woke early and took a moment to enjoy the sound of rain falling gently outside her window. Her fourth-floor apartment back in Sydney was too high off the ground for her to hear the rain and the tile roof so far above her that listening to the rain had never been possible. But out here, in the peace and quiet of the outback, with a tin roof less than ten feet above her head, the steady pitter patter of raindrops was both loud and strangely soothing.

Then there was the smell. She'd slid open her window the evening before to let in some fresh air, and her bedroom was now filled with the sweet scent of wet grass and earth. She breathed in deeply, taking a moment to appreciate the crisp, clean air. No exhaust fumes, no smog. Just fresh, uncontaminated, rain-and-flower-scented air. No wonder people loved living out here.

The thought brought her up short. She'd always been a city girl. Had never contemplated life outside the city limits until she'd started working on *Outback Bride*. It was only after meeting various people through her job that she'd discovered a whole new world west of the heavily populated metropolitan areas. Even still, she'd never considered living so far from the city, but recently she'd begun to see the appeal.

One thing about the rain, it would wreak havoc on their filming schedule. No outdoor activities today. The paddock outside her window had already turned into a muddy mess and from the look of the heavy gray clouds, the rain wasn't going to abate anytime soon. Hopefully, Cayd had some board games on hand for just this very occasion. What else did he do on a rainy day?

Throwing off the covers, she padded barefoot into the kitchen, where she'd left her phone charging on the counter. She checked the screen and swallowed a sigh of disappointment. She'd called Alex again before going to bed and had once again been directed to his voicemail. She hated that when she needed him the most, he was unavailable to her.

No, that wasn't fair to Alex. He had no idea how much she was missing him on this trip. The irony was, he was used to her going away for weeks at a time and hardly checking in. She was normally too busy working to find the time to talk to him. If anything, he was the one who called.

But this trip was different. Though she was busy, her unwelcome attraction to Cayd meant that she was desperate to reconnect with her fiancé and reassure herself that being his wife was exactly what she wanted.

Of course, it's exactly what I want. What we both want. We've waited all our lives to be husband and wife. A fleeting attraction to a good-looking farmer isn't going to change that.

Heading back into the bedroom, she stripped off her pajamas and stepped into the shower. She'd always been an early riser, even when she was young. She loved getting up at least an hour before she had to be at school or work just so she could enjoy the quiet of the morning before anyone else was awake. Out here was no different. She might have the cottage to herself, but she still relished the idea of relaxing over a cup of coffee, inhaling the silence, gathering her thoughts, and organizing her day.

Throwing on a clean blouse—this one a blue-and-white check—and a fresh pair of jeans, she left the cottage and crossed the wide expanse of lawn to the homestead. She'd been assured there was always a fresh pot of coffee available whenever she wanted it. From the delicious smell emanating from the kitchen, today was no different.

She found Cayd's parents seated on barstools that had been pulled up to the kitchen counter. Both cradled large mugs of steaming coffee in their hands. They were alone in the room. The gloomy day had been brightened with an overhead light that cast a soft yellow glow around the room that created an air of intimacy.

Lily hesitated on the threshold, unwilling to intrude on their privacy. It was enough that they'd given up their house to strangers. Before she could beat a hasty retreat, Ellen looked up at her and smiled.

"Good morning, Lily. You're up early. Please, come in."

Lily smiled back. "Are you sure I'm not intruding?"

"Not at all."

Lily stepped farther into the room.

"Would you like some coffee?" Bob asked.

"Yes, that would be wonderful. It smells divine."

Cayd's father stood and poured Lily a cup and then handed it to her. "The sugar's in that small canister near the stove and there's milk in the fridge. Help yourself."

Lily murmured her thanks and after adding milk and sugar, took a grateful sip. "Oh, that's just what I needed. Thank you."

She took a vacant stool beside them. "And thank you for so generously opening your home to me and my crew. And the ladies. I really appreciate your cooperation, giving up your house for the show, and keeping out of the way. I promise you'll star on the small screen before too long. We like to wait until our farmers are down to the final two ladies before introducing the families. It's easier that way."

Bob shrugged. "Whatever you need. We're here to support Cayd. When he came to us about his plans to apply for the show, we encouraged him all the way. Not only did it sound like fun, we agreed with him that it could also be good for his new venture. Nothing like being all over national TV to rouse some interest." He winked.

Lily nodded. "I agree. I can tell you from experience that the rural areas we've featured in the past have experienced a real uptick insofar as tourism and the number of travelers passing through is concerned. People fall in love with the area on TV and want to see it for themselves."

"The rain's a good thing too," Bob said. "It will green everything up again. The outback is a picture in a good season. Much more appealing to tourists."

Lily commiserated. "From what I've been told, you've had some tough years. Three years of drought, followed by a flood. That must have been hard."

Ellen nodded. "Yes. It's a tough life. Not for the faint-hearted, but if you can take the ups and downs, it can be incredibly rewarding."

"I can see that," Lily said. "The sheer hard work that goes into running such a vast operation and yet, the rewards are also there. Increasing your stock numbers after those natural disasters, bringing the station back to life. Providing training and job opportunities for those who might not otherwise have the chance. I can see why Cayd loves it out here."

Ellen regarded her thoughtfully. "How's the cottage? Are you comfortable enough?"

"Oh, gosh yes! It's delightful! So homey. Not at all what I expected."

Both Bob's and Ellen's gazes sharpened on hers.

"What did you expect?" Ellen asked in a neutral tone.

Lily blushed. "Oh, please don't think I'm judging you. That's not what I meant at all. It's just that, being so far away from everything..."

Her words petered off. Best to stop talking right now before she embarrassed herself further. To her relief, Ellen took pity on her.

"You mean, being so far away from the creature comforts of the city, you weren't sure if the accommodations would be up to scratch. Don't worry, we understand. Most city folk have no idea how well we live out here."

Lily eased out her breath and smiled again. "Absolutely! When I first heard that I was heading to outback Queensland where the nearest town was an hour's drive away and that town only the size of a postage stamp, I didn't know what I was in for. I imagined no electricity other than generators, no running water, no indoor loo. I was ready for the challenge, but I won't pretend I wasn't relieved to discover life out here wasn't quite so archaic as I'd imagined."

Bob smiled indulgently toward his wife. "Don't worry. This place wasn't always so civilized. When Ellen first came out here more than thirty years ago as my bride, we didn't have running water or an indoor toilet. Same went for electricity.

We had a generator, but diesel fuel was expensive, so we only ran it when we had to, which was at night."

"We had a wood stove back then," Ellen continued, "so we didn't need electricity to cook meals. All we used it for was to provide enough light to eat and clean up after the evening meal. Then we switched it off and spent most of the time sitting in darkness by the fire."

"Yes," Bob added. "And in the summer, when it was too hot to light a fire, we'd sit outside on the veranda and enjoy the evenings. Or we'd turn in early." He winked.

Lily fought off another blush and slowly shook her head. "That sounds so romantic."

Ellen gave her husband a tender smile. "It *was* romantic. Sometimes I miss those days. No TV. No distractions. More time spent together, talking, sharing our hopes and dreams. I think that's what brought us closer. We only had each other to rely on and no one else for company until the children arrived."

"Weren't you lonely?" Lily asked.

Ellen shrugged. "I guess I was lonely at times, but not enough that it bothered me. I had Bob and, later, the children. I didn't need anyone else."

Lily wasn't sure whether Alex would ever be able to fulfill all her needs like that. She enjoyed an active social life that included not only her fiancé, but her friends. She was a regular on the social scene, most often the one who organized the parties and other events that filled her calendar when she was home. It was hard to imagine just her and Alex and, God willing, their children being enough to fill that space.

"Of course, that doesn't mean life out here is easy."

Ellen's comment drew Lily out of her reverie. "I can imagine you've had some difficult times," she murmured.

"You right," Ellen agreed. "It can get tough and the isolation isn't for everyone. It's important to have the right person by your side." She flicked Lily a sideways glance. "I've met Cayd's ladies. I'm concerned he might choose a girl who's not suited to this life."

"He's not obligated to make a lifelong commitment to any of them," Lily hurried to assure her. "All he's contracted to do is to choose one of the three for now for the benefit of our television audience. Of course, it's great for ratings if the couple genuinely falls in love, but that doesn't always happen, and neither is it expected. Don't worry. Cayd won't be forced into doing anything he doesn't want to."

Ellen gave her a curious look. "Are you married, Lily?"

Lily lifted her left hand and flashed her ring. "Engaged."

Ellen smiled briefly. "Congratulations. When are you getting married?"

Lily flushed and lowered her gaze. For some reason, she didn't want to admit she hadn't yet set a date. "Um, I'm not sure."

"How long have you been engaged?" Bob asked.

Lily silently cursed their curiosity. "Three years," she said as casually as she could manage.

Ellen's eyes went wide. She tilted her head to one side and gave Lily a searching look. "What's holding you back from making it official?"

On his way toward the kitchen, Cayd heard his mother's question and paused, curious to hear Lily's answer. He'd heard her talking with his parents, and knowing she was there had spurred him out of bed. Not wanting to waste time changing out of his sweatpants, he'd made a beeline for the kitchen so he could speak to her before she left. Now he waited out of sight for her response. Guilt pricked at his conscience for eavesdropping, but he couldn't for the life of him step away and reveal himself until he heard her answer.

"I'm not sure what's holding me back," she said slowly, as if choosing her words with care. "I don't think there's anything in particular. We're not in a rush. We're both busy at work. My fiancé is working toward a partnership in his accountancy firm, and for the past five years I've been flying all over the country with my job. It's hard to find the time to plan a wedding."

Cayd wasn't sure if her answer put him at ease or not, but it wasn't right for him to continue to eavesdrop on what Lily thought was a private conversation. Coughing loudly to warn her of his imminent arrival, he stepped into the kitchen and smiled.

"Good morning! How is everyone today?"

Lily flushed at the sight of Cayd. His sweatpants hung low on his narrow hips. The vast swathe of tanned, naked chest snatched her breath. With an effort, she averted her gaze and took refuge in her coffee.

She wasn't sure how much of the conversation he'd heard. Not that she had anything to hide, but still... Talking about her fiancé and why they weren't already married was a subject she was uncomfortable with. Not only with Cayd's parents, but everyone. It seemed everybody she met had an opinion on how long their engagement should be and most people she came across were surprised she and Alex had been engaged so long. Particularly her parents.

She understood their confusion. She and Alex had known each other forever. What were they waiting for? Still, the pressure to make things official only filled Lily with panic. It always had. So far, she'd refused to analyze why that was, and she wasn't about to begin now. Not with Cayd standing a mere few feet away from her, looking way sexier than any man at this hour of the morning had a right to look.

Though his striking blue eyes were clear and bright and twinkling with good humor, his thick, dark hair was rumpled from sleep and a three-day growth shadowed his cheeks. The sweatpants looked like they'd been slept in. An image of him in bed flashed through her mind. Heat exploded across her cheeks. She looked away again, but not before she caught Ellen's eye. A knowing look crossed the other woman's face.

Lily flushed again, climbed off her stool, and turned away on the pretext of getting more coffee. When she couldn't put off looking at him any longer, she drew in a deep breath and spoke.

"What are your plans for today? We're not going to be able to film outside in the rain. Do you have any board games?"

Cayd shrugged. "Probably. You'll have to ask Mum. I've never really been into board games. Besides, I need to spend a day in the office. I'm falling behind on the bookwork."

Lily ignored a stab of disappointment. "What about the girls?"

"They'll have to amuse themselves today. I'm sure you'll think of something to keep them occupied."

"I guess we could do some individual interviews. See how they're liking the station so far." She paused and then sent Cayd an impish grin. "See how they're liking their farmer."

He chuckled and didn't seem at all uncomfortable with her question. She wondered if that was because he was already confident in his appeal with the ladies, or whether he didn't care less either way how they felt about him. Either scenario required further contemplation. Perhaps she could probe the women for answers...

"Okay," she said. "I'll let the ladies know that we'll be doing a question-and-answer session with each of them and then they can take the rest of the day off. I take it you don't want them disturbing you in the office?"

Cayd nodded. "You have that right. I need a few hours of deep concentration to get done what I need to, and interruptions can be irritating. I'll let you know when I come up for air and it's safe to be around me again."

"Don't forget you need to spend some individual time with the girls."

"I've already spent alone time with Chelsea. Isn't that enough?"

"There's still Olivia and Marissa. They're entitled to your undivided attention too."

"But I still have a week and a half to go before filming ends," Cayd protested.

"Yes, but you also need to send one of the ladies home by the end of this week," Lily reminded him. "Our viewers need to see that you've given each of the girls an equal amount of your time. That's very important."

"Can't you edit things to make it look like that?"

"We'll certainly be doing some editing. At the end of the day, I'm paid to come up with the best show I can, but we need the footage first. If you can spare any time at all today, I'd like you to make an effort to spend some alone time with at least one of the other girls. Do you think you can do that?"

Cayd nodded and sighed. "Sure. I'll do my best."

"Great."

Lily hid her smile, but a part of her was unreasonably pleased that Cayd wasn't overly eager to spend time alone with any of his ladies. It was wrong of her to find pleasure in that, but she couldn't help it, and that worried her more than anything.

Chapter Eleven

♥

The sound of the rain as it continued to fall outside Cayd's office window brought a smile to his face. It was the most rain they'd had for months. Already, he could see a green tinge across the paddocks. No doubt the dams were filling up. It was a good feeling knowing they had secure feed and water for the next little while at least.

Reaching for his coffee mug, he discovered it was empty. "Damn."

He'd been there for three hours and had made decent headway. He'd sorted through the pile of invoices and had set up electronic payments. He'd also entered income receipts into the accounting software and had paid the wages. All in all, he was pleased with his progress, despite the fact his thoughts had kept returning to Lily and the conversation he'd overheard.

He was more pleased than he should have been that she wasn't in a rush to get married, but that made him wonder about her fiancé and why the guy wasn't hastening her down the aisle. There was no way Cayd would want to give her the chance to change her mind. He'd have set the date the same night he proposed.

It was obvious the guy was so secure in Lily's love and commitment that it didn't matter that they'd been engaged for three years with no wedding date in sight. Cayd sighed. It must be nice to know that kind of love, that kind of confidence in the other person's feelings. So far, he couldn't imagine experiencing that kind of certainty with any of his ladies. Definitely not with Chelsea. She was already in the friend zone. Their kiss had proven that. But even Marissa and Olivia had so far failed to stir him in the way he expected a soul mate would.

I need to give myself a chance to get to know them better. After all, I barely know anything about either of them. They could say the same thing about me. How are we supposed to fall in love with each other when none of us knows how the other ticks?

If he spent more time with them as Lily suggested, opened his heart to the possibility that one of them could be "the one," then he might begin to see things differently. Okay, so Chelsea was already out of the running, but there were two other contenders. Spending time with them and getting to know them better certainly couldn't hurt, and after all, the whole point of the TV show was to find a bride.

He was filled with a sudden spurt of determination. He had two beautiful ladies to choose from and they were there right now, on his farm. All he had to do was give them a little attention, share something of himself, perhaps a kiss and a cuddle, and see what developed. It might not work. Then again, it could. There was only one way to find out.

With that thought in mind, he collected his coffee mug and rounded his desk. He opened the door to his office and stepped blindly out into the hallway and slammed straight into Lily, who let out a yelp of surprise and flailed her arms as she came precariously close to falling over.

"Shit. I'm so sorry. Are you all right?"

His arms came around her automatically, and he held her firmly against him until she'd regained her balance. He tried not to think about how good she felt in his arms. In fact, he tried not to think at all.

Lily wriggled out of Cayd's arms and stepped away from him. Her face burned with a combination of awareness and embarrassment.

"I'm fine, I'm fine," she mumbled, keeping her gaze firmly fixed on the floor.

The feel of his strong chest pressed against hers even for a few moments was branded on her brain. The brief contact had set her heart racing and it was all she could do to get her breathing under control. Right now, it felt like she'd run a marathon.

She hadn't expected him to step out of his office at the exact same moment she'd gone there to see if he wanted to take a break. He'd disappeared hours earlier, and with nothing much to do but hang around in the house, she'd missed his company.

She'd been about to knock on his door when he'd appeared from nowhere. He'd plowed right into her without warning and had given her no time to step aside. It had felt like she'd run into a brick wall. All solid muscle and firm flesh. Then his arms had come around her, and she'd been drawn tightly against that wall of masculinity. The memory left her feeling weak.

His biceps had bulged. His pectorals had flexed. His T-shirt had been soft against her cheek. He smelled of some kind of spicy cologne that filled her head in the moments before she forced herself to pull away. Now she had to look him in the eye and pretend her equilibrium hadn't just been shot to hell.

Her mind floundered around for something to say. Belatedly, she noticed the coffee mug in his hand.

"Let me guess. You're out of coffee."

The comment was so awkward, so banal, she almost cringed, but at least it gave her something else to focus on.

He held up the mug and grinned. "Yes."

"You're in luck. Your mother just made a fresh pot."

"Sounds like it was good timing on my part. I've just finished paying the bills for another month. Time for a break."

She sighed. "I know how that feels."

"What?"

"Paying the bills. My parents used to own a small business. A café in Sydney. They worked seven days a week. They were always worried about paying the bills."

Cayd nodded. "It's not fun, particularly when money's scarce. Believe me, I know what that's like. We just went through some hard times. We came close to losing the station. Thank goodness we were able to get a cash injection, enough to keep us going until we can get back on our feet."

"It's a hard life," she said softly.

"Yeah, it is," he agreed just as softly, "but it's also a good life. There's nothing like working with your hands, building something for the future, something that will last, that can be handed down. We can trace our family all the way back to the original cattle barons."

His gaze took on a faraway look. "I want to do my bit to keep that story going. I want to raise my own family right here on the station, teach my kids about rural life. The ups and downs, highs and lows. That's life. I wouldn't want to be anywhere else."

She gazed at him, her mind filling with wonder. "You really love it, don't you?"

His expression remained somber. "Yes, I do."

Their gazes caught and held. Moments passed. Emotion flared in his eyes. Her palms turned sweaty. Her heart skipped a beat and then pounded a frantic tattoo against her chest. The moment was broken when Cayd's mother appeared in the hallway, a tea towel in her hand.

"Oh, there you are," Ellen said, taking a few steps toward them. "I was just coming to tell you I've made a fresh pot of coffee. There's also tea cake fresh from the oven. Would you like some?"

Cayd smiled and spoke in an even voice, as if the turmoil of the past few moments had never been.

"Thanks, Mum. Sounds great. We'll be there in a minute."

Ellen nodded and turned away, disappearing the way she'd come. Cayd started walking down the hallway. A bit miffed he could dismiss what had just happened so easily, Lily drew in a deep breath, straightened her shoulders, and, pretending a nonchalance she was far from feeling, hurried to catch up with him. Together, they walked into the kitchen. The smell of freshly baked cake made her mouth water.

A perfect English tea cake stood on a large round platter. Beside it was a knife and some smaller serving plates.

"Oh, Ellen. This looks delicious," she said with a grin.

Ellen shrugged and grinned. "I thought you might like something to go with your coffee. Besides, Cayd loves tea cake." She winked at her son. "Right, Cayd?"

"You know me too well, Mum."

All of a sudden, the kitchen was filled with Cayd's ladies as they crowded around the counter to look at the cake.

"We could smell that all the way from the living room," Olivia said.

"What kind of cake is it?" Marissa asked.

Ellen kindly informed her. "Do you bake?" Cayd's mother asked.

Marissa blushed. "Um, no. Isn't that what bakeries are for?"

Unperturbed, Ellen turned to the other two girls. "What about you, Olivia? Chelsea? Surely, one of you must know how to bake."

"Afraid not," Olivia mumbled. "I failed Food Tech in high school."

"Baking never interested me," Chelsea said dismissively. "I'd rather paint."

"At least you have some creative instincts," Ellen replied. "What kind of things do you paint?"

"Landscapes, mostly. I'm no good with faces. Same thing for animals. I just can't get the emotion right. That's why I stick with landscapes. There's no emotion in a mountain range."

"Then you haven't seen enough of the Carnarvon Ranges," Ellen said. "Especially right before sunset. It's like they're ablaze with fire." She paused and then added a little wistfully, "I wish I could paint."

Cayd put his arm around her shoulders and gave her a squeeze. "You don't have to be good at everything, Mum. Who needs to paint when they can bake like you?"

Everyone laughed. Ellen smiled at him. "You're a real charmer, you know that? You get that from your father."

While Ellen served up the cake, Lily went around and filled coffee mugs. When she got to Cayd, her hand trembled slightly at his nearness, but thankfully, she managed the job without spilling anything on either of them.

She drew him away from the crowd and lowered her voice. "What are your plans for this afternoon?"

"I'm going to spend some alone time with Marissa."

Lily tried not to let his words affect her. Something in her demeanor must have given her away.

Cayd frowned. "What? Isn't that what you've been telling me to do? Arrange some one-on-one time with my ladies?"

She flushed and looked away. "Y-yes, of course. That's exactly what we need. Just give me a few moments to get the crew organized. Don't say anything to Marissa yet. We need to get the cameras rolling first so we can capture the entire scene."

His lips twisted. "Of course. Alone time means alone with my lady of choice and you and the camera crew." He shot her a wry grin that did funny things to her insides.

She forced herself to grin back. "That's as alone as it gets."

He winked. "Whoever said five's a crowd didn't know what they were talking about."

She tried hard to stop her heart fluttering from his way-too-sexy grin. A whiff of his spicy cologne reached her nostrils, reminding her of their up-close-and-personal moment outside his office. Bombarded with memories, she stepped back, flustered.

"I better go and find the crew," she murmured.

Setting the coffee pot down on the kitchen counter, she beat a hasty retreat.

Cayd stared after Lily as she disappeared into the living room and then made a conscious effort to avert his gaze. His pulse still thumped in his ears after their encounter outside his office. It was so stupid to react like that. She wasn't one of his girls. More than that, she was well and truly taken. He needed to forget about how much he connected with her on so many levels, how she filled him with an unfamiliar yearning, and focus on his ladies. Starting with Marissa.

After finishing his coffee and setting his mug in the sink, he walked over to the window that looked out onto the backyard. He slid open the glass. The rain had eased to a slow drizzle. Though the sky was still dreary and gray, the temperature outside was quite pleasant. Definitely warm enough that he could take Marissa outside for some of that coveted one-on-one time Lily kept insisting on.

He wasn't sure that any amount of alone time with his ladies would change his mind, but going through the motions was a term of his contract and after all, they were only four days in. Way too early to decide that none of his girls would make the final cut. He owed to it everyone to give it his best shot.

With that thought in mind, he summoned up a vestige of enthusiasm and wandered into the living room. Lily and her camera crew had set up their equipment and were already filming. The girls had taken their cake and coffee there and were now sprawled out on the floor playing a card game.

Lily looked up and saw him and made her way over to where he stood. "So, you're going to invite Marissa to go for a walk or something?"

A whiff of her expensive-smelling perfume wafted toward him. He turned his face away. "Given that it's still raining, we'll probably just sit on the back veranda and talk. Will that suffice?"

"That sounds fine." She waited for the cameramen to stop filming and then said, "Guys, if you can focus on Cayd right now, that would be great." After they'd done as she'd requested, she nodded toward Cayd. "Go ahead, Cayd."

He cleared his throat. "Um, Marissa. Would you like to step outside with me for a few minutes?"

Marissa's face lit up. "I'd love to."

At the same time, disappointment clouded Olivia's expression. Chelsea also looked glum. Cayd bit his lip. He hated to see the women look so down, but there was nothing he could do about it. They all knew how the TV show worked.

The fact that he'd already decided to send Chelsea home also weighed heavily on his conscience. He forced the feeling aside. Someone had to be the first. Too bad it was up to him to dash someone's dreams. Now that the moment had become a reality, it was harder than he'd thought.

Oblivious to his thoughts, Marissa unfolded herself from the floor and stood. She wore a brief pair of denim shorts that showcased her long, toned legs. Her tank top clung to her generous cleavage, reminding him how physically attractive she was. All he needed was to connect with her emotionally and things would be dandy.

As she bounced toward him with a wide grin, he sent up a silent prayer that their time alone would be fruitful.

Lily followed Cayd and Marissa out to the back veranda. While the two of them got cozy on a love seat, she busied herself issuing directions to her crew. There was no doubt Marissa was a beautiful woman and knew how to dress to make the most of her assets. Lily wouldn't be surprised if Cayd chose her as his final one.

An instant and unwelcome surge of jealousy poured through her. Once again, she was disturbed by her feelings, and once again, she was just as determined to ignore them. While the cameras started rolling, Marissa started chatting about how much she liked the farm.

"What do like about it?" Cayd asked, appearing to be genuinely interested.

Marissa smiled. "I like everything about it."

Cayd lifted an eyebrow. "The heat? The flies? The dust? The isolation?"

Marissa giggled. "Okay, well, maybe not everything." She paused and scooted closer, then reached out and stroked Cayd on his bare forearm. "I just like being here with you. I like you, Cayd. I like you a lot."

Lily held her breath while she waited for Cayd's response. It came sooner than expected.

"I like you too."

Though it pained Lily to do so, she had a job to do. "How about a kiss, guys?"

Cayd's gaze locked onto hers. He shot her an inscrutable look. Lily flushed and looked away, unable to bear the questions she saw in his eyes. Then he shrugged imperceptibly, reached out and cupped his hand around Marissa's cheek. Slowly, their heads drew closer until finally, their lips touched. Lily looked away again, her face blazing.

What's wrong with me? Why do I care that he kisses another girl? Of course he's going to kiss his ladies. That's what this is all about. He's searching for a bride.

The feelings coursing through her were strange and disconcerting. Five seasons behind her and she'd never been affected like this. She was proud of the fact that all five of her previous farmers were still in a relationship with the women they'd chosen on the show. Four of the five had popped the question and three had already walked down the aisle. She couldn't be happier for them and the small part she'd played in their love matches.

So what was it about Cayd that made her wish *she* was one of the girls competing for his attention? That was crazy thinking. It made her head spin. She could only put it down to the fact that she'd barely spent any time with Alex these past months. It seemed she was always busy with preproduction, visiting possible locations, meeting farmers and their families, and then the actual filming.

This season, the farms were spread out across four states and though she'd only been assigned to Cayd, the fact she lived in Sydney and his station was located in a remote part of Central Queensland meant that there was lots of time spent commuting to airports and waiting for flights. Alex was busy too, with tax returns, financial statements, profit and loss calculations. She wasn't exactly sure what all of that contained, but she'd seen how tired and stressed and distracted he usually was this time of year.

Coupled with her chaotic schedule, none of that was conducive to good conversation and reconnecting. She needed to make a bigger effort on that score. She'd already given some thought to a short romantic getaway. Now she was determined to put that into action. She could give the crew a couple of days off and fly home for the weekend and surprise Alex. Hopefully, he could get the time off too. They could leave the world behind them for a couple days. That should do the trick.

Chapter Twelve

♥

Cayd moved his lips over Marissa's and tried to block out everything but the woman in his arms. It felt weird kissing someone with Lily and her crew looking on, to say nothing of the fact that a camera recorded every moment.

Okay, so he knew the whole purpose of the show was to find true love and a happily ever after—or at least, a happy-for-now—but he hadn't thought about how that would actually play out. Certainly, French kissing someone he barely knew for the whole world to see had never entered his mind.

With an effort, he shut out all other thoughts and concentrated on the kiss. Marissa's lips were full and soft and supple. She tasted of cinnamon and sugar, no doubt from the tea cake. The kiss was perfectly pleasant. His body reacted instinctively. Marissa's hand stole down and grazed his erection. She pulled back slightly. Her smile widened into a knowing grin.

Shit.

He wasn't sure how he felt about her. He didn't want to give her too much encouragement just in case she wasn't his final choice, but he had no control over his physical reaction to her nearness, particularly with her lips on his, her breasts brushing across his chest, and her tongue deftly stroking the inside of his mouth.

Lily woke the next morning feeling tired and irritable. She'd spent the night tossing and turning. In between, her dreams had been filled with a certain sexy, blue-eyed cattleman. It annoyed her to know that even in sleep, Cayd invaded her personal thoughts. No doubt that had something to do with the phone conversation she'd had with Alex the night before.

Though her fiancé had sounded pleased to hear from her, when she'd suggested they steal a couple of days away for themselves that coming weekend, his enthusiasm had dimmed.

"I'm too busy to go anywhere at the moment, Lily. I'm snowed under at work and if I want any hope of getting that partnership, I need to spend every waking moment at my desk."

"Surely not *every* waking moment," she'd teased, disguising her hurt behind a flippant tone.

"You know what I mean." His reply had been brusque, dismissive. She heard papers rustling and could tell his focus had already shifted to his work.

In an effort to hold his attention and cajole him out of his bad mood, she'd spent the next few minutes regaling him with stories about the outback, Marlowe Downs, and the Fairfax family. He'd made only vague responses and didn't once ask about the potential brides.

She was miffed at his apparent lack of interest in her job. After all, that was the main reason they spent so much time apart. It was also out of character. Normally, Alex loved hearing about the escapades the farmers and their city guests got up to around the farm. Their adventures were usually so far removed from his life, he took pleasure hearing about a world he could only imagine.

They'd ended the call with renewed declarations of love, but for Lily, the words had fallen flat. She didn't feel the usual yearning to be by his side or to extend the conversation long into the night. It left her feeling disgruntled and confused. She'd eventually fallen asleep still feeling out of sorts. No wonder she'd woken up in such an irritable mood.

Not that she had the luxury of sleeping late or doing anything other than putting on a happy face and getting on with her day. It was day five of the first week. In two days, Cayd would be sending one of his ladies home. He had yet to spend any time alone with Olivia. Lily needed to ensure this happened before Sunday afternoon. She had to do all she could to keep the viewers guessing about who the unfortunate lady Cayd bid farewell to would be. If he hadn't even had personal time with Olivia, it would be natural for the audience to assume she was the one being sent home.

With a groan, she stretched and then climbed out of bed and took a quick, invigorating shower. A peek out the window assured her the rain of the day before had dissipated, leaving a bright and sunny day in its wake. The smell of orange blossoms from the nearby Murraya tree wafted through the window, filling the room with sweet scent. She breathed in deeply and, not for the first time, marveled at the fresh, clean air.

She found Cayd and his ladies in the kitchen, eating a hearty breakfast of bacon, sausages, and eggs. A pile of buttered toast stood high on a plate.

"Someone's been busy," she commented.

"Help yourself," Cayd invited as she walked up to where he stood near the kitchen counter.

She smiled to hide the sudden rush of nerves his presence evoked. Snatches of her dreams from the previous night floated through her mind. In one of them, Cayd stood before her shirtless, all tanned and toned flesh, skin gleaming from sweat. She blushed and averted her gaze, praying frantically for the heat in her cheeks to subside before he noticed.

Busying herself at the counter, she filled a plate with food and took a seat at one end of the table, beside Nigel. The sound and lighting guys were on Nigel's left. Marissa and Chelsea were seated opposite. Olivia was nowhere in sight.

Lily greeted the two women with a friendly smile. "Good morning, ladies. How did you sleep?"

Marissa's smile was wide and instant. "Great! It's so peaceful out here. How could anyone not sleep well?"

Her gaze zeroed in on Cayd and paused on him for what seemed like eons. Though Cayd remained apparently absorbed in washing his plate up at the sink, Lily couldn't help but wonder if the farmer had made a nocturnal visit to the woman after the rest of the household had gone to bed.

Chelsea's loud groan drew Lily's attention away from Marissa and ended her speculation.

"I had a mosquito buzzing around my ears half the night," Chelsea complained.

"Oh, you poor thing!" Lily commiserated and then asked, "Where's Olivia?"

Marissa gave a half shrug. "She ate earlier. I think she went outside."

"Who cooked breakfast?" Lily asked, tucking into her bacon and eggs.

"Ellen," Chelsea replied. "She's such a sweetie."

Lily glanced at Nigel, who held up a hand. "Don't worry. We made sure she stayed out of the shot. We've done an excellent job of making the audience believe that these ladies are top-notch chefs. Right, Max?" Nigel winked at the sound technician, who grinned.

"Right," Max replied. "That's what this is all about, isn't it? Making sure the ladies are shown in their best light? We need to get fans rooting for them, don't we? Isn't that one of the things that drives the ratings up?"

Lily nodded. "You bet. You won't believe how popular the kitchen scenes are on social media. They spark discussion and debate like nothing else. Most of our viewers want the ladies to have some sort of culinary skills. It's like they forget that these farmers have been living solo for years and must have had the opportunity by now to learn how to cook themselves a meal."

"It never ceases to amaze me how many of our viewers want the girls to take a more traditional role on the farm. I thought that thinking went out of style decades ago," Nigel observed.

Lily, who loved cooking for her family and knew her mother still derived a good deal of pleasure serving up meals to her husband and children, laughed.

"Surely, we shouldn't still be governed by other people's ideas of what roles women should and should not play in their family? If you ask me, that's the kind of thinking that's archaic. These days, a woman should be allowed to choose whatever makes her happy, right?"

"Right," Cayd agreed, joining in the conversation. He shifted closer to the table and then propped a hip against one corner, disturbingly close to where Lily sat.

Flustered, she took refuge in her breakfast. Filling her mouth with food, she chewed slowly. To her consternation,

Cayd waited until she'd swallowed before asking his next question.

"So, tell me, Lily. Are you a feminist?"

She narrowed her eyes at him. "You say that like it's something to be ashamed of."

"No, not at all," he said hurriedly. "I'm all for feminism. I fully support equality between the sexes, and I believe women should be allowed to be whatever they want to be. I have four sisters. Every one of them is pursuing their dreams career-wise, and not a single member of my family has voiced opposition to that. In fact, quite the opposite. We're all completely in support of them doing whatever makes them happy. I guess you and I are on the same page about that."

Cayd's blue eyes were intent on hers. She flushed and once again cursed the heat that crept across her face. She didn't want to be on the same page about anything with Cayd. In fact, the less they had in common, the better. That way, she might not be tempted to think about how sexy he was, how easy he was to talk to, how he kept featuring in her dreams...

"What are you and the girls doing today?" she asked, deftly steering the conversation to a safer topic.

Cayd shot her a knowing look but answered her question. "I thought we might go and help finish off vaccinating the cattle. I spoke to Lachlan earlier. They still have about a thousand head to go. We could take the horses. That would be fun."

Marissa pulled a face. "Since when was horse riding fun? I don't think I could ride another horse if you paid me. My ass and thighs are still so sore, it even hurts when I sit on the toilet."

Everyone laughed.

Olivia appeared from nowhere and smiled. She rubbed her thighs. "I know exactly how you feel!"

"Okay, let's forget about the horses," Cayd said. "We can go in the vehicles." He looked at Lily. "When do you want to leave?"

She swallowed the last mouthful on her plate and scooted out of her chair. "Give me a few minutes to wash this up and get the crew organized. We'll meet you at the shed in ten."

"Sounds good." He clapped his hands together and grinned at his ladies. "Who's up for some vaccinating?"

"Yay!" the ladies chorused with varying degrees of enthusiasm.

Lily smiled. She was doubtful that Marissa's and Olivia's fancy manicures would survive a day vaccinating a thousand head of cattle. Still, it would provide good TV viewing watching them try. Gathering her crew together, she gave them their instructions.

It would be fun to watch the women try their best to impress Cayd while also lending their hand at something Lily had every reason to believe would put them way out of their comfort zone. Marissa and Olivia were city born and bred and though Chelsea had spent time on her grandparents' farm, Lily was betting that had never involved vaccinating beef cattle.

Still, standing back and watching the interactions between the farmer and his girls was all part of the fun and one of the reasons she loved her job so much. Provided she could keep her own traitorous feelings in check and focus on the only thing that was important: capturing unforgettable footage of a gorgeous farmer on his quest to find true love and the highs and lows that came with that.

How hard can that be?

Not hard at all if she put her mind to it. Determined to encourage nothing more than a friendly and professional relationship with the man who had the power to turn her insides to mush, Lily left the homestead with her crew and headed toward the shed. She busied herself with checking angles and lighting while the cameramen set up their equipment and the sound technician moved into position. When Cayd and his ladies strode down the front stairs and started crossing the wide expanse of green lawn, she deliberately turned her back on the foursome and gave the signal to her crew to start filming.

The girls chatted and flirted with Cayd. Lily gritted her teeth and forced herself to feel pleased when Cayd laughed at something Marissa said. The cameras kept rolling while Cayd approached one of the Toyota utes. He opened the driver's door and climbed in. Quick as a flash, Marissa headed around the opposite side and jumped in beside Cayd. Chelsea squeezed herself in the cab too.

Olivia came up short, realizing there was no more room. She stood by uncertainly until Lily took pity on her.

"You can ride with us, Olivia. My crew will ride on the back. Climb in."

While the cameramen and the other guys packed up their gear and loaded it onto the back of the ute, Lily slid behind the wheel. With a sigh and looking glum, Olivia climbed in beside her. She tucked a strand of red hair behind her ear. Her shoulders slumped.

"Cheer up," Lily said. "It's not all bad. There's still a couple of days left to impress Cayd. The farewell dinner's not until Sunday night."

"But he hasn't even asked me to spend time alone with him!" the poor girl cried.

"Hey, like I said. There's still time." She shot the girl a sideways glance. "You need to be a bit more forceful. Do something or say something to capture his attention so that he has no choice but to notice you. You need to set yourself apart from the other girls. Be different. Stand out."

"But how do I do that?" Olivia wailed. "Marissa's stunning from head to toe. She's like some golden Amazon woman. There's no way I can compete with that. Then there's Chelsea, who's so capable. Nothing about being on the station fazes her. She's cute and calm and competent. She'd make the perfect farmer's wife. Meanwhile, I break nails and fall over and get myself covered in mud."

Lily hid a chuckle behind her hand. The memory of Olivia's moment of embarrassment in the piggery had been humorous for everyone, but no doubt the poor girl didn't look at it like that. Lily needed to give her some reassurance before the girl threw in the towel way before the game was up.

"Cayd saw something in you that he liked right from the very beginning, or he'd never have invited you to the farm. He had ten lovely ladies to choose from, remember? And you made the cut."

Olivia looked at her with blue eyes that were wide with uncertainty, but as Lily's words began to sink in, her expression slowly changed.

"You're right," she said. "He *did* choose me. I was shocked, you know. I didn't think I stood a chance against the other ladies. They were all so beautiful and accomplished. And yet, he chose me. He chose *me*."

The wonder in her voice was reflected on her face. Lily's encouragement was having the desired effect. She needed to keep it going.

"He likes you, Olivia. For whatever reason, he hasn't gotten around to asking you for some alone time, but he will. I'm sure of it." She paused and then shot Olivia a grin. "It's not against the rules for you to approach *him*, you know. You could be the one to ask *him* for some alone time."

Olivia's eyes widened further. "You think?"

Lily shrugged. "Why not? We live in a world of equal opportunity, don't we? And Cayd's all for equality between the sexes."

"He *is*?"

"Yes. He said so this morning. He has four sisters, remember? He's been around women all his life, and no doubt that's had an effect on the way he views the world. If I were you, I'd come straight out and ask him to spend some time alone with you. I don't think he'd be taken aback by that. In fact, most men are attracted to strong, confident women. I think Cayd is one of them."

Hope flooded Olivia's face. "You think so? You don't think I'd send him running for the hills?"

"No, I don't. And don't forget, this is a competition for Cayd's heart, and you only have a very short time to win it. There are two other women vying for his attention. You need to do everything you can to ensure you get your fair share of his time."

Olivia nodded thoughtfully. "You're right. I need to step up my game. I need to stop waiting for him to ask me and just *demand* that he spend some time with me."

Lily wasn't quite sure that Cayd was the kind of man who responded to demands, but at least Olivia was now thinking along the right lines. As she negotiated a turn into the paddock that housed the cattle yards, she smiled at the girl.

"What do you have to lose?"

Olivia nodded again. Determination lit up her eyes. "Exactly."

As Lily pulled up a short distance away from the cattle yards, Olivia tidied her hair, opened the door and jumped out of the ute. With a ground-eating, confident stride, she made a beeline for Cayd. He stood talking with Marissa and Chelsea. Upon reaching his side, Olivia tugged on his arm and eased him away from the group.

Lily grinned. It appeared her pep talk had done the trick.

Let the fun begin...

Chapter Thirteen

♥

The familiar smell of cattle filled Cayd's nostrils. A thousand head of prime Droughtmasters stood shoulder to shoulder in the paddock, waiting to be herded into the yards. Normally, the yards would be full of red dust clouds, but thanks to the recent rain, they had to put up with mud instead. With so many cattle pounding the surface with their hooves, it wasn't long before the entire yard was a mess. Still, there was nothing he enjoyed more than being up close and personal with the livestock that was the lifeblood of Marlowe Downs.

Cayd was also relieved to see his brothers, two station hands, and the three Aboriginal girls gathered together in the yards. At least there were more people around to engage his would-be brides and keep them entertained. He'd been feeling under siege.

He'd spent the short journey there with both Marissa and Chelsea vying for his attention, talking over each other with one story after another, until his head spun. To make matters worse, Olivia now strode toward him, fierce determination glinting in her eyes that matched the fire on her head. Remembering Lily's directive to pay attention to all of his ladies, he swallowed a groan and plastered a smile on his face.

"How's it going, Olivia?"

She grabbed him by the arm and drew him away. "This is so exciting! I've never been so close to this many cows!"

He chuckled. "I'm glad you feel that way. If you were to live out here permanently, being around the cattle would be a daily occurrence."

She visibly faltered. Some of her excitement dimmed. "Really? Every day?"

He couldn't help but take pity on her. "No, probably not every day. My brothers and I spend most of our days out here, but I wouldn't expect my wife to do that."

Her smile returned at full wattage. She gazed at him with such adoration, it was almost embarrassing. Maybe it was the mention of the word "wife" that had put that look on her face. He hoped he hadn't gotten her expectations up. Right now, he didn't know where his feelings lay.

He shifted uncomfortably and glanced away, wishing the other girls were closer. He would have felt even better if Lily was with them. At least she was close by. She and her crew had pulled up a short distance away and were setting up their equipment. Somehow, her presence brought everything to life, brightened the colors, sharpened the sounds, centered him.

"What are we vaccinating against, Cayd?" Olivia asked, looking up at him with wide blue eyes filled with curiosity.

"Tuberculosis."

Chelsea moved closer, her forehead furrowed. "I thought that disease had been eradicated in Australia."

"You're right," he said, surprised by her knowledge. Then again, she did have some kind of farming background—if visits to her grandparents' hobby farm qualified.

"In Queensland, we eradicated the disease back in the late nineties. Unfortunately, from time to time, we still get an outbreak. Sometimes it's carried by wild deer who come into contact with the herd. Other times, it's imported in through stock brought in from another country. That's what happened to our neighbors recently. Unfortunately, half their herd got infected and had to be put down. So we decided to vaccinate our own herd, to be on the safe side."

Not to be outdone, Marissa also moved in closer. "How do you do it?" she asked.

"Pretty much the same way that humans get vaccinated. Each cow is given a single injection into the muscle."

"With a needle?" Olivia asked.

"Yes, but we use a special gun. It has a needle attached. Come with me and I'll show you how it's done."

With that, he walked over to the cattle yards and climbed over the high steel gates. He waited on the other side and assisted the girls over. Lachlan, Aiden, and two of the Aboriginal workers, Zana and Breeanna, were herding stock up the race.

The cattle bellowed, kicking up dust. It was noisy, dirty work but Cayd loved it. Grinning, he urged his ladies to follow him as he went up to the end of the race where the third Aboriginal girl, Khloe, secured cattle in the crush. Justin stood nearby, brandishing the injection gun.

"First, we muster the cattle into the paddock beside the yards," Cayd explained. "Then we herd fifty or so of them into the yards, as many as can fit. Next, we push them up the race. See how Lachlan and Aiden are doing it?"

The girls stared across at his brothers, who were waving their arms and shouting and whistling at the cattle, herding them into the race.

"How many do you inject at once?" Chelsea asked. "I've seen my grandfather go along a line of sheep in a race and drench a dozen or so at a time before releasing them. Is that how it works here?"

"No. Drenching's different to vaccinating. We can only inject one at a time. That's why it takes so long. Cattle are difficult to handle. Much more difficult than sheep. They're quite a bit larger, for a start, and more likely to hurt someone if they spook. We need to secure them in the crush before we can administer the injection and unfortunately, the crush can only hold one beast at a time."

Marissa and Olivia shot fearful glances toward the huge red beasts. There were at least fifty of them in the yards and another ten or so in the race. The rest of the herd grazed in the adjoining paddock, waiting their turn. Only Chelsea appeared relaxed.

"Oh, my goodness! You're right. They're so huge! Are you sure they're not going to charge us?" Olivia asked, turning pale.

"No, they won't charge you, but don't get too close to them," Cayd replied. "They're not all that used to being around people, and we don't want to spook them."

If anything, Olivia grew paler. Cayd did his best to reassure her.

"It's okay, Olivia. They won't hurt you. If it makes you feel any better, stick close to me. You'll be fine."

She breathed out a sigh of relief and shot him a wobbly smile. He glanced over toward where Lily stood beside the cameramen. Both men had their cameras pointed toward him, no doubt recording everything he said and did. It was like he was some rare and exotic insect to be pored over, dissected, examined from every angle. He swallowed a sigh and got on with doing what was required.

He directed his gaze toward Olivia. "If you come up to the end of the race here where Justin is, you can watch how he gives the vaccine. Straight into the back thigh, where there's plenty of muscle."

"How do you know how much to give them?" Olivia asked, looking both curious and terrified.

"We set the dose on the gun." He took the gun off Justin and showed it to the girls. "See? There are measurements printed along the side, and this dial here allows us to set a premeasured amount. When you pull the trigger, it releases the set dose."

Olivia remained glued to his side, but some of the tension around her mouth began to ease. "Do you think I could have a go?"

Cayd's initial instinct was to refuse, but then he glanced at Lily, who'd moved closer, along with her crew. She gave him an imperceptible nod. He looked back at Olivia and smiled. "Of course. Here, let me show you how and then you can have a go. How does that sound?"

"F-fine," she said a little shakily.

"I want a turn too!" Marissa said.

"Me too!" Chelsea said, not wanting to be outdone by her rivals.

Cayd laughed. "Don't worry, there are a thousand cattle to be vaccinated. No one's going to miss out."

Marissa crowded in, almost pushing Olivia out of the way in her attempt to get closer to Cayd. Her breast brushed against his arm. No doubt she'd gained enough confidence from their recent intimate encounter to stake her claim.

Not that he minded. This was a competition for his heart. He understood the need for the women to do everything they could to gain his attention, but it was a bit embarrassing, especially with Lily watching their every move. It shouldn't matter to him what she thought, but it did. He was annoyed that he was so aware of her. How was he supposed to grow closer to his girls with Lily consuming so many of his thoughts?

Impatiently, he took the gun from Justin and demonstrated to the ladies and for the TV viewers how to inject a cow. "You have to use a reasonable amount of force with the needle. The cow's hide is tough. It takes a bit of effort to pierce through it into the muscle, and that's where we want the vaccine to go."

He placed a practiced hand against the side of the cow, high up on her rump, and then stabbed the needle through the skin and deep into the muscle. Thankfully, the cow remained motionless as he depressed the trigger and administered the dose. When he was done, he stepped away, and Justin released the beast from the crush and opened the gate. She ambled forward and into another yard, where one of the station hands released her back into another paddock.

"One down, another nine hundred and ninety-nine or so to go." He grinned at his ladies. "Who wants to go first?"

"I will," Olivia said, releasing her grip on Cayd's arm and taking a tentative step forward.

Cayd showed her where on the cow's rump to inject the vaccine and then handed her the gun.

"Don't forget, you need to push the needle in quite hard in order that it pierces the skin. It's important we inject into the muscle, okay?"

Olivia nodded. She got herself into position. The cow shifted slightly, and Olivia reared back in alarm.

"It's okay. She's just a little restless," Cayd said. "Get yourself in nice and close and thrust the needle in, just like I showed you."

"She's so huge," Olivia gasped.

"Yes, but she can't go anywhere in the crush. Nice and steady movements. You'll be fine."

Cayd looked up and saw both cameras were focused on them. Lily stood a short distance away, watching the proceedings with interest. She didn't seem at all fazed by the cattle.

"I-I can't do it," Olivia wailed.

"Sure you can," Cayd encouraged. "Hold the gun steady, take aim, and then push it firmly in."

Olivia tried to do as he'd said, but her long fingernails made handling the gun difficult. Coupled with her fear, the task was beyond her. She handed the gun back to Cayd.

"Here, take it. I don't want to do it."

"That's okay. Don't worry about it. I understand. It's a bit daunting when you're not used to it." Cayd took the gun from her and quickly and efficiently administered the dose of vaccine. Justin released the cow from the crush and sent her on her way before locking the next cow in place.

"Does anyone else want a turn?" Cayd asked, looking around at the women.

Marissa stepped forward with a confident grin. "I'll have a go."

Cayd looked doubtfully down at her fingernails. They were every bit as long as Olivia's. "Are you sure?" he asked.

She gave him a quick smile, but doubt shadowed her eyes. "Of course."

Cayd swallowed a sigh. "Okay." He demonstrated for Marissa how it was done. "So, do you think you can do that?"

"I'm not sure, but I'll give it a try."

Cayd admired her spirit. He handed her the gun and helped her get into position. The cameras kept rolling. Marissa brought the gun in close to the beast's side and then thrust hard.

"Ouch!" she cried, pulling her hand back and sticking a finger in her mouth.

"Are you all right?" Cayd asked.

Tears formed in Marissa's eyes. "I think I broke a fingernail." She pulled her finger out of her mouth and held it up. The nail had snapped off close to the tip of her finger.

"Ouch is right," Cayd said. "I'm so sorry, Marissa. This kind of work is pretty hard on long fingernails. Are you going to be okay?"

She sniffed and popped her finger back in her mouth. "I'll think so."

"I think you might be best to sit this out," Cayd said. "I don't want to be responsible for breaking another one."

Marissa didn't look happy about his suggestion, but he could tell she also wasn't keen to suffer another injury. With a disgruntled sigh, she turned and stomped away to where Olivia had taken refuge in the shade of one of the utes. Both women stared at him with their arms crossed and frowns on their faces. Cayd sighed again. These two weeks couldn't end soon enough.

Lily finished the last of her evening meal and sat back with a satisfied sigh. The steak had been cooked to perfection. The vegetables that had been picked fresh from Ellen's garden were crisp and full of flavor. So different from those Lily bought in the store back home. The meal had been finished off with a freshly baked lemon meringue pie and homemade ice cream. She couldn't eat another bite.

It seemed like the others congregated around the table felt the same way. Conversation between the three women seated together near Lily was muted. Cayd and his brothers sat at the other end, talking about the day's events and the mammoth task they'd achieved. Vaccinating a thousand head of cattle in one day was no mean feat.

She'd been pleased with the rushes from the day. Watching such a large and noisy herd of cattle getting vaccinated wasn't something her viewers saw every day. It would play well to them. And so would the footage of Cayd.

At one point over the course of the afternoon, he'd pulled off his shirt and had used it to wipe the sweat off his brow. His taut, toned chest had once again been on display for all to see. There wasn't a female within a hundred yards who hadn't noticed what a fine specimen of a man he was.

Of course that hadn't included Lily. In fact, seeing Cayd half-naked, all perfectly formed muscles glistening with sweat, had barely registered with her.

Liar.

She ignored the voice in her head. What was getting increasingly harder to ignore was the way she felt every time she watched Cayd interact with his ladies. He was so patient with them, so kind and understanding. They were admirable qualities for any man to possess. His competence around the cattle was impressive, and yet, he'd never shown any irritation toward the women when their efforts fell short.

Despite the setback at the cattle yards, both Olivia and Marissa had been glued to Cayd's side all night. No doubt they were keen to make up ground, especially when Chelsea had proven herself so adept with the vaccine gun. After all, this was a competition and Cayd was not only looking for a wife, but someone who could help him on the station. So far, both Marissa and Olivia had proven less than adequate in that regard.

But Cayd continued to lavish attention on all three ladies, and Lily was curious whether having a helpmate was as important to him as she'd assumed. Or maybe he was just taking her directive on board that he pay equal attention to all three women. She didn't know, but it was clear that she needed some time away from the place to clear her head of thoughts of Cayd Fairfax and to immerse herself in her fiancé.

Alex might not have been too eager for her to interrupt his work schedule, but she was sure that once she arrived on his doorstep with the intention of whisking him away for some alone time, he'd change his mind. She might even convince him to indulge in some heavy petting for a change, or even go the whole way.

With that thought in mind, Lily cleared her throat and spoke above the murmur of conversation. "I just want to let you know we're taking the weekend off. You're free to do whatever you want over the next couple of days. No filming, no scheduled activities. No anything."

Cayd shot her a curious look. "What will you do?"

She turned to face him and tried not to get caught up in the brilliance of his cobalt eyes. "I'm catching a plane back to Sydney in the morning. There are some people I need to catch up with."

The frown on Cayd's face surprised her. She wondered what had put it there.

"You mean your fiancé?" he asked.

She blinked at his brusque tone. "Yes. Among others."

If anything, his frown darkened. "I'll drive you to the airport."

She shook her head. "Oh, you don't have to do that. I'm sure there's someone else who could take me."

"No," he said firmly, his gaze fixed on hers. "I'll do it. The road's bound to be muddy after yesterday's rain. I want to make sure you get there safely."

"Okay," she said slowly. "Thank you. I appreciate that."

She steadfastly ignored the little hum of excitement that zinged through her veins. Later that night, as she packed her bag, she told herself the throb of anticipation that now filled her heart had everything to do with seeing Alex again and nothing to do with the sexy cattleman she was going to spend a whole hour alone with in a car as they made their way to Roma.

Chapter Fourteen

♥

Lily gazed out over the vast paddocks and plains of Marlowe Downs and realized she was going to miss the place while she was away. It had only been six days since she'd arrived, but the station had wormed its way into her heart. She never could have imagined that a city girl would feel quite so at home in the bush.

She glanced across at the man beside her. She wasn't going to pretend that a lot of her contentment with the outback had to do with the cattleman who sat behind the wheel of the Toyota. With a quiet sigh, she pressed the button on her armrest and lowered the window of the ute. She could only hope her surprise romantic weekend getaway would reignite the fire between her and Alex and that all thoughts of Cayd would be extinguished once and for all.

They'd left straight after breakfast, even though her flight back to Sydney wasn't due to depart until lunchtime. Cayd hadn't wanted to risk her missing her flight. As he'd explained, there was always a chance they might get bogged, blow a tire, or otherwise be delayed. One could never be too certain in the outback.

She didn't mind. She'd woken early and was keen to get on the road. Extra time spent with Cayd also appealed—probably more than it should. She looked forward to spending the time getting to know him better, learning what made him tick. Only so she could better anticipate his decisions, stay one step ahead of him. That was the way to get the most out of his story that was playing out on their screens. At least, that's what she told herself.

As they left the wide double gates of Marlowe Downs behind them, Cayd depressed the accelerator. The ute leaped forward. A warm breeze lifted the ends of Lily's hair. She breathed in deeply, filling her lungs with the fresh, sweet air.

The recent rains had brightened everything up. It was as if the world had been washed clean. The low olive-green scrub that dotted the landscape, the tall eucalyptus trees with their long, thin, leaves and smooth, colorful bark, the fields of wild-flowers... Their colors were deeper, more vivid and intense.

Though the dirt road was marked with potholes that were filled with water, Cayd drove with a confidence that appealed to Lily. She'd never been much of a driver herself. Born and raised in the city, she was a fan of public transport. There was nowhere she couldn't go on a train or a bus or a ferry. Light rail was also popping up all over the place, making it even more convenient to get around. She didn't have to worry about traffic jams, angry drivers, tolls. She could use the commute time productively by sitting back and relaxing with a book, catching up on emails, or scrolling through her social media feeds.

But there was something very attractive about a man who was fully in control of a vehicle and even made the whole driving thing look easy. Cayd had his sleeves rolled up to his elbows. The firm muscles in his forearm contracted every time he changed gears. A sudden change in direction brought a whiff of his spicy cologne on the air, teasing her and bringing forth erotic images she did her best to ignore.

In an effort to distract herself, she cast around for something to talk about and seized on the first thing that came to mind.

"So, did you go to school out here? It must have been a decent bus ride into town. That's if there was even a bus available."

He flicked her a glance and returned his attention to the road. "You're right. There's a school bus, but the route ends about fifteen minutes up the road. Then it's a ninety-minute trip into Roma. That's why we were homeschooled."

Lily blinked in surprise. "Homeschooled? Wow. For how long?"

"Seven years. All the way through infants and primary school. Then we went to boarding school in Brisbane."

Lily shook her head in awe. "Your mother homeschooled ten children? I already thought she was amazing. I was wrong. She's beyond amazing. She's a superwoman."

Cayd chuckled. "You won't get any argument from me. It must have been difficult for her at times, especially when we were going through hard times on the station. We've seen more than our fair share of droughts and flooding rains. They all leave a lasting impact, both good and bad.

"As a kid, we didn't fully appreciate the impacts. All we knew was that Dad and Mum were less fun, less cheery during the drought, and there were a whole lot less trips to town. They weren't all that happier when it flooded, but at least when the floodwaters subsided, there were many benefits to be had from the rain. In between, they just got on with the business of running a station and raising a family the best way they could. There were plenty of fun times. Plenty of great memories. I wouldn't trade my childhood for anything."

His voice was thick with emotion and told her more than words how important his family was to him.

"Is that what brought you back here? Your family?" she asked.

He was silent for a moment, then he nodded. "I think so. I always thought it was the station—wanting to carry on the family tradition of farming—that kind of thing. But I could have farmed anywhere, and I chose to come back here, in the middle of nowhere." He paused. When he spoke again, his voice was husky and deep. "I've never really thought about it before, but yeah, that's what brought me back. My family."

A lump lodged itself in Lily's throat. She understood the strong ties that bound families together. She felt the same way about hers. She couldn't imagine life without her parents, her brothers. They might fight and argue every now and then and Michael's inability to hold down a job drove her insane, but nothing and no one would ever come between them. It would always be that way.

"What was it like at boarding school? Did you enjoy it?"

"Yeah, I did. It was great. I went to an all-boys school. Growing up with five brothers, I fit right in. Fighting over showers and who got to sleep in the top bunk. We went to school for six hours a day and then played organized sports every afternoon. I think the teachers did that on purpose so that we could blow off some steam. We were all too exhausted at night to get up to too much trouble."

"I can't imagine you were the perfect angel. Surely, there were a few pranks," she teased.

He winked. "Maybe one or two."

She laughed. "Do tell."

He grinned and wagged one finger. "Oh, no. An old boy never tells."

Her stomach clenched with desire.

Hell, he's so unbelievably sexy. I've never met anyone who makes me feel like this... Oh, God... I'm in trouble...

Forcing her thoughts away from such dangerous territory—especially because she was on her way to meet up with her fiancé—she cast around for something else to talk about and latched onto her job. That was safe and neutral ground and after all, that's what she was there for.

"So, this Sunday will be the first farewell dinner, when you'll have to say goodbye to one of your ladies. Are you ready for that?"

Cayd shrugged as if it were of no consequence. "I guess."

"It's a pretty big deal," she said, wanting to impress upon him the importance of the occasion. "There will be plenty of viewers who've already formed an opinion on the girls and who should stay or go. You need to give it proper consideration. You're not going to please everyone, and that's okay, but you have to give sound reasons for your decision, or the viewers will be upset. Are you still intending to send Chelsea home?"

Cayd did his best to ignore Lily's question. He was well aware that the farewell dinner was fast approaching. The truth was, he couldn't wait for it to get there. The arrival of Sunday night meant he was that much closer to having this whole thing wrapped up and over with and he could get back on with the business of running his life.

Not for the first time, he wished Lily was in the mix. Or that he at least liked one of his potential brides as much as he liked her. Today, she wore a sundress that floated just above her knees. The navy-blue and white polka-dot patten was cute, but it was the low-cut neckline that kept drawing his gaze.

Her ample cleavage filled the space nicely and the soft fabric conformed to the shape of her breasts. It was the first time he'd seen her in a dress. He wanted to think she'd worn it for him, but he wasn't stupid. She was on her way home to Sydney. Back to her fiancé.

He ignored the sudden stab of jealousy. He'd known from the outset she was taken. It was his own stupid fault that he kept hoping things were different or that something might change. It was just that she was so easy to talk to. She was a city girl, but somehow, she understood the country way of life, the highs and lows, the challenges.

There was so much out of anyone's control. A farmer's destiny was governed by the weather. Some years it favored them; some years it didn't. A farmer did the best he could under the circumstances. There were no guarantees. Like Lily's parents. They could work seven days a week, but there were no guarantees the customers would come, or in the numbers they needed to stay afloat. Only a certain kind of person was cut out to run a small business—hell, any kind of business, when it came to that. They all faced similar challenges.

Lily shot him an expectant look, and he was reminded that he hadn't yet answered her question. He sighed and pursed his lips in thought. The thing was, he liked Marissa well enough and was certainly attracted to her physically, but the conversation was vapid. Every time she opened her mouth, it was all about her. He hadn't spent enough time around Olivia to know what she was really like, and even though she'd expressed interest about the farm and how it operated, so far, he hadn't gotten the feeling that he couldn't be apart from her. Chelsea—well he already knew Chelsea wasn't the one.

"Yes," he said. "I dread the thought of hurting her, but I have to choose someone, right?"

Lily nodded. "Don't feel bad. They know one of them will be sent home. If Chelsea's your first choice, then so be it." She paused and then asked, "I'm curious, do you mind telling me why you've chosen to send Chelsea home? I thought the two of you were getting on well."

Cayd compressed his lips. "Sure. She's a great girl. She's willing to get her hands dirty, gives anything a go. She's also fun and attractive."

Lily frowned. "Okay, so that all sounds very positive. What did it come down to?"

He glanced across at her and then shrugged. "There was no chemistry."

Lily's eyes widened in surprise. "No chemistry? You looked like you were enjoying the kiss you shared with her."

"You're right. It was enjoyable. But there were no fireworks. When I kiss the woman I'm planning to make my wife, I want the world to tilt off its axis."

Lily gaped. "Oh, my goodness! Did you really just say that? I think you've been reading too many romance novels."

Cayd stared at her, now filled with disbelief. "What? You don't think your world should rock when you kiss the love of your life?"

The intensity in Cayd's gaze made Lily squirm, and that only served to irritate her. Just because Cayd felt that way didn't mean she had to. Her world had never been rocked by Alex's kisses. That didn't mean they weren't perfect for each other.

She looked at Cayd and shrugged, not bothering to hide her annoyance. "Not everyone feels that way. I'm sure there are perfectly happy couples who don't necessarily feel the world needs to tilt off its axis when they kiss."

If anything, Cayd's expression grew more intense. "Are you speaking personally?"

"That's none of your business."

A knowing look filled his gaze, only serving to irritate her further.

"Ah," was all he said.

Anger nipped at her heels. "Don't go judging me and my relationship. You know nothing about me. Or Alex. Or our relationship."

Cayd's expression remained unperturbed. "I know more than you think."

"Like what?" she challenged.

"Like I can tell he's not the man for you," he said calmly.

She gasped in outrage. "You're unbelievable! We barely know each other, and you don't know my fiancé at all, and yet you feel qualified to hold an opinion on our relationship. Talk about arrogant."

He merely shrugged. "It's not arrogance. It's the truth. If your world doesn't rock when you kiss your fiancé, something's terribly wrong. Like I said, you're not with the right man."

She blinked, trying hard to control the anger and resentment that now billowed up inside her.

"I'm sorry that you feel you know me and my fiancé well enough to come up with such outlandish statements, especially when you haven't even met him. That makes this...discussion even worse. You have no right to say such things. They're incredibly offensive, and I resent the fact you're implying there's something wrong with our relationship just because the world doesn't tilt. Don't you see how egotistical that is? How utterly rude? Are you trying to tell me that every single girl you've kissed has made you feel that way? Or even half of them?"

Cayd laughed. "Hell, no. The only time my world rocked off its axis during a kiss was in the eleventh grade. I was seventeen and kissed Emily Dwyer in the movies. She was seventeen too. I'd been in love with her all year."

"What happened?" Lily asked, curious despite herself.

"We graduated from high school and went our separate ways. I came home to the station. She went to university. Last I heard, she was living in Brisbane, married with two kids."

Despite herself, Lily smiled. "Wow."

Cayd chuckled. "I know, right? I was convinced we'd be together forever. That kiss... I guess it wasn't meant to be."

Lily pursed her lips. "So, the way I see it, your means of measuring the validity of your relationships is flawed. Your world rocked off its axis with Emily, and yet you seem okay about the fact she married someone else. So, the converse could be argued too. Just because a kiss doesn't rock your world, doesn't mean they aren't the right one."

To her annoyance, the look he gave her was filled with pity. Unwilling to continue the conversation, she folded her arms across her chest and turned to stare out the window. The never-ending landscape of low scrubby bushes and tall gum trees flashed past. It was a relief when Cayd pulled into the parking lot at the airport.

"Here we are, with plenty of time to spare," he said.

He was right. There were still a couple of hours until her flight, but she was keen to remove herself from Cayd's company. He made her think about things that didn't sit well, and he also made her mad. The sooner he left and returned to the station, the better.

"Thanks for the ride," she muttered as she opened the door and climbed out.

Cayd retrieved her suitcase from the back of the ute. She went to take it from him.

"I'll carry it for you," he offered.

"It's fine," she replied stiffly. "I can manage."

His eyebrows lifted in surprise, but he handed over the suitcase without further comment.

She drew in a deep breath and forced away some of her tension. They weren't yet one week in, with another week to go. She needed to keep relations between them civil.

"I'll see you on Sunday night," she said.

"What time's your return flight land? I can come and get you."

Lily quickly shook her head. "Thank you, but no. I'm sure you'll be busy enough with your ladies."

He frowned. "Are you sure?"

"Absolutely," she said firmly. "I'll get one of the crew to meet me."

He stood there, looking uncertain. He glanced toward the terminal. "I'll wait with you until your plane arrives."

"No, that's fine. I'm good. I have a few emails to check and correspondence to tend to. I'll do that while I wait."

He nodded, but looked far from convinced. "Okay, then. If you're sure."

She eyed him steadily. "Have a good weekend, Cayd. I'll see you when I get back."

Chapter Fifteen

♥

Lily opened the door to Alex's office with the key that his boss had laughingly given her a couple of years earlier, knowing that Alex spent more time at the office than he did at home. That's why she'd had the uber drop her off there. It was five o'clock on Saturday afternoon, but she was confident Alex would still be at work.

She left her suitcase in the waiting room and, on silent feet, walked down the carpeted hallway. She paused at the closed door to his office and listened, but all was silent. Swinging open the door, she shouted, "Surprise!"

Alex looked up from his keyboard, momentarily startled. His short, dark hair was mussed on top, as if he'd been scrubbing at it. His Clark Kent-style glasses were slightly crooked on his prominent nose. As he registered her presence, a distracted grin spread across his face.

"Lily! My goodness! Where did you come from?"

He stood and came around the side of his desk and kissed her chastely on the cheek. For once, she wished he'd take her in his arms and kiss her thoroughly and with enough passion to sweep her off her feet. But that had never been his way. She couldn't expect him to suddenly change.

It was all Cayd's fault. His comments about the earth shaking had messed with her head. She'd always been content with the way Alex kissed. Okay, so the kisses they shared were more sweet than passionate, but what was wrong with that? They'd known each other since they were children. It was no surprise there wasn't any burning passion.

What they had was better than that. A deep, abiding love. A respect and admiration for each other. Unwavering support, loyalty, a deep friendship. Those were the things that mattered. Passion came and went. It often burned brightly for a short time and then fizzled out. She'd read enough romance novels and watched enough TV soap operas to know that.

It was obvious Cayd gave the act of kissing a high degree of priority. No doubt he'd kissed more than his share of women. With looks like his, he wouldn't have to try very hard to find willing candidates.

The thought of him kissing a vast number of nameless, faceless, but oh-so-beautiful women irked her. Refusing to analyze her reaction, she pushed the feeling away. Even so, she couldn't help but wonder what it would feel like to be kissed in the way Cayd had so vividly described—with unrestrained passion; with such heat, such hunger that her world tilted.

She flushed with guilt and avoided Alex's gaze. It was ridiculous to think like that. To compare Alex to Cayd. One was all sunshine, tanned, outdoorsy, and practical. The other was quieter, paler, and more circumspect. Alex would never command the attention of everyone in the room, but he was intelligent, methodical, and reliable. The men were completely different, and there was nothing wrong with that. She loved Alex. She was going to marry him.

Aren't I?

Forcing the disquieting question aside, she watched as he returned to take a seat behind his desk. Plastering a smile on her face, she propped a hip up on one corner of the polished oak and leaned slightly toward him, ensuring he got a good view of her breasts as they peeked out of her low, scoop-necked dress.

"Are you nearly ready to call it a day?" she asked and then gave him a saucy wink.

His gaze rested momentarily on her cleavage, but then he gave a reluctant shake of his head.

"I'm sorry. I'm in the middle of something important. If I'd known you were coming, I'd have skipped lunch and worked right on through."

"I wanted to surprise you," she said weakly, swallowing her disappointment.

Alex smiled, and she was reminded of how good-looking he was. His olive skin was clear and unlined. Whiskers shadowed his strong jaw. His demeanor might not command attention, but he always made her feel safe and secure.

"Yes," he replied, "and it was very nice of you. It's just that your timing isn't so good."

Some of her disappointment must have shown on her face. Alex stood again and came around her side of the desk. She'd forgotten how short he was. They were almost the same height.

Drawing her into his arms, he gave her a brief hug before setting her aside. "Give me a couple of hours and I'm all yours."

She pouted. Though his reaction to her unexpected arrival wasn't altogether surprising, she was a bit put out that he didn't want to stop what he was doing immediately and spend every possible moment with her. They hadn't seen each other all week. She wasn't even there for the whole weekend. By mid-morning Sunday, she'd be on a plane back to Roma. She wanted to feel important to him, as important as his work. The thought made her frown.

What a silly ninny I'm being. I know how important this partnership is to Alex. I need to cut him some slack and most of all, I need to stop thinking about and comparing him to Cayd.

It was just that Cayd had this presence about him, like some kind of magnetic force that was impossible to resist. He was charming and sexy and funny, and he'd sparked some kind of physical yearning inside her that she'd never experienced. It left her feeling confused and uncertain and wanting more.

Perhaps it was just that she and Alex hadn't been intimate. Perhaps that had been a mistake. Perhaps she wouldn't be having such erotic thoughts about Cayd, or such unfamiliar yearnings, if she'd already experienced the pinnacle of excitement with her fiancé.

Maybe we should make love? Connect in the most intimate way. Make sure we're compatible. Make sure the world tilts...

The last thought snuck up on her, taking her unawares, but the more she considered it, the more credence it had. Cayd was right in one respect, at least. Sexual compatibility was important. She intended to spend the rest of her life with Alex.

I ought to be confident before I make any permanent commitment that he can satisfy me on that level, shouldn't I?

Though she had no personal experience, she knew enough to accept that satisfying one's partner sexually, and being satisfied in return, was an integral part of any relationship. She and Alex might not have a white-hot-can't-keep-our-hands-off-each-other relationship, but that didn't mean she was happy with a passionless marriage. The very thought made her shudder.

Dragging in a deep breath, she gathered her courage. Alex would be taken by surprise, but she hoped he wasn't too put off by the idea. In fact, though he'd been the one to suggest they wait until they were married before consummating their relationship, that had been such a long time ago she rather hoped he'd now be delighted with the turn of events.

She cleared her throat, reached out, and squeezed his arm. "Um, Alex? I've been thinking... What would you say if I told you I don't want to wait anymore?"

He frowned at his screen, his expression distracted. "Wait for what?"

Embarrassment burned across her cheeks. She lifted one shoulder in a casual half shrug and averted her gaze.

This is harder than I thought...

Then she remembered how important this was and tried again. "Um, you know. For the wedding night."

His eyes went wide. A second later, a smile broke across his face. "You're ready to set a date?"

She blinked. Her stomach clenched at the hope in his eyes. She slowly shook her head. "Um, no. That's not what I meant."

His frown deepened. "Then what *did* you mean?"

She drew in another deep breath. It was now or never. She stepped closer and placed her palm flat against his shirtfront. "I mean..." she said huskily and then kissed him full on the mouth.

He sucked in a startled breath. His lips were soft and pliable beneath hers. That gave her the courage to kiss him again. With heart thumping, she stroked his chest through his shirt and stared into his eyes. "I mean, let's make love."

Her lips found his again, and she kissed him for all she was worth. She was gratified when his mouth opened under hers and their tongues began to dance. He tasted faintly of coffee. She was pleased she'd freshened her breath with a mint on her way from the airport. Though she hadn't planned on propositioning him, she'd definitely had some heavy petting in mind.

Alex's reaction was all she could have hoped for. He angled his head and deepened the kiss, and for a moment, she was lost in the feel of him against her. Strong, solid, dependable. Everything she wanted. But slowly, Alex brought the kiss to an end and stepped away. The regret on his face nearly brought her to tears.

"I'm sorry, Lily. I respect you too much not to wait until we're married. We've waited all this time. What's another few months? Maybe you'll finally be ready to set a date."

The smile she gave him felt brittle. It was all she could do not to scream aloud her frustration. While she admired his principles, a part of her wished that he wanted her with such hunger, such passion, that he couldn't wait. *Wouldn't* wait.

She wanted him to lose control. She wanted him to tear off her clothes, to clear the desk with one fell swoop, and bend her over the polished oak.

They were wild fantasies and wholly without precedent. In fact, later, when she took the time to analyze everything that had happened, she'd be shocked at her wayward thoughts. But right now, all she felt was a crushing disappointment. She pecked him on the cheek and turned to leave.

"I'll see you later?"

She clenched her jaw at the hope in his eyes and sent him another plastic smile. "Of course."

Though Cayd had spent the weekend keeping busy and doing his best to entertain his ladies, by the time he woke on Sunday morning, he was relieved the weekend was almost done. The clock on his bedside table told him it was a little after seven. In less than twelve hours, he'd be sending Chelsea home. The time couldn't come quickly enough.

Out of the three, he was probably most drawn to Marissa, but whenever he allowed himself to think about the future, his thoughts kept returning to Lily. He missed her more than he'd expected. They barely knew each other. He'd spent less time with her than he had his potential brides, but that didn't seem to matter.

Sighing, he rolled over onto his back and tugged up the sheet. The rain from earlier in the week had kept the temperatures unseasonably cool, and a fresh breeze filtered in through his open window, bringing with it the scent of orange blossom and honeysuckle. Stacking his hands behind his head, he stared up at the ceiling.

It was the last day of the first week. One more week to go. When he'd signed up for the show, spending two weeks with three beautiful women of his choosing had seemed like a walk in the park. Though it would interfere with some of his farm duties and would mean he'd have to work extra hours to catch up after they'd departed, how uncomfortable could things get?

He hadn't counted on the ladies developing real feelings for him, each hoping to be the chosen one. He hadn't counted on how difficult it would be to make the decision to send one of them home. Though he was comfortable about choosing Chelsea, that didn't mean he wasn't dreading the moment when he had to tell her. And every agonizing moment of it would be filmed for consumption by a national TV audience. Next week, another lady would be sent packing, and he'd be forced to go through this all over again.

He groaned aloud at the thought and scrubbed his hair.

How did I get into this mess? How did I ever think it would be easy? Fun, even?

His introspections were interrupted by a knock on the door. "Come in," he said, and then smiled in surprise as the door opened and revealed his older sister, Maggie, standing on the other side.

She was dressed for work in a pair of worn Levi's, dusty, battered boots, and a pink-and-white-checked work shirt. Her long blonde hair was pulled back into a loose ponytail that only emphasized her high cheekbones, just as the brown leather belt emphasized her narrow waist.

"Cayd Fairfax! Still in bed at seven in the morning! What kind of farmer do you call yourself?"

Her teasing grin put lie to the harshness of her tone. Cayd reached for a pillow and tossed it at her. She caught it easily and laughed before perching on the end of his bed.

"Seriously, Cayd. What are you still doing in bed? The others were up hours ago. They've just come in for breakfast. Mum sent me in here looking for you. She's concerned you might be coming down with something."

As she finished, Maggie rolled her eyes. "I told her you were twenty-seven years old and well able to look after yourself. Just because you still live at home doesn't mean she has to fuss over you like a baby."

Cayd grinned and propped another pillow behind him. He sat up and leaned against the headboard. "You're just jealous because you're not here long enough for Mum to fuss over you."

Maggie poked her tongue out and then shot him a rueful smile. "You're right. Sometimes I wonder why I didn't stay right here on the station, having all my meals cooked, my washing done, my every need seen to."

This time, it was Cayd who rolled his eyes. "You carry on with such nonsense. I've done my own washing before."

"Only when our parents went away for that week to the Gulf, and you only did it then because you had no choice. Don't worry, I heard all about it from Lachlan. He confessed that he and Aiden and Justin didn't have a clue how to start the washing machine."

"At least they knew how to cook," Cayd mumbled.

Maggie scoffed. "That's if you call microwaving frozen TV dinners cooking."

"What are you doing here, anyway? Besides busting my chops for no good reason?"

Maggie threw herself back on Cayd's bed with a dramatic sigh. "My life as I know it is over."

Cayd chuckled. "Sounds overly dramatic. What happened?"

"Arthur Hetherington died."

"Your boss?"

She grimaced. "I'm not sure I'd call him my boss. He only came out to the station once or twice a year. But he was the one who paid my salary and who I reported to whenever he felt so inclined as to inquire about what was going on. Which wasn't often."

"So why do you think your life is over? He barely interfered while he was alive. I can't see him doing much now that he's gone."

She shook her head and groaned. "Don't be so obtuse. Don't you get it? Arthur's left his entire holdings to his nephew. That's according to the lawyer who arrived at the station in a shiny silver Mercedes coupe yesterday to bring me the good news. Of course, it wasn't quite as shiny after driving along thirty miles of dirt road." She smirked.

Cayd chuckled. "Who drives a Mercedes coupe to the outback? Is he crazy?"

"More like a slick city lawyer who spends his days behind a desk and doesn't have a clue how we live out here. Or how bad the roads are. It's just lucky he waited long enough for the recent rains to dry up, or else we'd have been towing him out of a bog."

"What did he say?"

She sighed again. "Just that Arthur had died and had left the station to his nephew. A man, according to the lawyer, who fully intends to dispose himself of the farm just as soon as he can put it on the market. That means I'm out of a job."

"Not necessarily," Cayd responded. "The new owner might want you to stay on. They won't find a more hardworking manager than you. They'd be crazy to let you go."

She flushed with pleasure. "Thanks. That means a lot. Unfortunately, you don't have any say in the matter." She compressed her lips. "I've worked there since I left high school. I've given that station ten years of my life. Blood, sweat, and tears, and I wouldn't have wanted it any other way. To think it might be over and I'll be forced to move on..."

Her voice had thickened with emotion. Cayd leaned over and awkwardly patted her arm. "Hey, you'll be fine. You don't know what the future has in store. If it's not at Hetherington Station, it'll be somewhere else. There are plenty of station owners who'll employ you. Once word gets out that you're looking for a job, they'll be knocking down your door."

"I hope you're right."

"Of course, I'm right. Besides, you could always come back to Marlowe Downs."

She gave him a dubious look. "You'd appoint me station manager?"

He flushed. "Well, no. We already have a station manager."

"Right. You."

"That's right," Cayd said briskly. "But we're always on the lookout for hardworking station hands."

Maggie sat up, looking appalled. "A station hand? I've been managing one of the largest cattle stations in Central Queensland and you want to demote me to station hand?"

Cayd threw up his hands. "Okay, okay. Forget about it. I didn't mean it as an insult." He paused. "Something will come up. You'll see."

Maggie flopped back down across the bed. "I just hate that my life's been turned upside down like this. I feel so...unbalanced. Like everything's spinning out of control."

Feeling sorry for her, Cayd did his best to distract her. "Talking about life being turned upside down, have you met my ladies yet?"

Maggie sat straight back up, her face filling with curiosity. "What ladies?"

Chapter Sixteen

♥

C ayd grinned. "My potential brides."

Maggie gaped. "Get out of here! *Brides?* What are you talking about?"

"Didn't anyone tell you?"

"No, they didn't! I can't believe they kept something like this from me! Then again, I've been kind of busy these past few months. The recent floods did as much damage to the Hetherington fences as they did to yours. That's why I called in, by the way. We're out of fencing wire. I've got some on back order, but it hasn't arrived in time. I need to borrow some from you if that's all right?"

Cayd waved her question away. "Of course, that's all right. I know you're good for it. Although... Now that the station is about to change hands, perhaps I should wait until I meet the new owner. He might not be as generous as old Arthur." Cayd followed through with a wink.

"Arthur had nothing to do with it, as you know darn well," Maggie retorted. "I've been running that station for years, with only minimal staff. *I'm* the reason you know you'll get your fencing wire back in as short a time as possible and without any fuss."

Cayd laughed and once again held up his hands in a sign of surrender. "Okay, okay. Don't be so touchy. I'm only teasing."

Maggie glared at him. "Then don't. Until I know what's going on and whether or not I still have a job, I won't be in the mood for anything lighthearted, and probably not even then."

"Boy, haven't you woken up all grouchy," Cayd said unrepentantly.

Maggie narrowed her eyes. "It's not hard to guess why you're so chirpy. Apparently, you have a bevy of potential life partners lined up waiting for you to pop the question. Tell me, have you chosen one yet?"

Cayd threw himself back against the pillows and sighed. "Do you know anything about the TV show *Outback Bride*?"

Maggie shook her head. "I don't have much time for watching TV. By the time I've finished dinner and cleaned up, I'm ready to hit the hay."

"What an exciting life you lead, Maggie Fairfax."

"Cayd..." Both her narrowed eyes and her tone held a warning.

He merely chuckled. "Okay, so this is how it works. It's basically a dating show for farmers. I thought the exposure I'd get from being on TV would help my fledgling farm stay business, so I put in an application and was chosen to be one of the farmers in search of a wife. Nearly one hundred ladies sent in video applications. I had to cull them down to ten."

Maggie's eyes widened. "You have *ten* ladies staying here? Where the hell have you put them all?"

"No, I don't have ten ladies staying here. I met ten at a function set up by the TV station. It was at a winery in the Hunter Valley, about three hours north of Sydney. Very swanky. Great food. And the homestead... It was amazing. It—"

"Can we get to the part about the ladies?" Maggie cut in.

"Sure. Well, after speed dates with all ten ladies over the course of the day and into the evening, I had to choose three to take back with me to the station."

"So you have three ladies staying here?"

"Yes."

"Where? They'd better not be in my room. I still have a heap of stuff in there. If anyone's touched my books—"

"Your room's fine. They're not staying in the house," Cayd interrupted. "I had the shearer's quarters renovated."

Maggie looked impressed. "Wow! You've been busy. I'm impressed."

Cayd shrugged. "Yeah, well, it's all part of the farm stay project I'm hoping to get off the ground. At the moment, there are eight rooms, each big enough to hold a double bed. They're all air-conditioned and have ensuites. I'm hoping to add at least three or four family-sized cabins and set up some camping grounds out near the bore well."

Maggie's eyebrows rose above a grin. "My, my! I had no idea you had such big dreams for the place. Congratulations."

Cayd ducked his head, both embarrassed and pleased by the praise. "I'm just doing my bit to add an extra stream of revenue. We came so close to losing the farm. If it wasn't for the loan from Isabella, who knows what would have become of Marlowe Downs." He couldn't suppress a shudder.

Maggie nodded somberly. "This place means a lot to you, doesn't it?"

"Of course! Why wouldn't it? This station's been in our family for generations. I don't want to be the one who's responsible for losing it."

"No one blames you for what happened. They're called natural disasters for a reason," Maggie said softly.

Cayd compressed his lips, a familiar feeling of dread sinking into the pit of his belly. "I know. But it would be disastrous if we were forced to sell, no matter what the reason. I want to do my bit to make sure that doesn't happen."

Maggie nodded approvingly. "Good for you. And for what it's worth, I'm glad you feel so passionate about the station." She looked around his bedroom. "I love this place too. Just because I choose to work elsewhere, doesn't mean Marlowe Downs isn't close to my heart."

"Then why did you leave?" Cayd asked, curious.

Maggie stared down at his bedspread. "I had to forge my own path. I always wanted to live and work on a cattle station. Like you, cattle are in my blood. But I knew I would have had to fight to be heard over four brothers. It was clear you, Lachlan, Aiden, and Justin weren't going anywhere, and that's fine. I completely understand. But I didn't want to be tagging along behind you or having to prove myself over and over again.

"By striking out on my own, I've still had my fair share of battles, particularly when I cross paths with a man who underestimates my ability to get the job done, but I've built up a reputation all on my own of being a trusted and respectable station manager who's the equal of any male in the same position."

"You're head and shoulders above most of the competition," Cayd said. "Everyone who knows you admires you for all that you've achieved. You're only twenty-eight. It's an amazing effort to be running a station of that size at your age and doing it so well. I'm proud of you, sis."

She blushed, but looked pleased. "Oh, that's so sweet of you. So, tell me. Have any of these ladies caught your eye? Could there be a proposal in the wings?"

Her comment heated his cheeks. He looked down and slowly shook his head. "I don't think so. In fact, tonight, I'm sending one of them home."

Maggie perked up. "Ooh, do you know which one?"

"Actually, I do."

"Tell me about them. Then I can decide whether you've made the right decision."

Cayd laughed. "Right. Like you've had so much experience when it comes to matters of the heart. Remind me again, how many relationships you've had?"

Maggie pretended to hit him. "Hey! Not fair. It's not my fault eligible bachelors are rather thin on the ground out here. Or haven't you noticed?"

"Not as scarce as the eligible women," Cayd said. "Why do you think I went on the show?"

"I thought you said it was for the publicity?"

Cayd merely laughed. "Okay, do you want to hear about my ladies?"

"Yes, please."

Cayd shifted into a more comfortable position and tugged the sheet higher up his chest. "Okay, so the first one is Marissa. She was my first pick. She's tall, blonde, and beautiful."

Maggie frowned. "Why can I hear a 'but' coming?"

He silently cursed his sister's keen intuition. She knew him far too well. Still, he didn't feel like setting out the reasons why Marissa might not be the perfect fit. It would make him sound ungrateful, especially after Maggie's complaint about the lack of eligible men in the district.

"No 'but.' We get on well. She's certainly a strong contender."

Maggie grinned. "Wow, Cayd. That's so exciting! What do Mum and Dad think?"

He waved the question away. "Let me finish. My second choice was Olivia. She's a gorgeous redhead. Sweet and sassy and keen to experience life on the farm."

"She sounds promising. Do you like her?"

"Sure," he said noncommittedly.

Maggie shot him a shrewd look. "And lady number three?"

"That would be Chelsea. She's short and petite. She has shiny brown curls with a nice smile. She's been a big help already on the farm."

"But you're looking for a wife, not a station hand."

Cayd nodded. "You're right. And that's why I'll be sending Chelsea home tonight. She's a lovely girl, but she doesn't light my fire. Do know what I mean?"

Maggie nodded somberly. "Of course. Chemistry's important. Without that, you're just friends. You need both from your life partner, or it won't last. At least, that's what Mum's always told me."

They both laughed.

"So, how's *your* love life?" Cayd asked. "Surely, you must be thinking about settling down. I seem to recall you always said you wanted at least half a dozen kids. You might need to make a start on that if you don't want to still be popping them out in your forties."

"Cayd!" Maggie protested halfheartedly, and then sighed. "You're right. My biological clock's ticking louder every year. I'm not against finding a husband and settling down, but that's easier said than done out here. Where do I find an eligible bachelor in the middle of the outback? All the men I know are either my underlings or jealous of my position. I need a man who's my equal in every respect and who also lights my fire. That combination's proving hard to find."

He nodded sympathetically. "Yeah, I get it. I really do."

She smiled softly. "I know. And thank you. If anyone understands the challenges we face out here, it's you." She winked. "Lucky for you, there are three potential mates just waiting for you to decide. Chelsea might not be your soul mate, but who knows? Marissa might just be the one. Or Olivia. You're spoiled for choice. Lucky you."

Cayd forced a smile as his thoughts once again returned to Lily. "Yeah. Lucky me."

If only she was in the running. If only I could convince her to give me a go. If only she wasn't engaged...

Still, engaged wasn't married. Engagements were broken all the time. Perhaps he should try harder to convince her that they were made for each other? It was definitely something worth considering.

Lily was quiet as Nigel drove her back to Marlowe Downs on Sunday afternoon. The cameraman appeared lost in his thoughts as he negotiated the dirt road. Conversation had been kept to a minimum from the time she'd greeted him at the airport, and for that she was grateful. Her thoughts were in turmoil. Polite conversation was beyond her right now.

Her surprise visit to Sydney hadn't gone down quite as she'd planned. Alex had torn himself away from his work long enough to take her to dinner, but even the familiar ambience of their favorite Italian restaurant and the superb Sauvignon Blanc that Alex had chosen to accompany their linguine couldn't distract her from the funk she'd fallen into upon leaving his office. For the first time, she'd begun to find fault in all the things that had previously endeared him to her.

His hair was too short. His glasses were too heavy for his face. He was too serious. Even at dinner, though they'd been apart all week, it was clear his mind was still focused on his work. He'd told some lame jokes. Not so long ago, she'd have found them amusing. Last night, it seemed his efforts only irritated her.

She'd made another attempt to seduce him that had also fallen flat. She was well aware that was the real reason behind her discontent. Even now, fifteen hours later, lingering flames of embarrassment heated her cheeks. There was nothing more humiliating than being rejected by the man she loved.

She arrived back at the station feeling tired and irritated. The fact she was looking forward to seeing Cayd again only made things worse. She wished her visit with Alex had been everything she'd wanted it to be.

No, that's not fair.

The truth was, Alex was as lovely and attentive as he usually was. It wasn't his fault she'd suddenly felt the need to make their relationship physical. It wasn't his fault she now found herself wanting more. More excitement, More spontaneity. More fun. More passion.

After mumbling thanks to Nigel and assuring him she'd be ready to start filming within the hour, she climbed out of the ute. Hoisting her suitcase off the back, she made her way to the cottage. She'd already taken the first step onto the front veranda when she spied Cayd sitting in one of the Adirondack chairs not far from the door. Macey sat at his heel.

Her heart leaped with surprise and excitement. She pressed a hand to her chest to slow it down.

"Cayd!" she managed, annoyed that she sounded so breathless. "You startled me."

"Sorry," he said with a complete lack of repentance. "I didn't realize you hadn't seen me."

"No, I... My mind was on other things."

A single dark eyebrow rose. "Do tell."

He grinned, showing a full row of straight, white teeth. His eyes lit up with mischief. She was reminded how incredibly attractive he was. With an effort, she dragged her gaze away and occupied herself with patting the kelpie.

"How was your weekend?" he asked, stepping forward to take her suitcase. "Did you have a nice visit with your fiancé?"

Lily flushed. There was no way she was going to talk to him about Alex. Besides, it was none of his business.

"My weekend was fine. How was yours?" she asked, deflecting his second question. She gave Macey a final pat and straightened. "Are you ready for the farewell dinner tonight?"

Cayd nodded. "Yep. Mum's been busy in the kitchen all afternoon."

Lily groaned. "Can you at least *pretend* you've done the cooking? Our viewers love it when the farmers cook. It makes them swoon."

Cayd shot her another mischievous look and then stepped much closer than she was comfortable with. His voice lowered to a husky, conspiratorial whisper. "What about you? Do you go all weak at the knees over a man who cooks?"

She took a step backward, almost overwhelmed by his nearness and the smell of his spicy cologne.

"As long as he does his fair share, that's all I care about," she muttered.

Cayd threw her an inscrutable look. She wasn't sure if he believed her, or if there was something else behind the challenge in his eyes. Close to panic, she centered her thoughts on Alex. He was most definitely a good cook. He'd grown up spending a lot of time in the kitchen, learning from his Greek mother and grandmother. His specialty was Greek pastries—sweet and savory alike. They both loved baklava, and it was a must-have addition to any family meal, but she suddenly realized that Alex's expertise in the kitchen didn't get her as hot and bothered as it should.

She'd watched him many times measure and pour and beat and stir and create magnificent dishes, and yet, it had happened so often over the years that now it almost seemed commonplace. She certainly couldn't remember ever feeling aroused by the experience. And yet, what she'd said about some of the women who watched their show was true.

The TV station received countless emails from viewers about how sexy it was to meet a man who knew his way around a kitchen. Those scenes were real ratings winners and tended to trend on social media for days: #realmencook was just one of the hashtags she remembered. It was weird that she'd never looked at Alex's skills in the kitchen that way. In fact, she'd never thought of Alex as being sexy at all.

Handsome, hardworking, ambitious. Kind, gentle, understanding. A quiet achiever who didn't need to trumpet his own worth. Someone who got the job done without fuss or bother. Stable, reliable, dependable. All great qualities in a life partner. Moreover, they were qualities she admired. It was only after meeting the dynamic and charismatic Fairfax cattleman that she'd begun to yearn for something more.

Dammit. This is all Cayd's fault. I was perfectly content with my life before I met him...

Except, she'd been dragging her heels on setting a wedding date and she hadn't been able to pinpoint why.

Maybe I wasn't as happy as I thought? Maybe that's why I've been so reluctant to walk down the aisle...?

The realization brought her up short. Suddenly overwhelmed by a confusion of emotions, she was forced to swallow a gasp. Cayd shot her a look that was filled with questions. It was obvious he could tell something was awry. Frantically, she struggled to compose her face into a neutral mask.

This was no place to contemplate raw revelations or what they might mean for her future. Right now, she had a job to do. Another week on the station and then she could turn her back on Marlowe Downs and its way-too-sexy resident cowboy and get on with the rest of her life. Whatever that might look like.

With a gargantuan effort, she fixed a smile on her face and met Cayd's way-too-observant gaze.

"Give me a few minutes to unpack and freshen up, then I'll get the crew together and we'll get ready to start filming again. I assume the girls are busy preparing for tonight?"

"Yeah."

"Good. I want everyone in their Sunday best." Her eyes raked over his dusty jeans and stained work shirt. "How about you? Are you going to change for dinner?"

He glanced down at his clothes and then gave her an endearing grin. "Do you think I should?"

Her heart tumbled over at the sheer sexiness of his smile. As their gazes locked and held, a frisson of awareness arced between them. The air was suddenly charged with tension.

She drew in a surreptitious breath, desperate to slow her heart rate. Schooling her features, she managed to keep her voice from betraying the turmoil that raged inside her.

"Yes," she replied primly. "I'm sure our viewers would like to see you in something other than work clothes. A jacket and tie would be nice. Let's mix things up a bit. It keeps things interesting for everyone."

"Does that include you?" he asked in that same husky tone.

She blushed. It was as if he could see the traitorous feelings that coursed through her veins. She averted her gaze and ignored his question. Slowly, deliberately, he brushed past her and set her suitcase just inside the door. Then he turned and gave her a mocking salute. "See you soon."

As she watched him walk away, Macey padding beside him, she exerted every effort to stop the trembling that had started in her limbs the instant they'd touched. Her skin burned from the brief contact. Her heart pounded like she'd sprinted a mile. For a moment, she was tempted to throw caution to the wind and go after him and tell him how she felt, but thankfully, as her heart rate and breathing returned to normal, the madness passed. Forcing herself to turn her back on him, she stepped inside and closed the door firmly behind her.

Chapter Seventeen

♥

Cayd did his best to pretend he was enjoying the delicious roast dinner prepared by his mother. Of course, Lily had insisted they capture footage of him bringing the piece of prime roast beef out of the oven so that for their viewers, it was at least implied that he'd had a hand in cooking it. He'd gone along with the charade because that was what was demanded of him, but the whole pretending thing was getting irksome. He lived with his family. His mother and father and brothers. So what? Why was that such a big deal?

He grimaced. He was being unfair. He'd known at the outset the terms and conditions he'd signed up to. Lily had made it clear that they wanted to portray him as a bachelor running solo who was in desperate need of a wife. She'd assured him it wouldn't be forever. That day couldn't come soon enough.

But first, he had to get through the farewell dinner. The girls were uncharacteristically quiet. Conversation around the table was muted. No doubt the knowledge that he was about to send one of them home was playing on their minds as much as it played on his. He would rather have told Chelsea before dinner, but then she wouldn't have gotten to eat. The rules were that she had to leave immediately after being told it was over. He hated dragging the whole thing out, but it was out of his hands.

He glanced at Lily who stood off to one side, watching the proceedings while the cameras rolled. There was something different about her. A restlessness that hadn't been there before. He wondered if she was eager to wrap up shooting and get back to her fiancé permanently. He scowled at the thought.

Maybe now's the time to make my move? To let her know how interested I am. Take my chances with her and see how it plays out. But what about the show?

Shit.

There was no way he could continue to pretend to be into the other women once he'd made his feelings clear to Lily. That kind of acting, that kind of deceit was beyond him, no matter the consequences he might face for breaching his contract. And then he remembered the details of those consequences, and his frown deepened.

There was a significant monetary penalty that would be extracted from him if he failed to abide by the terms of the agreement. It was money neither he nor his family could afford. That meant biting his tongue and going along with the status quo—at least for the moment.

Damn.

Lily noticed the frown on Cayd's face and was struck by a pang of sympathy. She'd been around enough farmers to know that the farewell dinners were always tough. Cayd was a decent guy. That was just one of the things she liked about him. Chelsea would be disappointed and upset about being sent home. No doubt Cayd was unhappy about hurting her, no matter that the girls were all aware that this was how things went and that by the end of the second week, only one girl would remain.

The meal was nearly over. Taking care to keep out of sight of the camera, she gave Cayd a sign that it was time to get this over with. Almost immediately, a mixture of dread and relief flooded his face. He bent his head toward Chelsea, who was seated on his left.

"Chelsea. Would you like to come outside with me for a moment?"

Fear held Chelsea's face momentarily frozen before she forced a stilted smile. "Of course."

The other two ladies watched on, both looking slightly less apprehensive than they had a moment ago. Earlier, Lily had suggested that Cayd take the women who were staying out for separate chats, just to keep the suspense going a little longer, but he'd flatly refused, telling her that he wanted to get the unpleasantness over with as soon as possible.

"It's not fair to them to drag things out like that," he'd argued.

She'd silently agreed, although she wasn't sure how well her boss would take the change in procedure. The more drawn-out, the more dramatic, the better, he would say.

Drawing in a deep breath, Lily signaled her crew to follow them. By the time they'd reached the back veranda, Cayd and Chelsea were seated in the pair of matching rocking chairs. As the crew got into position and gave Lily a nod, she gave Cayd the go-ahead to start speaking.

"It's been so great having you here on the farm, Chelsea. I hope you've enjoyed yourself."

She gave him an uncertain smile. "I've loved every minute of it. I could really see myself living here. Tending to the pigs and horses. Weeding the garden. Looking after the stock. Just don't put me in charge of feeding the chickens."

A brief smile passed over Cayd's expression before he compressed his lips. Lily could tell he was choosing his words carefully.

"I'm glad you've had a good time. When I invited you out here, it was with a view to showing you my home, my life, and seeing where things went. The fact that you've taken to station life is great, but..."

One camera zoomed in on Cayd's face. The other focused on Chelsea. Her bottom lip trembled. It was almost as if she knew what was coming. And perhaps she did.

Cayd drew in a deep breath and then reached for Chelsea's hands. He took them in both of his and squeezed gently.

"You're a great girl, Chelsea, but I'm not the man you're searching for."

Tears formed in Chelsea's eyes. She bit her lip and nodded bravely. "I understand."

"I hate that it's come to this, but I can't pretend there's a future for us," Cayd continued earnestly, looking almost as miserable as Chelsea.

"That's all right, Cayd. I understand." Chelsea's voice trembled. It was obvious she was moments from a complete breakdown.

Cayd shot an urgent look in Lily's direction, but she had no words of wisdom or advice. This part of the show always sucked, no matter who was on the receiving end.

With another deep breath, Cayd drew Chelsea into his arms and hugged her before gently setting her aside.

"Your farmer's out there, Chelsea. You'll find him one day. I promise. Thank you for coming out to Marlowe Downs. I really loved having you here."

Chelsea ducked her head and swiped at her eyes and then stood and hurried away. The cameras followed her along the veranda, until she disappeared inside the main house. Lily closed her eyes briefly. Her shoulders slumped.

One down, one to go...

Cayd's expression was closed and resigned. As Lily approached him, he glanced up and then looked away again.

"That was one of the hardest things I've ever done," he muttered.

She dropped into the recently vacated chair and sighed. "Yes. I've watched that scene play out so many times and it never gets any easier."

Cayd scoffed quietly. "You imagine how hard it is to be part of it. Watching from the sidelines is child's play."

She tensed with anger and then forced herself to relax. Cayd was right. Compared to the emotional upheaval he'd just gone through, watching it as an interested observer was easy. The fact he cared so much about hurting Chelsea only reinforced what she already knew about his character. His kindness and decency only made her like him more.

She realized with a jolt how much he'd come to mean to her. She could now see with a clarity that surprised her that her visit home had been made not so much to reconnect and spend time with her fiancé, but as a desperate attempt to reassure herself that her burgeoning feelings for Cayd were nothing more than a temporary aberration brought about as a result of their close proximity and would dissolve away to nothing once she was away from him.

Long hours of filming. Evenings spent together with the group, swapping stories and sharing tales around the firepit. Their enforced closeness had generated an intimacy that didn't exist outside the world of the TV show. At least, that's what she'd been telling herself.

But now, in the muted light that shone from the windows and illuminated the planes and hollows of Cayd's face, she could no longer deny the truth. She'd thought about him almost constantly while she'd been in Sydney. She'd compared him to Alex and had found her fiancé lacking. She'd tried to seduce Alex in the desperate hope of erasing thoughts of Cayd from her mind. Now she was relieved Alex had resisted her advances.

It wouldn't have been fair to her kind and loyal fiancé if they'd made love while she was fixated on someone else. He'd done nothing to deserve the kind of betrayal she'd committed in her mind. Okay, so nothing had happened between her and Cayd, but that didn't mean she hadn't thought about it. Or wanted it. Alex deserved better. He deserved a woman who was committed to him one hundred percent. Who didn't think about sexy cowboys and wonder what it would feel like to kiss them...

Caught up in his own dark thoughts, Cayd appeared oblivious to Lily's feverish musings. After a few moments, he stirred himself and stood, muttering something about having to go and see to his remaining ladies.

Alone on the veranda, except for Macey, Lily took a moment to appreciate the stark beauty of the outback. The sun had set long ago, bringing with it an absolute darkness that she'd never seen before she'd arrived there. No city lights. No high-rise buildings, with their hundreds of illuminated windows. No headlights from passing cars. No light at all, except for the blanket of stars that covered the night sky.

She stepped off the veranda and tilted her head back to better appreciate the tiny pinpoints of light that sparkled like diamonds against the velvety sky. She searched for familiar constellations and found the southern cross and the saucepan. She could remember a long-ago camping trip with her parents and brothers when they'd spent part of the summer holidays camping in tents on a river north of Sydney. She couldn't even remember exactly where they'd gone, but she remembered the sheer beauty and magnificence of the evening sky.

That was the first time she'd seen the sky filled with stars. The city sky didn't lend itself to such magic. Too many tall buildings and too much light. But out in the country, along the banks of a gurgling stream, her father had pointed out the constellations and she'd been filled with wonder at the sight.

As she began to wander across the wide expanse of lawn that led around the front of the homestead with Macey trotting beside her, the same kind of peace and wonder filled her again. She'd always considered herself a city slicker. Was completely at home among the crowds and noise and traffic. She felt alive in the city. But here in the outback, she was more relaxed than she'd ever been. She'd shed tension she hadn't even been aware of, like an old skin, no longer needed, and it had left her feeling renewed, refreshed, reenergized.

She'd put the feelings of euphoria down to Cayd. After all, there was a lot about him that inspired excitement. Whenever she was around him, she came alive. But now she realized it was more than that. Sure, Cayd was a huge part of it and though, until now, she'd refused to acknowledge that her feelings for him ran deep, she'd also fallen in love with the outback, his home, his family, his way of life.

What a pickle I'm in... Falling for a man who's not even available... Worse still, falling for a man while I'm engaged to someone else... What does that say about me? That I'm a terrible person? That I ought to be ashamed? Yes, and yes.

But it was hard to feel ashamed in such beautiful surroundings, with the clear night air filled with the sounds of crickets and other nightlife. A lone owl hooted in the distance. A tawny frogmouth swooped low in the sky, searching for prey. The quiet neigh of a horse as it sought out its foal. Macey's gentle panting as the dog padded beside her.

Giving Macey a pat, Lily slowly climbed the wide stone steps that led to the front door and sighed. Too bad there was nothing she could do about her burgeoning feelings. She was there to film a TV show about a farmer in search of a bride and that bride didn't include her. As she thought about the outrage that would erupt if she confessed to everyone that she wanted to throw her hat in the ring, a reluctant smile turned up her lips.

"What's so funny?"

The woman's voice came from somewhere in the darkness. Lily blinked and as her vision adjusted to the dimness, she saw Cayd's sister, Maggie, seated on an Adirondack chair at the far end of the veranda. Heat rushed into Lily's face. She was pleased the darkness concealed her discomfort.

"Come, sit with me for a while," Maggie urged, patting the matching Adirondack chair beside her.

Lily paused, in two minds about whether to join Cayd's sister or politely excuse herself and head inside. Her revelations about Cayd were still so new. She wanted time to properly analyze them, in particular how they affected Alex. Even though Cayd might be out of reach, there was one thing she knew for certain: She couldn't marry Alex. She loved him dearly and always would, but not in the way she instinctively knew she should love the man she was going to marry. Alex was more like a beloved brother, someone who'd always have her back. Someone she could trust and confide in, but who'd never set her heart on fire.

Maggie patted the empty seat again, and Lily swallowed another sigh and dropped down in the chair beside her. They'd swapped small talk over dinner, but that was all. They were virtually strangers. Maggie was the manager of a large cattle station that adjoined Marlowe Downs. Lily was a city girl who worked in television. They had nothing in common. She wasn't sure what they'd talk about.

Still, she didn't want to be rude. She supposed she could spare a few minutes and then make some excuse to escape. A well-timed yawn and some hints about the long plane trip from Sydney to Roma via Brisbane should do the trick.

With that thought in mind, Lily smiled. "It must be nice to catch up with your family. How often do you get home?"

Maggie grimaced. "Not as often as I'd like. We might share a common boundary, but that's fifteen miles from here. It's another thirty miles to the homestead where I live."

Lily laughed in surprise. "Oh. When you said you worked on the adjoining station, I imagined it was only a few minutes' drive away."

Maggie chuckled. "No one's geographically close out here. Not even the neighbors. The station I manage is to the west of Marlowe Downs. We have other neighbors north, south, and east of us, but all of them are at least a forty-minute drive away. Longer when it's wet and some of the roads become impassable. Once, during the last flood, we were marooned for more than three weeks."

Lily's eyes widened in disbelief. "Marooned? As in, you couldn't go anywhere?"

"That's right. We were surrounded by water. An island in the middle of the flood."

"What did you do for food?"

"Fortunately, we're always well-stocked as far as food goes. We also have a decent vegetable garden. Not as good as Mum's, but good enough. Of course, that went underwater when it flooded, so all that food was wasted."

"What did you eat?"

"We had plenty of meat. We live on a beef cattle station, after all. As for perishables and other things, we got them delivered by helicopter."

Lily shook her head, trying to get her thoughts around the idea of having to rely on food delivery by helicopter to survive.

"It's a different world out here, isn't it?" she murmured. "People who live in the city have no idea what you go through. They take for granted being able to stop in at the supermarket anytime they feel like it. They never expect to have to plan for more than a day or two at a time. They wouldn't know how to cope if they were told the shops would be closed for more than three weeks." She shot Maggie a look filled with admiration. "No wonder you guys are so resilient."

"Yep," Maggie said cheerfully. "That comes with the territory."

"You say that as if it's nothing. Do you ever think about living somewhere else? Somewhere closer to civilization?"

Maggie chuckled. "I went to boarding school in Brisbane for six years. That was enough civilization for me."

"So, you hated the city?"

Maggie shrugged. "I wouldn't say I hated it, but I was born and bred in the outback. It gets in your blood. I don't mind visiting the city, but this is where I'm happiest. And my family are only just down the road. What's not to like about that?"

Lily laughed. "Of course. Because forty-five miles away is just down the road. I love how casual country people are about distances. Like driving forty-five miles to go to dinner is nothing."

"It's a matter of perspective—and necessity. To get anywhere, you must drive long distances. You've just come back from a trip to Sydney. You know how far away everything is."

"How do you cope with the isolation?" Lily asked, curious.

A pensive look filled Maggie's face. "I grew up with it. I think that helps. Besides, most of my family are out here. I have two younger sisters and two older brothers who live in Brisbane, but they visit reasonably often. And we take a trip to the city every now and then. The city's great for shopping and eating out, but this is my happy place."

"Good for you," Lily said. She paused. "It's funny, but I know what you mean. There's something about the outback that draws you. It's like nowhere I've ever been. The wide blue skies that stretch on forever. The vast open plains. The mountains, the underground streams, the hot bore baths. It's all so exotic and beautiful."

Maggie grinned wryly. "It sounds like you've fallen in love with the place."

Lily nodded, realizing in that moment that what Maggie said was true. "You're right. I love it out here. I feel a level of peace I've never experienced. I've spent all my life in the city, and I love the hustle and bustle, the noise, the vibrancy, but I didn't realize how all that filled me with a tension I wasn't even aware of until I came out here.

"The first time I traveled those miles from Roma to Marlowe Downs, I could feel the tension falling away. It was weird. I felt the same way this afternoon. The farther I got from civilization, the more relaxed I became."

Maggie chuckled. "Sounds like you were meant to be one of us—a woman of the outback." She winked.

Lily flushed with pleasure. For a moment, it felt like they were coconspirators in on a secret that no one else was aware of.

Is this what it feels like to have a little sister?

Chapter Eighteen

♥

As much as Lily loved her brothers, it wasn't the same as confiding in a woman. Someone who thought the way you did. Who looked out on life with a similar attitude. Who experienced the same roadblocks and challenges and who was determined to conquer them all.

Maggie was making her way in a man's world, and by all accounts, she was killing it. Lily admired her grit and determination and the courage it must have taken to climb to the top of a traditionally male-dominated world.

"Tell me about your family," Maggie asked quietly.

Lily smiled. "I'm the oldest of five. I used to think that was a big family until I met yours."

Maggie laughed. "Yes, it's not often you come across a family with ten children. I don't know what my parents were thinking!"

Lily joined in the laughter. It was obvious to anyone how much Maggie loved each of her siblings.

"How many brothers and how many sisters?" Maggie asked, shifting to a more comfortable position.

"No sisters."

Maggie's eyes widened in surprise. "You have four brothers?"

"Yes."

"Do they all live in Sydney?"

"Yes. The twins are nearly thirty, but they're still at university. They share a tiny flat together. Honestly, it's hardly bigger than a shoebox. They never have any money. Thank goodness my parents don't live too far away. They eat at home most of the time."

Maggie smiled. "I bet my youngest sisters wish they were closer to home. Marnie's just graduated from university. Thankfully, she has a job, but she's on the lowest rung of her career and is earning peanuts. Skyla's still studying. She's always complaining about how broke she is."

"Oh, yes. I remember those days well. I remember eating breakfast cereal three meals a day. It was the cheapest food I could find. I could make a box of cornflakes and a bottle of milk last all week."

Maggie laughed. "And Emma. Well, she's most at home in the sky. We only see her on the odd occasion when she has a day or two off in our vicinity. She works with the Flying Doctors."

Lily nodded. "That sounds exciting."

Maggie chuckled. "It is for her, at least. What about your other two brothers? Do they still live at home?"

Lily grimaced. "One of them does, but not the one everyone thinks. Sam's twenty-seven, the same age as Cayd. He's legally blind, but that doesn't stop him from achieving his dreams. He's a computer programmer. He has a special Braille keyboard. He works part-time and lives in a group home with five other people. My other brother, Michael, is still trying to work out what he wants out of life. He's twenty-eight, so he should have some idea by now, but he's in and out of low-paying, unskilled jobs. He's the one who still lives at home." She shook her head and smiled. "I'm not sure where my parents went wrong with him."

"Every family has their black sheep, right?" Maggie teased.

"Absolutely. Who's yours?"

The question came out before she could stop herself. Fortunately, Maggie merely chuckled.

"Probably Marnie. She just finished a law degree and is interning at a slick firm in the city, but I'm not sure her heart's in it. She keeps talking about returning to Marlowe Downs and helping out on the station."

"Still a country girl at heart?" Lily winked.

Maggie sighed. "I guess so. It wouldn't be a terrible thing for her to come home. I'm sure Mum could do with some more regular female companionship."

Lily laughed. "Yes, she's rather outnumbered by the men in her life, isn't she?"

Maggie grinned. "You've got that right. A bit like your own mother. Her only daughter spends her time all over the countryside. I bet she misses you when you're away on location."

"Yes. She hates it when I go away. My father's in his seventies. Mum just turned sixty-six. Neither of them is in good health. Dad has diabetes, which affects his eyesight and a host of other things. Mum had a bad fall a couple of years ago and broke her hip. The bones didn't mend very well. She uses a walker most of the time to get around. These days, she rarely leaves the house."

"Oh! That's too bad," Maggie replied, looking genuinely distressed.

Lily compressed her lips and shrugged to ward off a rush of emotion. "Yeah," she choked.

"Does your brother take care of them when you're away?"

"Michael does his best. After Mum's accident, I arranged for homecare to come in a couple of times a week. They clean and cook and do other light household duties. Without that, they'd be doing it really tough. Especially when I'm away so much. And even when I'm home, I live in an apartment about twenty minutes away. Between long hours at work and the commute, I can't get there every day."

"What about the twins? Do they help out?"

Lily smiled ruefully at the thought of her brothers. They were only a year younger than she was, but they were more like rambunctious puppies who preferred to spend their time goofing off rather than doing anything serious.

"They help when they can, but they live an hour away from our parents and they're busy too. Between their university commitments and their part-time jobs, there's never a lot of time to spare."

"Do they help out financially?"

Lily averted her gaze and shook her head. "I'm the oldest. I earn the most. I pay the bills."

Maggie's eyes widened in surprise. "For everyone?"

"For my parents, at least. And Michael. That's why I work so hard." Her lips twisted. "Homecare doesn't come cheap."

"But that doesn't seem fair. You have four siblings. The burden shouldn't fall on you alone."

Lily shrugged. "I don't mind. I've always been family oriented. I'll look after them for as long as I have to."

"That's very generous of you. A lot of people would resent that kind of burden."

"Hey, they're my family. They mean everything to me."

Maggie fell silent. She gazed out across the dark expanse of front lawn to where ancient gum trees and fragrant Murrayas grew near the fence. The sound of male voices interspersed with female tones carried clearly on the still evening air. Lily recognized Cayd's deep voice along with Marissa's and one of Cayd's brothers. She wondered what they were talking about and then silently cursed her curiosity. It didn't matter what they were talking about. Cayd wasn't hers and never would be. He was none of her business.

In the dimness, Maggie shot her a sideways glance. "How are you finding my brother? How does he compare to the other farmers you've had on your show?"

Lily blushed again. She tried out a casual shrug. "He's okay. Easy enough to get along with. Happy to take directions. That certainly makes my life easier."

"He's *okay?* Is that all?"

Something about the intensity of Maggie's gaze made Lily shift uncomfortably in her seat, but she did her best to ignore it. There was no way Cayd's sister could know how she felt about him. She hadn't told anyone, and she'd gone to great lengths to conceal it. Maggie was merely probing, testing the waters. Nothing more.

"He's a great guy. What else do you want me to say?" she replied, trying hard not to sound defensive.

Maggie shot her a knowing look. "You don't fool me."

Lily's stomach dropped on a wave of nervousness. "W-what do you mean?"

Maggie regarded her steadily. "I saw the way you kept looking at him tonight. You like him a lot more than you're letting on."

Heat exploded across Lily's face. It was all she could do not to make a hasty retreat. But that would only prove Maggie's point, so she forced herself to sit there, and pretend Maggie's words hadn't turned her insides upside down.

"I... I..." She shrugged helplessly. "He's looking for love with one of three gorgeous, handpicked women. He's the star of the show. I'm just the producer. Who he chooses to enter into a relationship with has nothing to do with me."

"Except you wish you were in the running, and from what I've seen of my brother whenever he's around you, he wishes you were too."

Lily's jaw dropped. She stared at Maggie in shock. "What are you talking about?"

Maggie waved Lily's question away. "Oh, come on. Don't look at me like that. You must know how he feels about you. You've been living in close quarters all week, haven't you?"

"Yes, but I'm not one of his potential brides. I'm not part of the show," Lily sputtered.

"Perhaps. But that doesn't mean Cayd doesn't like you. It was so obvious over dinner. He barely took his eyes off you."

Lily flushed. Maggie was right. Every time Lily had looked up, she'd found Cayd's gaze upon her. She'd been nervous and jittery all night, not knowing what it meant, but had deliberately refrained from hoping it was anything more than coincidence. After all, he'd been preparing to send Chelsea home. Lily was certain that was all that had been on his mind. The fact that their gazes clashed more than once during the course of the meal meant nothing.

Then again, Maggie seemed to think that wasn't the case.

Could it be true? Could Cayd feel something for me? Something more than friendship? Something that goes beyond our professional relationship?

She hated that she so desperately wanted the answer to be yes.

She risked a quick glance in Maggie's direction. The woman regarded her with exasperation. "When are you going to admit you like my brother as much as he likes you?"

The air of command in Maggie's tone momentarily took Lily aback, but then the tension went out of her shoulders and she sighed in capitulation.

"You're right," she said, and relief poured through her. "I do like your brother. Much more than is appropriate, given I'm not one of the participants. I have no right to harbor feelings for him. Not only because of my position, but because I'm engaged."

She held up her left hand and showed Maggie the diamond that winked in the light that spilled out of the front window. Maggie's expression turned grim.

"What a pickle you're in, Lily. I wouldn't want to be you for quids."

Lily grimaced, feeling just as grim as Maggie looked. "Thanks. I was kind of hoping you might have some helpful advice."

Maggie regarded her solemnly. "How long have you been engaged?"

"Three years."

Maggie started in surprise. "Three *years*?"

Lily ducked her head. "Yes."

"So, I take it this man isn't the love of your life."

"Why would you say that?"

"Because no one waits three years to walk down the aisle if they've found the love of their life, especially at your age."

"Are you speaking from experience?" Lily asked, filled with curiosity.

"No. But that doesn't mean I can't see this for what it is. You're obviously not in love with your fiancé. Not in the way you should be."

Lily compressed her lips and nodded. "You're right. Although, in my defense, I only discovered that recently." She explained how she and Alex had come to be together. "It was only after I met Cayd that I began to question all that."

It was Maggie's turn to sigh. "You've fallen in love with my brother, haven't you?"

Lily closed her eyes briefly. "I'm not sure."

"Well, whatever you're feeling for him, it's way more than you feel for your fiancé, right?"

"Right."

"And that's a bad thing. For your fiancé, anyway."

"Right. That's why I've decided to break off the engagement. It's the only fair thing to do. Alex deserves better."

"You're right. He does. I'm glad you've decided to do the right thing. But what about my brother?"

"What about him?"

"He likes you. He likes you a lot. More than he likes any of the other women."

"But he chose those women to come here. He picked them out himself from a group of ten others."

Maggie waved away Lily's words impatiently. "I don't care what he did. He doesn't feel the same way about them as he feels about you. Trust me. I've known him all his life. He can't hide that kind of thing from me."

"I'm not sure I agree with you on the depths of Cayd's feelings, but even if what you say is true, there's nothing I can do. He's taking part in a TV show. He's under contract. We still have a week of filming to go. At the end of it, he gets to choose one of the two remaining women to share his life. I'm not part of that equation, and I never will be."

Maggie regarded her steadily. "You're in a difficult situation, that's for sure. Only you can decide what to do. Then again, life goes on after the cameras stop rolling. Who knows what will become of Cayd and his ladies then."

Lily blew out her breath on a heavy sigh. "I guess we'll have to wait and see."

With that, she stood and excused herself. She needed some time alone. Walking down the front steps, she took off across the lawn toward the guest cottage. Macey padded loyally by her side.

Lily was being pulled in two directions. On one hand, there were her obligations to the show and putting on something the viewers expected to see—to say nothing of the demands of her boss. Then there were her fledgling feelings for Cayd. The two were most definitely not compatible.

The best thing she could do was to keep her distance. Remain professional and polite, but nothing more. No more casual conversations. No more flirtations. One thing for sure was that she couldn't remain engaged. Alex deserved a woman who was into him one hundred percent. A woman who was as passionately in love with him as he was in her, and that wasn't how it was between her and Alex. It never had been.

They'd been thrown together by loving parents who thought that they'd be perfect for each other. And in theory, they were. But matters of the heart didn't always play by the rules, and no one could help who they fell in love with. Lily would love Alex for the rest of her life, but it was clear to her now that she'd never been *in* love with him. There was an important difference, and now that she'd opened her eyes to the truth, it could no longer be ignored.

But she couldn't tell him over the phone. He meant too much to her to do that. He deserved to hear it from her in person. The only trouble was, they still had another week of filming. She didn't think she could leave it that long. Not now she'd made her decision. She couldn't bear the thought of speaking to him over the course of the week ahead and pretending everything was normal.

But neither did she have the liberty of taking more time off. She'd just had leave over the weekend. There was no way her boss would approve another absence. Not when they only had one week of filming to go.

She sighed quietly as she stepped onto the veranda of the cottage. She patted Macey, who dropped to her usual position on the doormat. Lily reached for the doorknob. There was nothing for it. She'd have to call Alex. Right now. While she was feeling brave enough.

The conversation with Alex was as difficult as she'd envisioned. He was as upset as she'd thought he'd be. He kept pleading with her to reconsider, that she was wrong about the passion thing. That what they had together was special. At one point, she was tempted to agree with him, but then she thought about Cayd and the way he made her feel with the slightest touch, a glancing look, and she knew she was right to insist it was over.

With a heavy heart, she slowly prepared for bed. She brushed her hair, flossed and brushed her teeth, applied eye cream and moisturizer and dabbed perfume on the insides of her wrists. It was a ritual she completed every night, and the normalcy of it brought with it a sense of peace. Last of all, as she slid beneath the cool cotton sheets, she took off her engagement ring. Setting it on the bedside table, she turned her back on it and did her best to fall asleep.

Chapter Nineteen

♥

Cayd woke the next morning determined to focus on his remaining girls, particularly Olivia. He'd spent less time with her than he had with Marissa. He needed to change that. It was the start of a new week and while it had been tough sending Chelsea home knowing how hurt she was, he was glad it was over with. With her gone, he could now spend more time with the other two.

By the end of the week, he'd be making the decision about which girl he wanted to build a relationship with. Seven days within which to make the most important decision of his life.

Don't be so dramatic, you ass. There's no obligation to make any permanent commitment... Thank God.

As he rounded the corner into the kitchen, he was pulled up short by the sight of Lily and the camera crew. Marissa and Olivia were nowhere in sight, but the crew were already seated at the breakfast table, drinking coffee. A plate of buttered toast and a dish piled high with scrambled eggs sat on the kitchen counter, alongside a pan of sizzling bacon. His mother had obviously been up early.

After taking a plate, Cayd filled it with food and then made his way to the table. Deliberately, he took the seat opposite Lily and gave her a bold grin.

"Good morning. How are we all?" he asked, looking around at the gathering.

There were murmured greetings. Lily picked up her coffee cup and took a sip. Cayd's gaze zeroed in on her hand.

She's not wearing her ring.

For the whole time he'd known her, the impressive solitaire diamond affixed to the simple band of gold had been taunting him, reminding him that she was taken. But this morning, it wasn't there. He wondered if she'd misplaced it, or whether there was something more significant going on.

Questioning her with his eyes, he stared from her face to her left hand and back again. She flushed before averting her gaze. Just as quickly, she glanced back at him. He could tell she knew that he'd noticed her missing ring and that he wanted to probe the discovery further.

The problem was the room was full of her crew, and he didn't want to embarrass her or raise something that personal in front of everyone. He was about to suggest they step outside for a breath of fresh air when Marissa and Olivia traipsed in from the hallway and the opportunity for private conversation was lost.

Resigned to quizzing Lily about it later, he shifted his chair to allow Olivia room to sit beside him and gave her an engaging grin.

"Good morning, Olivia. I hope you slept well. How would you like to spend some one-on-one time with me after breakfast?"

Her answering smile lit up her face. It was all Cayd could do not to groan.

Lily stuffed her mouth full of eggs and tried to ignore Cayd across from her. Thankfully, he was now in conversation with Olivia, and though that gnawed at her insides, it was better than being put under the microscope by his way-too-observant gaze.

She could tell the instant he'd noticed her bare finger. His gazes had widened, and questions had immediately filled his eyes. Thankfully, he'd remained silent. The last thing she wanted was to discuss her private life in front of everyone.

Her ring finger felt bare, but she also felt strangely free. For the first time in her adult life, she was a single woman, free to love as she pleased. Though she felt sad for Alex, knowing how upset he was, she'd done the right thing by both of them, and she'd never regret that. She had no doubt he'd make someone a wonderful husband, just not her. And she was perfectly okay with that.

After breakfast, Cayd took Olivia outside. With the cameras recording their every move, they walked over to the stables and perched on a couple of hay bales. Lily stood a short distance away, watching.

"So, how do you like the farm so far?" he forced himself to ask.

Olivia beamed. "I love it!"

Cayd frowned. "Could you see yourself living out here, so far away from everything?"

"Absolutely! As long as you're here."

His frown deepened. "What would you do?"

"I don't know. Whatever you want me to do. Cook, clean, garden. Maybe not get so involved with the stock work, but I'd be happy to check the fence lines."

"Do you like it enough to trim your fingernails? Long nails don't work so well on a station."

Olivia laughed. "Are you kidding? Do you know how long it takes to grow nails like this?" She giggled.

Cayd couldn't tell if she was joking or not. Idly, he picked up a stick and started drawing in the dirt. Olivia continued speaking.

"I'd love to raise kids on a farm. It's such a wholesome life, so different to the city. You do want kids, don't you?"

"Sure I do. But what about your family? Wouldn't you miss them? We're a long way from Sydney."

Olivia's expression turned earnest. "Of course, I'd miss them, but we could go back to visit whenever we want, right?"

Cayd compressed his lips and grimaced. "Um, sure. Sometimes. But this is a working farm. Me being around the house so much isn't normal. I'm usually out in the paddock, dealing with the cattle or whatever else needs my attention. In fact, later today, we're mustering the cattle and moving them into another paddock. Are you up for that?"

Uncertainty flashed in Olivia's eyes, but she gave him a tremulous smile. "Sure."

From the corner of his eye, Cayd spied Lily step in a little closer.

"How about a kiss, Cayd? Is that all right?" Lily asked.

Cayd swallowed the instinctive "no" that threatened to spill from his mouth. Olivia beamed. She leaned across and squeezed Cayd's thigh. "I'm keen if you are."

He shifted his body and angled his head toward her. As he drew nearer, Olivia's eyes fluttered closed. Her lips were soft and pliable beneath his. She opened her mouth in an unspoken invitation, and for a moment, his tongue swept the warm recesses of her mouth. Conscious of Lily and the cameras, he kept the kiss brief.

After it was over, he admitted it had been pleasant, but nothing fantastic. Certainly not earth-shattering. As he set her gently aside and smiled at her for the benefit of the camera, on the inside, he couldn't help but wonder if he was going to be able to bring himself to choose either of the girls to stay after filming came to an end.

As she watched Cayd kiss Olivia, Lily's stomach twisted with jealousy and her heart was filled with lead. It had been her suggestion that they share a kiss. After all, that's what her viewers expected. She hadn't realized her reaction to it would be even worse than before. Now that she was no longer engaged, it was like she'd given her feelings free rein. *She* wanted to be the woman in Cayd's arms. *She* wanted to be the one enjoying his kisses, running her fingers through his hair, clinging to his shoulders.

This is not good.

With a concerted effort, she shifted away and deliberately focused on the scenery behind her. A horse and foal had come up to the fence, curious about the happenings. She reached out and patted the velvety-soft nose of the mare.

"Hey, girl," she crooned. "How're you doing?"

The horse nickered and nuzzled her hand. Slowly, the heaviness in her heart eased. She drew in a deep, calming breath. As the scene began to wrap up, she forced herself to turn back around to face the group. Her smile felt brittle, but she kept it firmly in place while she gave suggestions for the next round of filming.

"I was speaking with my brothers this morning," Cayd said. "We're moving cattle from the north pasture and into an adjoining paddock," Cayd said. "We could take the horses."

Olivia paled, but Lily merely smiled again. "Great idea. Our viewers love seeing the horses. There's nothing quite so romantic as a farmer and his women on horseback. We'll follow in the vehicle."

Cayd barely glanced at her. "Great."

Cayd was flanked by Marissa on one side and Olivia on the other. Neither girl looked comfortable on their mares, despite Cayd's reassurances that they were perfectly safe.

"Just don't do anything to spook them," he advised. "They're as placid as can be, but stay alert. Occasionally, quail might fly up in front of them. That sometimes gets tricky."

If anything, both girls turned paler than they had been before. "Maybe I could leave Ronnie here and ride in the vehicle?" Olivia suggested.

Cayd looked around them at the wide-open spaces with the nearest tree more than four hundred yards away and grinned. "Where do you suggest we tie her up?"

Olivia blushed and looked resigned. Cayd took pity on her. "Hey, if you really want to climb off, I'll lead her beside mine. What do you think?"

"That sounds like a good idea," Marissa said. "Go and ride with the film crew. You'll be more comfortable there." She dug her heels into the sides of her horse and trotted closer to Cayd.

Olivia narrowed her eyes at the other woman and then straightened in the saddle. "No, that's all right. I'll manage."

Cayd hid his amusement. While he didn't care that much for either girl, it was kind of fun watching their rivalry in their quest to win his heart. He glanced behind him. Lily and the crew followed slowly in a vehicle. Justin, Lachlan and Aiden were also helping out. Lily had instructed them to hang back so that they remained out of the frame. This segment was all about Cayd and the girls.

As Olivia bounced along, looking increasingly uncomfortable, Cayd was concerned she might fall off. The reins hung loosely in her hands as she tried to protect her long nails. She was giving the horse no direction. It was fortunate the little mare was as placid as she was, or Olivia might very well have been in trouble.

Marissa was faring slightly better, but he could tell she wasn't exactly enamored of the cows. They'd arrived at the paddock where the livestock were contained. Five thousand bellowing cattle were snorting, stomping their feet, and sending up dust clouds so thick, it was difficult to see. On top of that, they were smelly. Cayd loved everything about his cattle, but he appreciated that not everyone felt that way.

Once again, he found himself seeking out Lily. She hung out of the window on the passenger's side a short distance behind them, grinning widely and looking like she was having the time of her life. He caught himself grinning back at her, though he wasn't exactly sure she could see him through the dust.

A surge of longing went through him, so strong it almost bent him double. It wasn't fair that the only girl he was truly interested in wasn't his for the choosing. At least there was a possibility she was no longer engaged. He didn't know for certain, but the lack of an engagement ring surely pointed to something awry in that department. Of course there could have been a much simpler explanation, like she'd lost it.

He much preferred that she'd broken off her commitment to the faceless fiancé in Sydney. After all, the ring went missing the very next morning after her return. Could her visit back home have been a turning point? A realization she no longer felt as strongly about her lover as she had before. Or was all this wishful thinking and by tomorrow, the ring would be back where it had come from?

A yelp of alarm cut through his musings. He looked up in time to see Olivia half sliding, half falling from her horse. Moving quickly, he cantered over to her and reached for her just before she hit the ground. With one arm, he hauled her up in front of him. With the other, he struggled to calm his mount. As Olivia clung to him and began to sob, Cayd took a moment to speak quietly to his horse.

Calypso was a brute of a stallion who needed a firm hand to keep him under control. Fortunately, he was also well-trained not to balk at unexpected situations. Carrying two riders in the manner that had just occurred fell squarely within that definition. Though the horse was jittery and danced around, he didn't buck, which was a bonus. Once Calypso had calmed, Cayd turned his attention to Olivia.

"What happened?" he asked gently.

"I don't know," she sobbed. "One moment I was walking along, the next I was slipping off. I did all I could, but the stupid horse wouldn't stop. I hate it. I hate everything about it. I hope I never see another horse again."

Cayd should have been shocked at her outburst. The fact that he wasn't indicated how much he'd already come to accept Olivia wasn't cut out for station life. This only reinforced that.

Signaling to one of his brothers and telling Marissa to stay where she was, Cayd held Olivia tightly against him and cantered toward the vehicle. The driver brought it to a halt and waited for him to reach them.

"What's the matter?" Lily asked, climbing out of the ute and striding up to his horse.

"Olivia wants to go back to the homestead. Could someone drive her back?"

"I want to go home!" Olivia wailed. "I can't stand this place! It's so hot and dusty and awful! The cows are so noisy, and they smell *horrible*! If I'd known it was going to be like this, I'd never have come!"

Chapter Twenty

♥

At Olivia's impassioned outburst, Lily's stomach clenched with panic. They still had six more days of filming. There was no way the girl could leave now, or it would mean the end of the show. Marissa would become the chosen one by default. There was no suspense in that. Their viewers would be merciless on social media. Lily had to make Olivia see sense.

"Hey, Olivia," she said in a mild tone. "You're going to be all right. Let me take you back to the house."

As Cayd helped her slide off Calypso and onto the ground, Olivia's face filled with relief. She grabbed Lily by the arms. "Take me back to the house and book me on the first flight back to Sydney. I don't want to spend another night in this place."

Lily glanced at Cayd before drawing Olivia away. His face reflected a mixture of disappointment and bemusement. She wasn't sure what to think of that, but right now, she had more important things to deal with. Like convincing Olivia to stay until the end of the week. By all accounts, that wasn't going to be easy.

The camera crew had climbed out of the ute and were setting up their equipment well clear of the bellowing cattle.

"See what footage you can get," Lily told them over the noise. "Get some shots of Cayd. He looks the real deal up there on that horse. Our viewers will eat that up. I'll take Olivia back to the house and get her settled and then I'll be back."

Nigel grinned. "No worries. We've got this sorted. We'll get plenty of footage of the herd and your cowboy." He winked.

Lily fought a blush and quickly turned away so her cameraman wouldn't notice. He'd known her for more than five years. She wondered if he had any clue how she was struggling against a strong attraction to Cayd. He was her sixth farmer and the first time she'd felt anything like this for one of the participants—or any man, for that matter. Wasn't that why she'd broken off her engagement?

After bundling Olivia into the ute, Lily climbed behind the wheel. She started the vehicle and turned it in the direction of the homestead.

"Thank God I'm getting out of here," Olivia exclaimed. "I had no idea it would be so awful."

Lily shot her a look. "Really? Has it *really* been that awful?"

"Of course it has! Who wants to be surrounded by a herd of smelly, noisy cattle?"

"You did apply to be considered by a cattle farmer," Lily said dryly. "What kind of stock did you think he'd be running? Pigs? Oh, that's right, you don't like those either."

Olivia glared at her. Lily glared right back. Then she pushed her anger aside. She needed Olivia willing and compliant. She needed Olivia to want to stay.

She forced herself to apologize. "I'm sorry, Olivia. That was out of line. What I meant to say was, I'd like you to reconsider. Okay, so you don't like horses. That's all right. You don't have to ride another one."

"That's not the only thing I don't like!" Olivia cried.

Lily closed her eyes briefly and prayed for patience. "Do I need to remind you about the contract you signed? You agreed to spend up to two weeks on the station. You're only released from that obligation when Cayd decides it's time for you to leave. Not before. If you leave without our permission, you'll be in breach of contract and you'll run the risk of being sued by the TV station. Do you understand?"

"But you told me I could go home!"

Lily fought to keep her tone even. "No. I said I'd take you back to the homestead."

Olivia's mouth thinned into a mutinous line. She looked like she wanted to argue further, but remained silent.

Lily pressed home her advantage. "We have six more days of filming. That's not such a long time. You've already been here for more than a week. Look how fast that's flown. While we're filming, you need to look like you want to be here, like you want to be with Cayd. That's what you came here for, right? To find a husband? To fall in love?"

Olivia gave the tiniest nod. "Yes."

Lily eyeballed her as she swung into the house yard and brought the ute to a halt. "Then I suggest you pull yourself together and get out there and fight for him, because right now, Marissa has most definitely gotten the upper hand. You don't want her to win Cayd's heart, do you?"

Cayd took a seat at the breakfast table the next morning and was surprised when Olivia joined him there. She drew her chair up right against his, so close that when she sat down, their thighs brushed. He frowned, confused. She was the last person he expected to see there, let alone having her get so up close and personal with him.

What the hell's going on?

He glanced across at Lily, who was seated on the other side and a few chairs to his right. Her face was a picture of innocence, as if she didn't have a clue what he was trying to telegraph with his eyes. Olivia drew his attention back to her with a warm hand on his jean-clad thigh. She squeezed his leg and smiled.

"I'm sorry about my outburst yesterday, Cayd. I don't know what got into me. I'm so embarrassed. Please don't send me home. I love the station. I love everything about it. I'd be devastated if you made me leave."

Cayd shook his head, even more confused. He didn't know what had brought about the sudden change in Olivia's attitude. It was like she'd morphed into someone completely different overnight. She'd even trimmed her nails the tiniest bit.

He shot her a bemused look. "Hey, forget about it. No more talk about going home. We all have our moments. I'm proud of you for wanting to stick it out."

She gave him a brilliant smile and patted him on the arm. Meanwhile, Marissa shot daggers at the two of them from across the table. It was clear she wasn't happy with the most recent turn of events. No doubt she'd been looking forward to having him all to herself.

He bit back a sigh. Not for the first time, he wished the week was over already and he could go back to his uncomplicated life. He still hadn't had a chance to speak to Lily about her lack of an engagement ring. The fact her ring finger was still bare this morning gave him a fresh surge of hope. As she pushed away from the table with her coffee cup and started heading outside, he quickly excused himself and hurried after her. Finally, it seemed he'd get his chance to satisfy his curiosity.

As she wandered across freshly mown lawn and past newly clipped shrubs, Lily sipped her morning coffee and admired Ellen's garden. The carefully tended beds were awash with color. Hot pink, light pink, and white Azaleas, mauve chrysanthemums, and blue-and-yellow forget-me-nots. Brightly colored fuchsias, pansies of the deepest purple, dark-red poppies, and a wall covered in sweet peas of every color. Their scent hung heavily on the light breeze. She bent low and drew in a deep breath, filling her nostrils with perfume.

It was another beautiful day. The sky was clear and blue above her; the bright sunshine was pleasantly warm on her face. She breathed in deeply of the fresh air, cleansing her lungs of the smog that permeated the city. She'd always been at home living in Sydney. It was the only place she'd known. It was where she'd grown up, gone to school. Where her family lived.

But after spending a week in the outback, she realized she might very well be a country girl at heart, like Maggie had said. It surprised her, given her background, but it also felt right. Like she was where she was meant to be.

"There you are."

Cayd's comment startled her out of her reverie. She was immediately beset with nerves. Only last night, she'd decided to avoid any alone time with the man who'd come to mean so much to her and yet, here they were, alone in his mother's garden, well out of view and hearing of anyone else.

"I'm just finishing off my coffee. It's such a beautiful day to be outside, don't you think? The air is so fresh and clean this time of day."

She was rambling, but there was nothing she could do about it.

Cayd merely quirked an eyebrow in amusement. "Olivia seems to have had a miraculous change of mind overnight."

Lily's stomach dipped. She couldn't tell from his mild tone whether he was displeased about Olivia's sudden change of heart, but whether he was or not didn't alter anything. She needed Olivia in the picture, at least until the end of the week. She told him as much.

He grimaced. "Yes. I figured that was the case. Is it fair to force her to stay?"

"We talked. She came on the show to fall in love. She's still keen to make that happen."

Cayd's expression darkened. "No one can force love. It doesn't work that way."

"True, but she's willing to stay and give it her best shot. That's what this is all about, right? A show about finding true love?"

He gave her an inscrutable look. Nerves once again swirled in her stomach. Her gaze raked over him. His overlong, dark hair was messy, as if he'd run his fingers through it in lieu of a brush. His firm jaw was covered in a five o'clock shadow, making him look even sexier than usual. He was dressed in his customary work clothes: a royal-blue button-up shirt with the sleeves rolled up to his elbows, exposing his tanned, muscular forearms; a pair of faded Levi's that emphasized his narrow hips and molded to his long legs; dusty work boots that seemed so much more masculine, so much more appealing than Alex's expensive Italian loafers.

As her gaze met his, heat flared in his eyes. Nerves and excitement battled inside her, leaving her slightly dizzy. Her chest went tight. Oxygen was suddenly in short supply. She hated that her traitorous heart seemed determined to beat itself out of her chest at his nearness, but there was nothing she could do about that either.

"You're not wearing your engagement ring."

She cast around for something to say and then settled on the truth. "I broke things off. Being out here made me realize I want more from my life."

He went still. "More what?"

"I don't know. More excitement, more passion, more living. Everything's so vast out here. It put things into perspective."

She paused to draw in a breath. "Being out here has made me realize I'm a mere speck on the universe. Unimportant. Ordinary." Emotion lodged itself in her throat. She swallowed and continued. "The thing is, I want to live an extraordinary life, and I'm not sure I can do that with Alex."

"Alex. Is that your fiancé?"

She stared at him. Her face was aflame with a mixture of passion and embarrassment. She couldn't believe she'd revealed so much personal information to someone she barely knew. But Cayd had that effect on her. He made her feel comfortable, like she'd known him forever.

She held his gaze steadily and then slowly broke into a smile. "Don't you mean my *ex-fiancé*?

Cayd's heart thumped at the look in Lily's eyes. Acting purely on instinct, he took her hand and drew her farther into the garden. They came to a halt inside the orange grove. The smell of citrus blossom filled the air. Once again, Cayd's gaze zeroed in on her. She'd been giving every sign that she was as into him as he was into her, but he needed to make sure.

"Did breaking off your engagement have anything to do with me?"

Her eyes flashed with emotion. Her gaze dropped to his lips, his chest, and back up again. When she looked at him, her brown eyes glowed with desire.

She nodded. "Yes."

Adrenaline surged through him. The woman who'd turned his life upside down had feelings for him! He wanted to shout with joy. Instead, beneath the shade of the orange grove, he set her coffee cup aside and took her in his arms and kissed her. Gently at first, tasting, teasing, exploring. Her lips were as soft as the clouds that floated above them. She opened her mouth, and his tongue slid in. She tasted faintly of coffee.

Desire ignited inside him. His heart pounded with need. On a groan, he drew her closer, pressing her against his hard cock. He angled his head and deepened the kiss. Her arms crept around his neck. She pressed herself even closer, as if she couldn't get close enough. He didn't mind. He wanted to bury his cock in her sweet warmth and find relief from the fire that raged inside him. In fact, he was a little concerned that if they didn't stop now, he might disgrace himself.

Lily moved her lips over Cayd's, loving the feel and taste of him. She couldn't believe she was kissing him. His lips were warm and supple. His tongue had taken possession of her mouth. He kissed like a man who knew what he was doing, and no doubt he did. His erection pressed against her stomach, sending molten heat to her core. She'd never wanted anyone like she wanted him. She clung to him, needing his strength and support to keep her upright.

Alex had never made her feel like this. Not even when they'd engaged in heavy petting. It had been enjoyable, nice even. But it had never tilted her world off its axis, and that's exactly how she felt right now.

To think what I'd been prepared to settle for!

Thank goodness Cayd had come into her life. Even if they didn't end up together, he'd shown her what true passion felt like. From now on, she'd never be satisfied with anything less.

The kiss went on forever. It was like fireworks bursting across the sky. She was breathless, dazed, filled with awe at how wonderful kissing could be. An overwhelming desire to tear his clothes off and make love to him overcame her. It was a feeling so strange, so foreign, but persistent just the same. In a mindless whirlwind of desire, she reached for the buttons on his shirt.

The cotton was soft beneath her fingers. His sculptured pectorals were firm and perfectly formed. Her fingernails scraped across the hard nubs of his nipples. His gasp penetrated her fog.

On a sudden intake of breath, she crashed back to reality. The garden came back into focus. The scent of orange blossoms and sweet flowers filled the air. As the fog of desire evaporated, it was replaced by a clarity that had her immediately pulling away.

At Lily's sudden resistance, Cayd dropped his arms to his sides. He stared at her. They were both breathing hard. He was inordinately pleased that she looked as dazed and bemused as he felt.

"That was amazing, magical," he whispered, his voice still husky with need. "In fact, I'd go so far as to say it was earth-shattering."

He smiled a little as he said it, waiting anxiously for her to respond. As the moment stretched out, his nervousness ratcheted up a notch.

Surely, she feels the same way. It couldn't just be me...

Lily stared up at Cayd, aghast at what had just happened. Desire still darkened his eyes. His chest heaved from exertion. She drew in a deep breath and worked hard on slowing her heart rate.

"I'm sorry. We shouldn't have done that."

His expression fell. His lips tightened. Disappointment clouded his eyes.

"I take it that wasn't as good as for you as it was for me?"

She shook her head, not wanting him to misunderstand. "No, not that. Never that. That's the problem. It was too good. I never wanted it to stop. It was amazing. The best kiss I've ever had. And that's the problem."

He frowned. "I'm sorry, I'm confused. If that was the best kiss you've ever had, then what's the problem?"

She blew out her breath on a weary sigh, hoping he'd understand. "I'm sorry. I overstepped. Let my professionalism slip. I find you incredibly attractive, but you're here to find a wife, and I'm not part of that lineup. Our viewers have certain expectations. I have a job to do. Don't take this personally, but the show must go on."

Cayd bit back a curse and shook his head. "So that's it? You're just going to walk away?"Lily regarded him steadily, her expression somber. "Yes."

"The show's that important to you that you're willing to give up something so special, something that might turn into the most amazing experience of your life."

Her gaze didn't waver from his. "Yes."

He tried to keep the hurt and disappointment from his voice but was unsuccessful. "You're unbelievable."

She merely shrugged. "My job's important to me. Why would I put that at risk for someone I barely know?"

He winced. Anger licked at the inside of his veins. "I see. Well, don't let me get in the way of your job. After all, I'm no one."

He turned away before he completely lost it, but was halted by her words.

"Don't forget you signed a contract. Your obligations don't end until next Sunday."

Slowly, he turned to face her. She stood with her arms crossed over her chest, her expression hard.

"We expect you to do everything in your power to show your remaining ladies a good time," she continued in a dispassionate voice. "We owe it to our viewers to keep them guessing right until the very end. I'm sure we can count on you to keep up your end of the deal, right?"

He glared at her. He couldn't believe that only moments ago, this cold and somber woman had been liquid fire in his arms, kissing him for all he was worth and enjoying the same attention from him in return. She'd turned into an icy stranger, one that was all business.

He wanted to stand his ground and argue, remind her of the earth-shattering experience they'd just shared. But from her closed expression and her defensive posture, he could tell that it wouldn't do any good. For whatever reason, she'd chosen her job over them.

Now that he knew what it was like to kiss her, he had no idea how he'd be able to keep up the subterfuge with the other two girls, but Lily had given him no choice. At least until the end of the week when filming would wrap up. A contract was a contract, as she'd so succinctly reminded him.

A surge of determination went through him, diminishing his hurt. Icy anger settled in his gut. If she wanted him to hold up his end of the deal, then so be it.

Chapter Twenty-One

♥

Pale, early morning light leached in through the bathroom window. Lily stared at her reflection in the mirror. There were dark shadows beneath her eyes. No surprise, given that she'd tossed and turned all night. She still couldn't believe she'd kissed Cayd Fairfax! What a stupid thing to do. She'd known from the outset that she was attracted to him. She'd also known that he was off-limits.

It had been easier to remain distant while she was safely engaged to Alex, but now that fallback protection had been torn apart by her own hand, she had no one to blame but herself for the fact she'd fallen in love with a man she couldn't have.

She'd spent the night reliving their kiss. Every glorious, passionate moment of it. The feel of his soft, supple lips. The solid wall of his chest. And his erection. That wonderful rock-hard pressure against her stomach that had sent liquid need to her core. If it had gone on for too much longer, she was pretty sure she would have combusted in a shower of sparks and red-hot desire.

The fact that she'd never felt that way and wasn't sure if she ever would again was daunting. She'd had no choice but to shut down Cayd's suggestion that they act on the attraction between them. They had four more days of filming. Four more days and they were done. Cayd would make his final choice and everyone else, including her, could go home.

No!

She felt the silent protest from way deep down inside her. She didn't want him to choose one of the other women. She didn't want to tell him goodbye. She wanted to explore what was between them, get to know him better, see where it might lead. Most of all, she wanted to kiss him again.

The sound of her phone ringing brought her out of the bathroom. She padded barefoot into the kitchen and retrieved it from the counter where she'd left it charging overnight. Checking the screen, she bit her lip. It was her boss.

"Good morning, Gerald. How are things?"

His gruff response sent Lily's heart plummeting. She forced herself to keep her tone upbeat.

"We've been getting some great footage out here. Horses, cattle, and pigs. It's got a little bit of everything."

"I've seen the first week's rushes. I'm not impressed."

Her shoulders slumped. Nerves swirled in her stomach. One word from the boss and her job was toast.

She made herself speak. "Oh, that's a shame. Is there any-thing in particular you weren't happy with?"

"There's not enough drama. Everyone's getting along too well," he barked.

Lily closed her eyes briefly and drew in a calming breath. "The people out here are like that. They're decent folks. Hard-working, respectful."

"That might be so, but none of that interests our viewers. They tune in for the fireworks. I shouldn't have to tell you that. Get in the ears of those ladies and pit them against one another. Hell, tell lies if you must. Whatever it takes to increase the ratings."

"Gerald, I'm not sure I should—"

"You know how these things work, Lily. It's nothing person-al."

"But we're playing with their feelings. People are going to get hurt."

"They know what they signed up for. They'll get over it," her boss replied dismissively. "Besides," he added, "they signed a nondisclosure agreement. No one will ever get wind of it."

"I just don't think lying to them is a good idea. It's so underhanded."

"Your contract's up for renewal at the end of this season, isn't it?"

Her mouth snapped closed on another protest. The un-spoken threat was clear. After assuring him she'd do what she could to increase the drama, she ended the call on a sigh. Though it went against her sense of decency, she had no choice but to do as she'd been ordered. She also needed to distance herself from Cayd, at least until the show was over. She'd fallen in love with him and watching him flirt and frolic and kiss and canoodle with Marissa and Olivia was more than her heart could bear. She wasn't that much of a masochist.

Cayd sought Lily out over breakfast, but it seemed she was preoccupied with her crew. She sat with them at the farthest end of the table and appeared engrossed in conversation. She interrupted herself for the briefest of moments to acknowledge his morning greeting, but that was all. Later, when he and the ladies went out to feed the horses and chickens, Lily hung back with the cameramen. Each time Cayd smiled at her, she looked away. It was obvious she was avoiding him.

As the day wore on and she continued to keep her distance, his anger resurfaced. It didn't matter that he was prepared to explain to Marissa and Olivia that he'd fallen in love with someone else. Lily continued to make it clear she had no intention of exploring the fledgling feelings between them. For her, the show came first.

If that's the way she wants to play it, so be it...

Raising his voice loud enough that everyone could hear, he called to Marissa and Olivia. "Hey, who wants to have some fun?"

"I do!" Olivia cried.

"Yes!" Marissa shouted.

From across the way, Lily's expression registered interest. "What did you have in mind?" she asked.

"I thought we could drive into Roma and go to a local bar. Have a few drinks. Play some pool. Who's in?"

He was met with a chorus of cheers from the ladies. The cameramen and sound crew grinned.

Lily nodded briefly. "Sounds like a good idea. How about you take the girls with you? The crew and I'll follow you in another vehicle."

Cayd shrugged as if her suggestion was of no consequence, but he would have much preferred that Lily spent the hour-long journey with him. Now that he knew what it felt like to kiss her, he wanted to spend as much time with her as possible. Unfortunately, he wasn't in a position to argue, and she knew it.

Nearly two hours later, after Marissa and Olivia insisted they needed time to get changed and prepare for the outing, they finally bundled into two vehicles and headed out. They arrived in Roma when the last of the lunch patrons were leaving. Cayd greeted the ones he knew with a friendly smile and a handshake. Spying the TV crew, most of them stopped to ask what was going on.

"I'm taking part in a TV show," he admitted. "Ever hear of a show called *Outback Bride*?"

"No, mate," a farmer friend of his father replied. "What's that about?"

Cayd blushed. "It's about a group of outback farmers who are all in search of a wife. It's just a bit of fun, really. Nothing too serious."

The older man eyed him quizzically. "You're on the lookout for a wife, are you? I wish you'd told me. My niece's been hanging out for a wedding ring for years. She's nudging forty now, but that's not too old for you, right? She's a good cook and a hard worker. You wouldn't be disappointed."

Cayd's gut tightened with panic as he cast around for a polite way to decline. He knew the niece the old man referred to. Not only was she more than a decade older than him, but she was also short and squat and balding and owned a set of rotten, protruding teeth.

"I... Thank you, Jack. I appreciate the offer, but..."

The old man cackled with laughter. "You should see your face..."

Cayd's relief that the man had only been teasing was instantaneous. He grinned back and introduced the ladies, who stood a short distance away. "This is Marissa and Olivia. They've been staying out on the station."

Jack eyed them up and down and then whistled his approval. "They look very nice, Cayd. Do you get to keep both of 'em?"

Cayd chuckled and shook his head. "No. I have to choose between them. That's part of the rules of the show."

Jack pursed his lips and nodded. "Well, I can't say that would be an easy decision. A good problem to have, right? Lucky you."

As Jack wandered off, Cayd escorted his ladies inside the bar. A few more locals raised their heads long enough to send curious gazes their way. He acknowledged them with a brief wave and headed to the bar.

"Hey there, Paulie. It's good to see you again," he said, greeting the manager behind the bar.

"Cayd. It's been a while. How've you been?"

"Not too bad. Nice drop of rain."

"Yeah, mate. Sure was." Paulie nodded toward the women and the camera crew who'd filed in behind Cayd. "What's going on?"

Cayd explained again about the show. "Do you mind if they do a bit of filming in here?"

"Will it be on TV?" Paulie asked, his eyes lighting up with glee.

"Maybe. I don't have any say over the final cut, but you never know... It might help put this bar on the map." He winked at the barman.

"You do all the filming you want. And stay as long as you like. What are you and your friends drinking? The first round's on me."

While Cayd placed an order for drinks, he was conscious of Lily and her crew setting up their equipment in one corner.

He wanted to go and ask her what she was drinking, but he didn't want to be given the cold shoulder again. He was also still mad at her. In the end, he turned his back on her and ignored her, choosing instead to focus on his women. After all, that's what Lily wanted.

After collecting the drinks, he took them over to Marissa and Olivia. All three sipped their beer.

"So, this is your local hangout," Marissa commented.

Cayd looked around at the original pressed metal ceiling, the weatherboard walls with their peeling paint, the faded carpet that used to be a red color, but now looked more rusty-brown. The barstools, with their cracked vinyl and the smell of stale beer in the air. It was like many of the bars in outback Queensland: original, ancient, and well-loved.

"Yes, I guess."

"How often do you come into town?" Olivia asked.

"As often as we need to, but we try not to come in more than once a week. Mum comes in to do the shopping and she usually picks up anything we might need. I'm sure you can appreciate the distance involved in a round trip. It's not like popping around the corner for a carton of ice cream."

Marissa chuckled, but Olivia's answering smile was strained. Cayd was pretty sure her earlier outburst more accurately reflected her attitude toward farm life than the display of eagerness she'd put on the next morning and continued to display. Her anger and frustration two days earlier had been too heartfelt not to be genuine. Somewhere between then and morning, she'd made the decision to at least pretend to want to be there. At least that made it easier on him when it came time to send one of them home. In the meantime, he was forced to go through with the charade for the cameras.

Four more days and that's it. Might as well give them what that want...

He entertained the ladies by giving them a bit of history about the local town, how it was founded circa 1867 and named after the wife of the Queensland governor at that time. Though they both asked a couple of questions, Cayd could tell they weren't all that interested.

"Who's up for a game of pool?" he finally asked.

Both girls cheered, and Marissa warned him she was an ace with a pool cue. Cayd chuckled. Though kissing Marissa had paled in comparison to kissing Lily, he reacted favorably to Marissa's confidence.

"So, you're a pool shark, are you?" he teased.

Marissa gave him a bold look. "You'd better watch out, buddy. I'm gonna wipe the table with you."

He laughed. "Oooh, I'm scared."

Marissa smiled. "You ought to be."

From the corner of his eye, he saw Lily scowling. A burst of satisfaction went through him. He hoped she was jealous.

Serves her right...

He deliberately continued flirting with the ladies as they chalked their pool cues and racked up the balls.

"Okay, you and Olivia against me. How does that sound?" he asked.

"Fine with me," Olivia replied.

Marissa took the first shot. The white ball made a cracking sound as it contacted the others. Balls flew in every direction. Two of the small numbers fell into the pockets.

Cayd's eyebrows rose. "I'm impressed."

Marissa winked. "I warned you, didn't I?"

Cayd chuckled, amused despite himself. "That you did," he murmured and lined up to take his shot.

Lily had shifted to the bar. The bartender set a glass of beer in front of her. She smiled and handed over some money. One of the local lads sidled up to her and started chatting. Though Cayd couldn't hear what was being said, it was obvious from the man's body language that he was coming on to her.

A surge of jealousy rushed through him. It was all he could do not to toss his pool cue away and storm over to them.

Get a grip, you idiot. She wants nothing to do with you, remember? In fact, she told you to put all your efforts into your ladies.

"Come on, Cayd. Take your shot."

Marissa's remark registered. Drawing in a breath, he calmed the turmoil coursing through his veins. Giving both girls a bold wink, he did as she asked. One of the balls rolled into a side pocket.

"Yes!" he cheered.

Marissa smirked. "Lucky shot."

"Looks like you're not the only one who knows how to shoot pool," Olivia murmured.

She took the pool cue from Marissa and lined up for her shot. It was immediately obvious that she wasn't much of a player. She struggled to hold the cue properly and when she tapped the white ball, it barely rolled a few inches forward.

Marissa scowled at her. "You call that a shot?"

Olivia flushed with embarrassment and ducked her head.

Cayd frowned at Marissa. "Hey, no need to get nasty. If you're as good as you say you are, you shouldn't need Olivia's help."

Olivia jumped in. "Yeah, Marissa. Show us what you've got!"

Cayd took his second shot and popped another ball in the pocket. His third shot went awry. He turned to Marissa. "Your turn."

As the woman leaned over the table and lined up her shot, Cayd's gaze was once again drawn to Lily. Her uninvited companion had taken a seat at the bar next to her. From his animated expression, he was deep in conversation. Lily looked equally engaged. Jealousy once again reared its ugly head. Before Cayd could stop himself, he set the pool cue aside and strode over to where they sat.

"Cayd Fairfax," he said, holding out his hand toward the stranger. "I don't think we've met."

Lily fought a wave of embarrassment as the two men shook hands. Their greeting was friendly enough, but almost immediately, she sensed an undertone of tension as each man sized the other up and gauged each other's importance to her.

While a part of her was flattered by Cayd's need to stake his claim, she was also embarrassed by his presence. What was he doing there? She had a job to do, and so did he, and it didn't involve getting jealous over attention paid to her by a stranger. Even worse, Marissa and Olivia were only a few yards away.

Lily dreaded the possibility that they might cotton on to Cayd's interest in her. That would be disastrous. It was hard enough to convince Cayd to keep up the charade, let alone two women who had nothing to gain and everything to lose if they got an inkling that Cayd's heart was no longer in it for either of them. She was also acutely aware the cameras were still rolling, capturing every moment for all the world to see. She had to try to distract him.

"Cayd. Why don't you return to your pool game? Your ladies are waiting for you."

Lily glanced over her shoulder. It was as she'd expected. Both Marissa and Olivia stood watching them, their expressions a mixture of curiosity and suspicion. Panicked nipped at Lily's heels. She tugged Cayd by the arm, trying to herd him in the girls' direction.

Resisting her attempts to move him on, Cayd stubbornly remained where he was. "I don't want to play pool. I want to dance. With you."

Belatedly, she realized someone had put a song on the jukebox. Before she knew what was happening, Cayd pulled her upright and led her toward the makeshift dance floor. She squeaked in alarm.

"Cayd! Stop it this instant," she hissed.

But Cayd was having none of it. Instead, he pulled her onto the small square of wooden flooring and took her in his arms. Lily was forced to consider her options. She didn't want to cause a scene, but neither did she want Cayd's ladies and the crew asking awkward questions. No doubt they'd be wondering what the hell was going on. Why was the producer dancing up close and personal with the star of the show?

She was grateful when Nigel lowered his camera. Though his gaze was full of questions, at least he'd stopped filming. Her second cameraman followed suit. As if aware they were no longer on film, Cayd's hands went to her hips. He drew her in close. She did her best to maintain some distance between them, but it wasn't easy.

As they swayed to the beat of the music, the gazes of the other two girls bored into them, confusion and a growing resentment in their eyes. Cayd was supposed to be romancing *them*. Lily wished she could deny how good it felt to be in his arms. He was a confident dancer. She liked that. In fact, there was a lot she liked about him.

She'd never imagined falling for one of her farmers. Over the course of five seasons, she'd never even come close. Now she'd fallen for Cayd and with a speed that snatched her breath away.

As if sensing her thoughts, he smiled down at her. It was a slow, sexy smile that crinkled the corners of his eyes and lit up his beautiful blue eyes. The intensity in those sapphire orbs had the power to curl her toes. He was too sexy for his own good. Much too sexy for her peace of mind. It was too bad they weren't free to explore their feelings. She had a sudden yearning to know what it felt like to be with someone who had the power to tilt her world off its axis.

As he drew her closer, she brushed against his erection. Molten heat shot through her veins and centered in her core. Desire hardened her nipples. She stifled a gasp.

Oh, God.

He shot her a knowing look. Somehow, he could tell how aroused she was.

This is madness. What am I doing?

Without warning, she came to a halt and wrenched herself out of his arms.

"I'm sorry. I can't do this."

Turning on her heel, she left him standing on the dance floor, a look of surprise and disappointment on his face. With her thoughts in turmoil, she barely registered that Marissa swiftly took her place. With reluctance, Cayd started dancing again.

"Get those cameras rolling again," she said to her crew as she passed them on her way outside.

"Sure thing," Nigel murmured.

He shot her a searching look, but she ignored it. Keeping her head down, and avoiding all eye contact, she strode across the barroom to the exit and made her escape.

Chapter Twenty-Two

♥

C ayd wanted to follow Lily outside, but he didn't get the chance. No sooner had she abandoned him on the dance floor than Marissa slid into his arms. Draping her arms around his neck, she pressed herself against him and began moving to the slow love song that had just started on the jukebox.

He knew the instant she became aware of his erection. She stilled momentarily and her eyes went wide. Then she smiled with a confidence that was reflected in the knowing gleam in her gaze. Cayd cursed under his breath. Of course Marissa would assume he was aroused because of her. Why wouldn't she? She was a beautiful woman, well used to attention from men. Not only that, it wouldn't occur to her that his arousal had anything to do with Lily. She was only the TV producer, after all.

Marissa pressed ever closer against him. When she touched her lips to the side of his neck, he suppressed a groan. Not wanting to offend her, he maintained the charade of dancing together and ignored her tongue that had now stolen into his ear. Trying not to tense, he counted down the excruciating minutes before the song came to an end. As soon as it did, he extricated himself from her grip as politely as he could and, with a murmured apology, escaped to the restroom where he could hide out for a while in peace.

After taking the time to restore her equilibrium, Lily headed back inside. Marissa leaned on the bar with a drink in her hand, talking to one of the crew. Olivia sat alone on a stool farther down the bar, poking at the ice in her glass with a straw and looking for all money like she didn't have a friend in the world. Cayd was nowhere in sight.

Lily suppressed a sigh. She'd been ordered to create drama. The only drama she'd created was for herself. If she wasn't careful, Gerald would be back on the phone, chewing her out for failing to deliver.

When did my job become such a drag?

When she began falling for Cayd, that's when. And as much as this season had become so difficult through her own making, she couldn't afford to mess up now. She needed her job, and that meant keeping her distance from Cayd. She'd resolved to do that before, but now she was even more determined to shut down any fledgling feelings and get the job done.

Four more days... That's all. Four more days to keep up the subterfuge and then we can all go home.

In the meantime, she had to up the ante, increase the drama, get some conflict happening. Tell lies if she had to. She made a beeline for Marissa and plastered a smile on her face.

"Hey, Marissa. Do you have a minute?"

Not waiting for the woman to respond, Lily drew her to one side, far enough away that no one could hear them. They were partially hidden behind a potted palm.

"What is it?" Marissa asked a little sulkily.

Lily leaned her head in conspiratorially. "I was just speaking with Cayd. He's confessed that he's really into you. Isn't that great news?"

Marissa's eyes widened. She gave a yelp of excitement and grabbed Lily's arm. "Are you sure?"

"Of course I'm sure. The thing is, he's a bit uncertain how you feel about him."

"How could he be uncertain? I've made myself very clear. Anyway, if he needs me to spell it out..."

"Yes, yes! Spell it out! Why don't you declare your love for him!" Lily urged, almost choking on her words.

Marissa's answering smile was supremely confident. "I *knew* he liked me more than he said!" She looked down at her body. Her close-fitting dress displayed her numerous charms. "After all, who could resist this?"

She shimmied her shoulders and grinned. Her bountiful breasts almost spilled out over her low-cut neckline. It killed Lily to push Marissa into Cayd's arms, and she was wracked with guilt over her deception, but what choice did she have? It was obvious out of the two of them, he was more attracted to Marissa than Olivia, and Lily had been ordered to spice things up. If she walked away with a broken heart as a result, then that was the price she had to pay. If nothing else, it would certainly provide good TV viewing, and that's what mattered most.

Cayd sat alone in one of the rockers on the back veranda and brooded in silence. Dinner had been a noisy affair, with both Olivia and Marissa vying for his attention. Particularly Marissa. Dancing with him at the bar had emboldened her. She'd squeezed herself beside him at dinner, brushing up against him whenever she could. In between mouthfuls, she stared up at him adoringly, batting her eyelashes and then looking away coyly, as if they were engaged in some kind of unspoken courtship.

Meanwhile, Lily sat as far away from him as she could and ignored him, barely speaking to him, and then only when asked a direct question. It irked him that she could discount so easily all that lay between them, not the least the white-hot passion that ignited between them whenever they touched. And for what? A TV show. What a disgrace.

He wanted to rail against her, shake her and tell her to wake up to herself. The kind of passion between them didn't come often. It might not ever be like that for either of them again. They ought to be grateful that they'd been blessed with the gift of each other, not setting it aside in favor of something as inconsequential as a TV show.

With a weary sigh, he leaned forward and rested his elbows on his knees. The evening air was warm on his face as a gentle breeze floated through the trees. The cicadas that were almost deafening in the daytime had settled down to sleep. Only the howl of a dingo in the distance broke the silence.

The sound of a sliding door opening caught his attention. He looked up, hope blooming in his chest. He swallowed his disappointment as Marissa stepped out onto the veranda and made her way toward him.

She'd changed out of the body-hugging dress she'd worn to the bar and was now dressed in a floaty, floral summer skirt and short-sleeved white blouse that was tight enough across her chest to remind anyone who cared to notice that God had been more than generous in that department. He'd noticed. Of course, he had. He was a flesh-and-blood man. But as she settled herself in the chair beside him, he discovered his body was strangely unmoved by her presence.

"Here you are!" she said brightly. "You disappeared after dinner. I wasn't sure where you'd gone."

He offered her a tight smile that felt more like a grimace. "Nowhere special. Just here."

She smiled, and then her gaze darted away. She looked out across the backyard. "It's such a beautiful evening."

"Yeah. This is one of my favorite times of day. I like to come out here and take advantage of the solitude to recharge."

He hoped she'd take the hint but was disappointed when she merely smiled again. Then she looked down at her lap and began pulling at a loose thread in her skirt. He frowned. If he didn't know better, he'd guess she was nervous.

No, that can't be right. Marissa's supremely confident in her appeal. There's no way she could be nervous. Besides, she's sought me out, not the other way round.

A moment of silence fell between them. She kept pulling at the thread. Then she cleared her throat. He found himself instinctively bracing himself against what she was about to say.

"I need to tell you something," she said, glancing briefly in his direction.

He kept his tone light. "What is it?"

She compressed her lips and looked away and then blurted, "I've fallen totally in love with you, Cayd, and I hope you feel the same way."

If she'd said she wanted to be a bronc rider and compete in the national rodeo, he couldn't have been more surprised. Blinking, he tried to come up with the words to let her down gently. Though he very much doubted she was in love with him, she believed that was the case. He might not feel the same way about her, but that didn't mean he wanted to hurt her.

She shot him a pleading look. "Please, Cayd. Say something."

He drew in a deep breath. "Okay. Well, to say that I'm flattered is an understatement, but I'm sorry. I'm afraid I don't feel the same way. You're a beautiful, accomplished woman, and some day you're going to make some man a wonderful wife. But you're not the woman for me. I'm sorry. I wish you were. Life would be so much easier, believe me."

He smiled wryly, hoping to lighten the mood, but Marissa's eyes filled with tears.

"But Lily told me you were in love with me! She told me that it was only because you didn't know how I felt that you'd been holding back."

Cayd stared at her in shock. "Lily told you that?"

"Yes! She told me while we were in Roma today. She led me to believe you were only waiting for a sign from me to declare your love."

An icy fury took hold of Cayd. He was angrier than he'd ever been in his life. Beneath the fury was a hurt so powerful, he wasn't sure he'd ever get over it.

How could she? Knowing how I feel about her? How could she?

But first, he had to deal with Marissa's hurt feelings. Taking her hands in his, he squeezed them gently.

"I don't know why Lily told you that, Marissa. It's simply not true. You're a lovely girl and so fun to be with, but I'm not in love with you."

Marissa gasped on a sharp intake of breath. Struggling awkwardly to her feet, she buried her face in her hands and stumbled away. In the sudden silence, Cayd became aware of someone behind him. He swiveled around and spied the red glow of a camera. He cursed long and loud.

The whole awful scene had been captured on film for the world to see. His gaze shifted. Behind the cameraman stood Lily. He got to his feet so forcefully, the rocker went skittering away from him.

As Cayd strode toward her, his face as black as a thunder-cloud, Lily braced herself for whatever was to come. She had a fair inkling. She'd heard every word Marissa had uttered. No wonder Cayd looked fit to kill.

Unwilling to have the conversation with so many curious onlookers, Lily beckoned to him with movement of her head and then turned and struck out across the back lawn. She'd reached the fence that bordered Ellen's vegetable garden, well away from curious eyes and ears and, more importantly, the cameras, before she came to a halt. Cayd was right on her heels. Slowly, she turned to face him.

Anger held his face taut. "Why the hell did you tell Marissa I was in love with her?"

"First of all, I didn't say that. I told her you were into her."

"And why would you say that when you knew it wasn't true?"

She averted her gaze. "How would I know it wasn't true? You seemed interested enough in her while you were kissing her, or have you forgotten about that?"

If anything, Cayd looked angrier. "For fuck's sake! You *told* me to kiss her!"

Frustration surged through her. She threw her head back and groaned. "For heaven's sake, Cayd! This is a game. You chose three women to compete for the prize. Only one of them is going home with it. In case you've forgotten, *you're* the prize.

"Of course hearts are going to be broken, feelings trampled along the way. That's par for the course. But everyone knows the gig. Everyone knows that only one will be chosen to stay. Ramping up the suspense, keeping our viewers guessing is all part of it. We have to fulfill their expectations. Back home in their living rooms, they're barracking for this one or that. Everyone will have a favorite, and they'll want their favorite to win. They want to know that their lady has an equal chance at winning your heart. Otherwise, what's the point?

"It's my job to facilitate that. If that means putting ideas in someone's head, or giving one of them a little push, then that's all part of it."

Cayd shook his head slowly back and forth. "So, this is all just a game to you."

Lily closed her eyes against another surge of frustration. "It's a game to everyone. Yes, that's what this is. A game."

Hurt flashed in his eyes. Her stomach clenched. The last thing she wanted to do was hurt him.

"And what about you and me?" he asked bitterly. "Were those feelings real, or were they all part of the game? Just another way to increase the ratings?"

Lily was appalled. "No! Of course, my feelings were real. But what would you have me do? Tell your would-be brides that sorry, you see, Cayd and I have a thing going. Neither of you stand a chance. Best pack your bags now and get it over with, because guess what, he's with me. Of course, I couldn't say any of those things!"

With her breath coming fast and her heart thumping, she took a moment to drag in some deep breaths before speaking again. This time, she managed to take a slightly calmer tone.

"I'm contracted to getting this series over the line. That means a happy-ever-after or at least a happy-for-now with one of your *chosen* ladies. Did you hear what I said? *I'm* not one of them."

"You don't need to remind me of that!" Cayd shouted. "How is it my fault that I've fallen in love with the wrong woman?"

His words shocked Lily into silence. Her mouth opened, but no words came out. When she finally found her voice, it came out in a whisper.

"You... You're in love with me?"

Her voice was so hoarse she barely recognized it.

Cayd's expression turned stony. "Yes. I'm in love with you. Does that mean anything at all to you?"

Filled with agony, she shook her head slowly from side to side. "I'm sorry, Cayd. I didn't ask for this to happen. I have obligations. I have no choice but to finish this series in the way everyone expects, especially my boss."

She grimaced. "I wish things were different, that we'd met under different circumstances, but that didn't happen, and there's no point living with regrets or getting upset about that. No point at all." Her voice choked on the final words. Any minute, she might burst into tears. She couldn't let that happen. She *wouldn't* let that happen. Clenching her jaw tight and fisting her hands, she stared Cayd down.

Cayd glared at Lily. The white-hot fury of only moments ago had receded, but it had been replaced by an icy calm. He was still angry at her for lying to Marissa, and all for the benefit of a stupid TV show. The game. The fucking *game*. To make matters worse, she hadn't even bothered to address his declaration of love.

"Listen, Lily, and listen well," he rasped. "Playing with people's emotions has *never* been a game to me. Yes, I understood the rules of engagement, but I always intended to play fair. Deceiving the ladies into thinking I care more for them than I do was never part of the deal."

He continued to eyeball her. "Then there's us. You're lying to yourself if you think there's nothing special between us. It's been there from the very beginning. The only reason I didn't make a move earlier was because you were wearing a fucking engagement ring. I'd never stoop so low as to steal away another man's fiancée.

"But then the ring went AWOL, and you told me you'd broken off the engagement. That's all the encouragement I needed to try to convince you how I felt. And you felt it too. But apparently, even that isn't as important to you as your damn TV show."

Emotion threatened to overwhelm him. Hurt and pain rose inside him, choking off his breath. He shook his head, trying to dislodge it. "I can't believe you think so little of me, of *us*, that you're willing to throw another woman at me, all for the sake of your ratings."

She opened her mouth to protest, but he'd already heard enough. With a vicious movement of his hand, he cut her off. "You know what? Save it. I'm done."

With that, he stormed away.

Lily watched Cayd stalk away and felt like her heart was breaking. His parting words flayed her. His coldness, his icy rage filled her with despair. She had no hope that he'd ever forgive her. She hated that things had come to this. She'd fallen in love with him. But what good was that now when he despised her?

She cursed her job for putting her in such a predicament, and cursed her boss, too. She couldn't leave now no matter how much she might want to. She needed to see out her contract, which meant seeing out this series. If she left now, there would be no hope her contract would be renewed. Gerald would see to that.

She'd have to convince Cayd to fake it for the cameras, no matter how angry he was with her, and she'd have to ignore the shards of her broken heart and continue on as if there was nothing wrong. She wasn't at all confident Cayd would be on board, but she had to give it her best shot. All she could hope was that by reminding him of his contractual obligations to see out the series until the end and pointing out the consequences to him, and potentially to his dream of setting up a farm stay business if he didn't, would be enough.

Chapter
Twenty-Three

❤

Cayd climbed astride Calypso and dug his heels into the massive stallion's side. Somehow the beast sensed the turmoil that continued to writhe in Cayd's gut. The horse took off at a gallop, shaking his head and kicking up dust in their wake.

Cayd turned Calypso toward the west and onto a long straight path that stretched for miles, giving the horse his head. They galloped nonstop for what felt like hours and were both in a lather of sweat when Cayd finally eased back on the reins and slowed Calypso to a walk.

"Easy, boy. Easy, now."

He patted the horse's shoulder while the two of them caught their breath. A little farther on, they took refuge beneath the shade of a huge gum tree. Cayd slid off and patted the horse reassuringly once again. Calypso snorted and nudged Cayd with his head, as if seeking an apology.

"You're right, old boy. I'm sorry. I shouldn't have ridden you so hard. I don't even have any water to give you."

When he'd hastily thrown on the saddle and climbed astride the stallion, his only thought had been to get the hell away from everyone, especially Lily. Packing water had been the last thing on his mind. Fortunately, the morning sun was still pleasantly warm on his skin and a refreshing breeze blew in across the plain.

Securing the reins to a nearby gum tree, he pulled off his Akubra, wiped the sweat off his brow, and then found a spot to sit. He leaned back against the trunk of another gum tree and gave his thoughts free rein. He was furious with himself as much as Lily. He was furious that he'd fallen in love with her and furious that she repaid him by wanting him to continue with the charade.

What a joke.

Yes, he knew what he'd signed up for, and at the time, though he had a few reservations, he was open to falling in love. Was still open to that. He'd never imagined he'd fall in love with the wrong woman. A woman who cared more for her TV show and its ratings than she cared for him. It was infuriating, as well as hurtful. He wanted to believe that she loved him as much as he loved her, but it appeared he was only deceiving himself in that regard. Surely, if she truly felt as strongly as he did about them, she wouldn't be able to do what she had.

She'd alluded to her own contractual obligations, namely her job. But how did keeping a job stack up against what could be a perfect love? She must have been in love before. She'd been engaged. But perhaps it had come so easily to her that she didn't understand how rare true love really was?

Not that there was anything he could do to convince her. She'd obviously made up her mind. She'd chosen her job and a TV show over him and that was that.

A fresh wave of anger, hurt, and disappointment washed over him. His hands tightened into fists. She wanted him to continue with the charade of falling in love with one of his ladies, and by God, that's what he'd do. What didn't sit well with him was having to deceive the women who were completely innocent in all this. Pretending he had feelings for either one of them was wrong. Besides, he'd already made it clear to Marissa that he didn't see her as anything other than a friend.

Then an idea came to him, and he couldn't help but smile. He'd come clean with Olivia and Marissa. Tell them the truth about how he felt. But he'd also tell them about Lily and what she'd forced him to do. He hoped both women would be as outraged as he was. So much so that they'd willingly get on board.

With a renewed sense of grim determination, he untied the reins and swung his leg over Calypso. As he turned the stallion toward home and settled into an easy canter, he was filled with anticipation. Lily Calimeris thought she held all the cards. She was wrong. He looked forward to playing her as ruthlessly as she'd played him.

Bring it on.

Lily pleaded a headache, and after giving instructions to her film crew about what footage they should take, she hid out in the cottage for the rest of the day. She was being a coward and that had never been her style, but after her last confrontation with Cayd, she hadn't felt up to being around anyone.

He'd arrived at the homestead covered in dust and sweat and smelling of horses. She'd briskly reminded him of his contractual obligations and, after enduring a searing, angry look from him, had made her escape.

When evening arrived, she asked Nigel to make her apologies for not attending dinner. Ellen organized a tray of food to be delivered, along with a glass of water and some pain killers. A stab of guilt went through her at the sight of them, but by that time, she had a headache for real and was grateful for Ellen's thoughtfulness.

As the early morning light filtered through the curtains, she struggled out of bed and forced herself to face the day. She couldn't hide out forever. Not only would people begin to get suspicious or be concerned there was something seriously wrong, she had a job to do, and it wasn't going to get done without her.

During the previous day, Nigel had followed her instructions and allowed Cayd's family to finally be introduced to their viewers. Though the girls had become well acquainted with Cayd's parents and brothers over the previous week, it was important for their audience to believe this was the first time the family had met Cayd's ladies. Lily had arranged with Ellen a few days earlier for a lunch to be prepared that everyone could partake in. This would give the audience a chance to watch how each girl interacted with the most important people in Cayd's life—his family.

Of course, the fact they all lived together was left out of the frame. Most of their viewers would prefer to think of Cayd as the lonely farmer, living his life in the outback doing what he loved, but longing for someone to share it with. It was a cliché to be certain, but that's what pulled the audience in, and at the end of the day, it was all about the ratings.

A knock at the door startled her from her reverie. Her heart leaped. *Cayd!* Though her stomach immediately swirled with nerves, she scrambled out of bed and hurried down the hall, not bothering to pull a robe over her summer pajamas. She opened the front door and blinked in surprise.

"Maggie! What are you doing here?"

"I came over last night for dinner. Mum said you weren't feeling well. I thought I'd come and check on you."

Lily stood back to let her enter. Maggie dropped onto the sofa. Lily perched on the matching armchair that stood opposite. Though her nerves had receded, they hadn't disappeared. After all, the woman knew how she felt about Cayd. Lily was curious about what had really brought Maggie to her doorstep.

"So, how's the filming going?" Maggie asked.

Lily shrugged. "Not too bad. We're in the home stretch. Only three more days to go and we're done."

"What happens then?"

"The footage gets handed over to the postproduction team. That's when the magic happens. They start by putting the material into a sequence. Then they use a variety of techniques including coloring, fades, sync, and jump cuts. Everything gets pieced together to make a coherent project. The editor works closely with the postproduction supervisor to create a rough draft. Once that's approved, a final cut is compressed and another season of *Outback Bride* is ready to be shown to the public."

"Wow," Maggie replied, looking impressed. "I had no idea so much work went into it."

Lily nodded. "Yep, and that doesn't count the hours of filming, directing, producing. We can film for three or four hours and only use a two-minute segment."

"Sounds incredibly tiresome." Maggie grinned. "I don't think I'd have the patience for that. I'm a big fan of efficiency and making a TV series sounds anything but that."

Lily laughed. Some of the tension inside her eased. "You're right about that."

There was a moment of silence, then Maggie said, "You're probably wondering what I'm doing here."

"I thought you came to check on me?" Lily winked.

Maggie chuckled disparagingly. "Of course. But there was another reason."

"Of course." Lily smiled. Despite her issues with Cayd, she liked Maggie. In different circumstances, they might even have been friends.

"Cayd's stomping around the place like a mad bull. He won't tell me what's got him all upset." She shot Lily a quick glance. "I thought you might have something to do with it, or at least know what's put my brother in such a bad mood."

Lily closed her eyes on a weary sigh and sat back against the chair. "Oh. I see."

"Care to explain?"

Lily debated briefly about what to say and decided on the truth. "It's as you said. Cayd likes me a lot. He says he's fallen in love with me. I... I've fallen in love with him too."

Maggie's face split into a wide grin. "I knew it! That's fantastic! I'd love to have you as my sister!"

Warmth spread through Lily at Maggie's words, but she remained somber. Slowly, Maggie's smile faded and was replaced by a frown.

"I don't understand. Why isn't this something to celebrate?"

Lily sighed again. "I wish it were that easy. See, Cayd's meant to be falling in love with one of his participants, not me. Filming doesn't wrap up for another three days. We have to keep up the pretense that he's going to fall for one of the women. That's what the viewers expect. That's what my boss expects. He's made it clear that he wants excitement, drama, and conflict right to the very end. I can't have Cayd coming out and declaring his love for me in public. It would ruin everything."

"You mean, it would ruin the show."

"Yes, the show. I'm the producer. It's my responsibility to make things happen the way my boss and our audience expect. My boss has made it clear my job's on the line if I don't."

"And you can't afford to lose your job," Maggie finished. She sighed. "I can see why you and Cayd falling in love isn't cause for rejoicing. Have you told him what's at stake?"

Lily eyed Maggie steadily. "He knows how important my job is to me. I have no choice. The show must go on."

Maggie sighed again. "I don't envy you your position. You're stuck between a rock and a hard place."

Lily managed to smile. "You sure have that right, but I appreciate your understanding. It's nice to have someone on my side." She paused and then added, "I don't know how often you come to Sydney, but if you ever find yourself in the city, give me a call. There's always a bed at my place."

Maggie's face was wreathed in smiles. "Thank you. I might just take you up on that."

"Please do. My offer's sincere. No matter how this all works out."

To show that she was genuine, Lily scribbled her address and phone number on a notepad that was lying on the coffee table and handed it to Maggie.

"Call me," she said. "Once this is all over and done with and the dust settles—pun intended—I'd love to catch up over a drink."

Cayd had put it off for as long as he could, but the time had come to tell Olivia and Marissa the truth. As he'd already had a conversation with Marissa, he drew Olivia aside first. They took a seat on a bench in his mother's garden. Away from the prying cameras, he told her as gently as he could that he'd fallen in love with someone else.

"It's Marissa. Of course it is." Olivia's voice was filled with resignation. "How could I hope to compete with someone as beautiful as she is?"

He shook his head. "It's not Marissa."

Olivia frowned. "But there's no one else left."

"It's someone I've met during the show."

Olivia's eyes widened in sudden comprehension. "Oh my goodness! You're talking about Lily! I've seen the way you look at each other. And that dance! I dismissed it because she was just the producer, but now it all makes sense."

Cayd compressed his lips. "You're right. It's Lily."

"Marissa and I never stood a chance, did we?" There was accusation in her tone.

Cayd grimaced. "I'm sorry, Olivia. I certainly didn't plan on falling in love with her. In the beginning, I was excited to see how things would develop between my chosen ladies. I felt a spark with all three of you. This thing with Lily, it just happened. I didn't start out to make it happen, but we don't have any control over who we fall in love with, do we?"

Olivia's shoulders slumped. She looked resigned. "I guess not. Thanks for telling me. I appreciate your honesty. I wish you and Lily all the best."

She got up to leave. Cayd reached out and grabbed her arm. "There's something else."

Olivia returned to her seat. "What is it?"

He explained how Lily had chosen the TV show over him. How, despite admitting she had real feelings for him, she wanted him to keep up the charade of being into the women until filming had wrapped.

"She wanted you to deliberately deceive us?" Olivia asked, her tone reflecting her shock.

"Yes. It's all about what their audience wants."

Anger glinted in Olivia's eyes. "Forget about the audience, what about *us*? We're flesh-and-blood people with real feelings and real hearts on the line. How monstrous of her to suggest such a thing!"

Cayd nodded. "Exactly. And that's where I need your help. After Lily threatened me with all sorts of dire consequences if I breached my contract, I agreed to keep up the charade, but I want you and Marissa to be in on it. I say we ham it up for the cameras, do everything we can to make Lily and her precious audience believe we're falling in love. I'll shower both of you with attention, so no one will be able to tell who I'm going to finally choose."

A grin tugged at the corners of Olivia's mouth. "Lily's going to be beside herself. If she really does have feelings for you, she's going to be eaten alive with jealousy."

Cayd winked. "That's the plan."

"That's the least of what she deserves," Olivia said, still miffed.

"I agree. So, are you in?"

Cayd stuck out his hand. Olivia shook it enthusiastically. "I'm in."

Next, Cayd drew Marissa aside and filled her in. Once she'd heard about what Lily had asked him to do and still feeling upset over Lily's earlier deception, Marissa was also keen to get on board with Cayd's plan.

"Just so you know, there are no hard feelings," she said. "It would have been nice to find love, but I was also motivated by the need to get publicity for my online fashion business. I only launched it six months ago, and something like this could give it a real shot in the arm."

Cayd looked at her in surprise. "We have more in common than you think." He told her about his farm stay project.

When he'd finished, Marissa smiled and linked her arm with his. "We're two of a kind."

He grinned. "You bet."

It was late in the afternoon when Cayd suggested he and the girls go to the hot artesian pool for a swim and to watch the sunset. Lily had done her best to avoid him all day, but her crew would expect her to go with them and give them some direction. It was going to be difficult to watch him frolic with Marissa and Olivia half-naked in the water, but she'd get through it. She had no choice.

By the time she arrived, the ladies were already in the bore bath. Their skimpy bikinis left little to the imagination. To her chagrin, Cayd seemed to be making the most of all that bare skin. He grabbed Marissa around the waist and lifted her against him before playfully tossing her away. Olivia pressed herself against his back. He swung around and pulled her close before pressing a kiss against her lips.

Hot shards of jealousy stabbed at Lily every which way. She had no one to blame but herself. After all, this was what she'd wanted. She didn't want to watch, but it was hard to drag her gaze away. Cayd looked magnificent wearing nothing more than colorful board shorts that emphasized his slim hips and cradled the noticeable bulge in his groin. His well-defined pectorals and washboard stomach glistened in the sun. Recalling the way his strong, broad chest felt against her, she yearned to run her fingers over his firm flesh and get as close to him as she could get. As close as his two ladies.

Once again, Marissa took the opportunity to press herself against him. Olivia climbed on his back. The three of them laughed and played and had fun. Taking a moment to make sure the cameras were capturing every second of the frivolity, Lily turned away and slunk back to the ute.

The next two days passed by for Cayd in a blur of activities, all of them instigated by Lily. There was footage of him and his ladies carrying out repairs to some of the outbuildings that had been damaged in the flood. There was more fencing and feeding of the farm animals. Lily kept her distance, but Cayd was painfully aware of her everywhere they went.

It was getting harder and harder to keep up the pretense of being attracted to his ladies. Having them in on the charade made it bearable, but knowing it was all for show left a sour taste in his mouth. He hated Lily for putting him in that position. There was only one day left before filming would be over and he could finish with this travesty once and for all. It couldn't come fast enough.

Lily watched as Cayd laughed and flirted with the women as they filled up the water troughs. Predictably, Cayd turned the hose on Marissa, who squealed in delight. It wasn't long before her T-shirt was soaked through, leaving little to the imagination. No doubt her male viewers would be just as impressed as Cayd obviously was with Marissa's bountiful display.

Not to be outdone, Olivia soon got into the fun. She stole the hose from Cayd and sprayed him with it. He pretended outrage, but it was clear he was getting as much pleasure out of it as they were.

Lily scowled. She hated how obsessed she'd become with watching him. It was like she was a masochist. She hated every minute he spent with the girls, but she couldn't look away. Knowing that it had to be this way didn't make things any more bearable.

Thank goodness there was the final farewell dinner was right around the corner. She was no longer sure which one he'd choose to stay. She'd thought Marissa was a front-runner, but lately, he'd been paying just as much attention to Olivia. Gerald had wanted to keep everyone guessing, and that was exactly what he was going to get. At least one of them would be happy.

Lily ought to be grateful Cayd had taken her at her word, but it was excruciating watching him acting all loved-up. She wanted to believe it was all an act, that he was merely pretending, but it looked so real. The kisses and holding hands, the private glances, whispering in each other's ears.

It all played well for the cameras, and that meant it would be great for the ratings too. But at moments like this, with Cayd and his ladies all over each other, she couldn't help but wonder if everything they'd shared was a lie, including his declaration of love. Not knowing the truth was driving her slowly crazy. Thank goodness they were nearly ready to wrap things up.

Chapter Twenty-Four

♥

From the corner of his eye, Cayd spied Lily standing in the shadows while the cameras rolled. He deliberately reached for Marissa and planted a kiss right on her mouth. She immediately brought her arms up around his neck and deepened the kiss. Long moments later, they finally drew apart. They grinned at each other as if there was nothing awry.

Cayd had never realized he was such a good actor. Marissa was also playing her part to the hilt. And he couldn't fault Olivia. Anyone watching would think she was the favorite for Cayd's heart. The whole thing filled him with disgust, and he hated Lily for forcing him into doing it.

It irritated him that despite his anger and hurt, his feelings for her hadn't changed. He was still in love with her. Every now and then, he'd see hurt flash in her eyes and that would kill him, but then he'd remind himself that this was what she wanted.

It was the night of the final farewell dinner. He'd already agreed ahead of time with Marissa and Olivia that it would be Olivia he sent home. She was fine with that. She'd confessed that she couldn't wait to leave the station and get back to the comforts of her city life. She'd agreed with him that she'd never have made an outback bride. They'd laughed about it together. He told her it had been an honor to meet her, and he couldn't wait to hear that she'd met her Mr Right. Cayd was sure it wouldn't be too long.

Marissa was happy to continue the charade for one more night. It made it easier knowing that at the end of it, they'd go their separate ways with everyone's heart intact. Well, at least as far as his ladies were concerned. Though Cayd's heart had never been in danger from Marissa and Olivia, the same couldn't be said for Lily.

He sighed. He couldn't wait for the filming to end and for everyone to go back to where they'd come from. He couldn't help but wonder if he'd ever see Lily again. Right now, he wasn't sure he even wanted to.

For Lily, it had been the longest couple of days in her life. All joy over the show had long since dissipated. Now she was just going through the motions. They'd gotten through the farewell dinner, with Cayd opting to send Olivia home. There had been plenty of tears and good-luck wishes, and finally,

Olivia had climbed into one of the vehicles and disappeared into the night.

That left Cayd alone with Marissa, the woman he'd chosen to stay to see where things might lead. The two of them had spent the rest of the night kissing and cuddling and holding each other close. Lily couldn't tell if their performance was just for the cameras or whether genuine feelings had developed between the two.

It's my own fault if they've fallen in love... I'm the one who insisted Cayd do all he could to give my viewers what they wanted... A happy ending. Too bad the ending's not so happy for me...

Still, she was a professional to the end and she smiled when it was expected, praising the loved-up couple, expressing happiness at the wonder of them finding each other and falling in love. That night, as soon as filming had wrapped up, she escaped back to her cottage and cried herself to sleep.

The next morning, with Cayd and Marissa all over each other at breakfast, Lily said her farewells. She bid Ellen and Bob a fond goodbye and thanked them for their hospitality. She also thanked Cayd's brothers for being good sports about it all. They wished her luck.

Cayd was still wrapped around Marissa when she stopped by him to say goodbye. She held out a hand toward him and he shook it, like they were nothing more than polite strangers.

"It was nice to meet you both. Thank you for being part of *Outback Bride*," she said.

Marissa smiled. "Thank *you*. Without you, we'd never have found each other."

Cayd merely nodded dismissively. His response was brief. "Safe travels."

She walked away disappointed. She'd been hoping for more. Hoping for some sign that he still liked her, loved her. But there was nothing. With a heavy heart, she hoisted her suitcase into the back of a vehicle and, after giving Macey a final farewell pat on the head, she left with her camera crew. She refused to look back.

Cayd gazed after the cloud of dust left behind by Lily's transport long after the ute had disappeared. He could still see the hurt and disappointment in her beautiful eyes as she'd told him goodbye, but he was a long way from forgiving her for what she'd ordered him to do.

Now that the cameras had stopped rolling, he gently disengaged himself from Marissa and stood.

"I guess that's it," she said with a small smile.

"I guess so." He paused. Hope flared in Marissa's eyes. He cursed under his breath.

"Thanks for being such a champion about all this, Marissa. I really appreciate everything you've done."

"That's all right, Cayd. I enjoyed pretending to be the love of your life."

Though she spoke lightly, he caught the shimmer of tears in her eyes.

Shit.

"You're a great girl. You know that don't you?"

"O-of course."

"If it makes things any better, I wish I'd fallen in love with you. Things would have been so much easier."

Marissa gave him another small smile and then averted her gaze. He hated being put in this position, but it was his own fault. He'd tried to be as honest as he could, but it seemed that wasn't enough.

"When do you leave?" he asked.

"Soon."

"Who's taking you to the airport?"

"Lachlan offered to drive me."

"Good. Great."

It appeared Marissa felt just as awkward as he. He was relieved when she stood on tiptoe and kissed him briefly on the cheek before waving goodbye and leaving the room.

His shoulders slumped on a sigh.

When had life gotten so complicated?

At least he now had the place to himself. Three women vying for his attention, a camera crew and a way-too-sexy producer had taken their toll. He was exhausted.

"Why do you look so down in the mouth? Anyone would think your best friend had just died."

The caustic remark came from his sister. Maggie appeared in the open doorway of the kitchen, shaking her head.

He frowned. "What are you doing here? Don't you have work to do? I thought you were worried about losing your job. You'd think you'd be doing all you could to impress the new owner before he decides to sell the place."

Maggie walked farther into the room and waved her hand dismissively. "Yeah, yeah, yeah. Whatever. We're talking about *you*, not me. I passed Lily in a Land Cruiser heading toward Roma. I take it filming's done?"

Cayd grimaced. "Yeah, thank God. I don't think I could have stood another day longer."

"So, how did you do? Did you choose one of your ladies to make your bride?"

Cayd shot her a sour look. "Does it look like it?"

"Ah, so that's why you're so grumpy. They all turned you down."

"They didn't turn me down!" Cayd protested. "I... I wasn't in love with any of them."

"Ah. Well, not any of your ladies, that's for sure."

Cayd frowned. "What the hell's that supposed to mean?"

Maggie shrugged. "You tell me."

"Maggie..." His voice was dark with warning.

She threw her arms up in a sign of surrender. "Okay, okay! Geez, someone's gotten up on the wrong side of the bed."

Before he could offer another retort, she spoke again.

"I know you're in love with Lily, and she's in love with you. This nonsense over the show is just that, nonsense. Now that the show's over, it's time to get over your bruised ego and tell her how you feel."

Anger licked along Cayd's veins. He narrowed his eyes at his sister. "You know nothing about what went on."

Maggie held his gaze. "In fact, I do. Lily told me."

"She *told* you. Then why aren't you as outraged as I am?"

Once again, Maggie dismissed his words with a casual wave. "Okay, so she chose her job over you, but what choice did she have? She needs the money. She supports her elderly parents. They're both in poor health. Her mother needs care around the home. Lily has been paying for that. She also helps to support her four brothers." Maggie gave him a pointed look. "Did you set aside your outrage long enough to think about that?"

Cayd reeled back in shock. He had no idea about Lily's situation with her parents or her brothers.

"Why didn't she tell me?"

"Would you have listened?"

"Maybe. I'd like to think so. Now we'll never know."

Maggie shrugged. "For whatever reason, she didn't. But don't blame her for that. Not all of us share personal details so easily. You can be pretty tight-lipped yourself. But I hope you can see why she might have chosen her job over you. At least in the short term. That doesn't mean she isn't in love with you, just like you're in love with her."

He opened his mouth to protest, but Maggie beat him to it.

"Don't bother denying it, brother. It's written all over your face. Now, if I were you, I'd go after her and beg her forgiveness and tell her how you feel. You know as well as I do that true love doesn't come by every day." She leveled him with her gaze. "That kind of love's worth fighting for."

Lily flopped down on her white leather sofa and flicked through the TV channels trying to find something that could hold her interest. She'd been back in Sydney for five days and was still trying to readjust from her time in the outback. The traffic noise and congestion were two of the things that were irritating her way more than they had before. So far, she hadn't come up with any idea how to deal with them.

She'd caught up with her parents on her first night back home. Thankfully, both were doing okay. The past couple of weeks had made her realize that her life needed a dramatic makeover, starting with her brothers. She'd had a full and frank discussion with Michael and the twins about the need for them to step up and do their bit to support their ailing parents, starting with Michael securing regular employment and all three of them contributing financially. She'd given Sam a free pass because he had enough challenges in his life, but to her surprise and delight, her youngest brother had insisted on doing his part.

She'd also taken some personal leave from her job to give herself time to recalibrate after what had been a hectic few months, not the least traveling all over the countryside with a film crew in tow, and breaking off her engagement, and falling for a man she couldn't have. She fully intended to pursue the fledgling idea that had taken root to open up an online interior decorating business.

Bringing her long-term relationship with Alex to an end hadn't been quite as traumatic as she'd expected. Though she thought of him fondly, she realized she didn't miss him like she thought she would. More evidence that she'd made the right decision.

One man she'd spent far too much time thinking about was Cayd. Thoughts of him filled her every waking moment and even some of her dreams. She hadn't heard from him since she'd departed Marlowe Downs, and it left her heartsick. She could only assume that he'd cut her out of his life for good and was enjoying his time with Marissa away from the cameras.

Though she'd thought about it more than once, she couldn't bring herself to call him. She didn't want her suspicions confirmed. It was pathetic, but she'd rather live in ignorance for just a little bit longer, while she healed, rather than have her hopes dashed forever.

She sighed. What she needed was a bottle of wine, or maybe two. She'd never been much of a drinker, but alcohol had recently taken on a whole new appeal. Drowning out her woes while watching something sappy on TV seemed like the perfect way to spend the night.

With that thought in mind, she stood and reached for her handbag. On the way out, she collected her phone off the charger and dropped it into her bag. Snatching her car keys off the hall table, she pulled open the door and stopped short in surprise.

"Cayd! Oh, my goodness! What are you doing here?"

His hand was poised as if he were ready to knock. Her heart started pounding a mile a minute. As nerves assailed her, she began garbling. The whole time, he stood on her doorstep and regarded her with a bemused smile.

Cayd did his best to hide his nervousness. On the plane to Sydney, he'd second-guessed his decision, convinced he'd made a mistake. In the taxi from the airport, he'd almost asked the driver to turn around. All the time, he was terrified of the reception he'd get; that Lily would take one look at him and ask him to leave. But she hadn't done that. At least, not yet.

"May I come in?" he asked, testing the waters.

She blinked and then gave a quick nod. A second later, she stepped back to allow him to enter.

"Sure. Come in."

He feasted his eyes on the sight of her. She looked wonderful in another low-cut, floaty summer dress, this one predominantly white and covered in splashes of bright pink hibiscus. The color brought out the delicious olive tones of her skin. Belatedly, he noticed her handbag strap draped across her shoulder. "You're on your way out?"

She touched the soft leather of her bag and nodded. "Yes. Um. I was."

"Don't let me keep you. I can come back later."

She flushed. "No, that's okay. I wasn't going anywhere important."

He cocked a single eyebrow. "Oh?"

Her blush deepened. "If you must know, I was on my way out to buy a bottle of wine. It felt like a wine kind of evening."

"Oh." He followed the single word with a smile. "Lucky I brought some with me."

From behind his back, he produced two bottles, one red, one white. "I wasn't sure which one you preferred, so I got both."

She laughed, and the musical sound of it was like a balm to his battered soul.

So far, so good...

She turned and led the way through a tastefully decorated apartment. The dominant color scheme was pale green and gray, with marble benchtops in the kitchen and mint green paint on the cupboards and walls. A large white leather sofa took up a fair amount of space in the adjoining living room and stood in front of a huge flatscreen TV.

"So, will you watch *Outback Bride* when it airs?" he asked, curious.

"Yes. It's the only time I get to see the finished product. My day comprises of hundreds of little scenes. I'm always keen to see how the postproduction team pull it all together."

"And are you usually pleased with the end result?"

She thought for a moment. "I'm not sure 'pleased' is the right word. You forget that I'm on the ground dealing with the reality of every day. Sometimes things get edited differently to how I remember them happening, but that's okay. It's done in the name of entertainment and that's our aim: to entertain."

"Do you think *I'll* be pleased with the final cut?"

She laughed again and wagged a finger. "Oh, no. You don't get to ask me that. The final product is out of my hands. I have no say in how things get edited, so I'm not going to hazard a guess as to how they'll turn out. You'll have to decide that for yourself."

He set the wine on the counter and then went back to the front door for his bag. He'd packed light. A single small duffel. He wasn't sure how long he'd be staying. By the time he returned, Lily had opened the bottle of red and had poured a generous amount into two glasses.

"I put the white in the fridge. It tastes better when it's chilled."

"Of course. I'm happy to drink either one."

"Me too."

She smiled shyly. An awkward silence ensued. They both took refuge in their wine.

"Where are you staying?"

"How have you been?"

They spoke simultaneously. Cayd issued a nervous chuckle. Lily gulped at her wine.

"I booked a room at a hotel a couple of blocks away," he answered.

"Oh, okay. Good." She buried her nose again in the glass.

"It's good to see you," he ventured.

"It's good to see you too. Where did you get my address?"

"From Maggie. I hope that's okay."

"Sure."

Another awkward silence descended. Cayd knew it was now or never. He had to find his courage and ask her straight out how she felt about him. It was the only way forward.

"I missed you, Lily. And I'm sorry. I acted like a spoiled brat. Will you forgive me?"

Chapter Twenty-Five

♥

Lily's heart skipped a beat at the intensity in Cayd's eyes. It was clear he was speaking genuinely, but there were so many unanswered questions.

"Where's Marissa?" she asked.

"I don't know. She left a couple of hours after you. I haven't seen her since."

"Have you spoken to her?"

"No."

"Texted?"

"No."

"Emailed?"

"I haven't had any form of communication with her since she left Marlowe Downs." She frowned. "I don't understand. You chose her to stay, to build a relationship with. She's your outback bride."

He shook his head. "No, she isn't, and she was never going to be my outback bride."

Lily's confusion deepened. "You're not making sense. I don't need to remind you how into each other you were. Are you telling me that was fake?"

His gaze remained steady on hers. "Yes."

She gaped. She'd hoped in her heart of hearts that he'd been pretending interest in the women for the sake of the cameras, but hearing him confirm it so definitively filled her with hope. Then she recalled the other reason she'd suspected he might be putting on a show.

"You did it to get back at me. You did it out of spite."

Once again, he didn't avert his gaze. "Yes. That was a part of it. I'm not proud of that. It was juvenile and very hurtful. In my defense, you hurt me too. You acknowledged you had genuine feelings for me, and then you ordered me to throw myself at other women."

"You already knew my reasons for doing that."

He grimaced. "Right. Your precious TV show. At least, that's what you told me."

She held his gaze. "There was more to it than that."

He nodded. "Yes. So I recently found out."

She frowned again. "What are you talking about?"

"Maggie told me your job was on the line if you failed to deliver what was expected for the show. She also told me you support several of your family members, in particular your elderly ailing parents. Why didn't you tell me?"

"We only had a few more days of filming. I didn't want to have to explain myself. I thought pulling rank and reminding you of your obligations was all I needed to do to get things over the line."

Hurt flashed in his eyes. "I wish you'd told me."

"Would it have made a difference?" she shot back.

"Of course, it would have."

"So, you would have faked your feelings for Marissa and Olivia right up until the very end and then broken their hearts?"

"That's what I did anyway, except no one's heart got broken."

"How can you say that? I caught up with Olivia as she was packing her bags to leave. She was very upset."

"No, she *appeared* to be very upset. She was pretending too. It was all part of the plan."

Lily shook her head, now completely confused. "What plan?"

Cayd sighed and took a sip of wine before answering. "When you ordered me to continue the charade with the ladies, I was mad as all hell at you for thumbing your nose at what we had between us and also at the circumstances that meant I had no choice but to comply. One thing I did have a choice about was deceiving two innocent women who deserved far better treatment than that. We'd all signed contracts and we were well aware of how the rules went, but that didn't matter to me. I wasn't going to deliberately hurt them like that."

"So what did you do?" she asked, curious now.

"I went to Olivia and Marissa, and I told them the truth."

Lily's eyes widened with shock. "You told them you weren't into them?"

"Yes. I also told them I was in love with you."

If she'd been shocked before, this time, she was rendered speechless. He'd told the two women vying for his heart that he'd fallen in love with someone else. It was unbelievable. It was also incredibly brave, honorable, and flattering. The full implication of what he'd just said suddenly hit her. As she contemplated asking him for clarification, her mouth went dry with nerves.

Still, she'd never know if she didn't ask. His presence in her kitchen gave her the courage to put the question to him.

"Do you still feel that way?"

His gaze burned into hers. "Yes."

He said it without hesitation and with complete conviction. Her face split into a grin. She felt like whooping and hollering and dancing around the room. She felt like throwing herself in his arms.

"Oh, Cayd," she breathed. "You won't believe how happy I am to hear that. I'm in love with you too! I have been from the very beginning. It just took me a while to recognize that. I'm so sorry for any hurt I caused. I hated being responsible for that, but at the time, I didn't have a choice."

"I understand that now. It helps."

With that, he set aside his glass and walked toward her. She did the same. They met in the middle and came together. She sighed as their bodies touched. Tilting her head backward, she waited for his lips to descend.

From the very first fleeting touch, she was gone. His lips were firm, his kiss was confident and familiar. She felt like she was coming home. His arms went around her and drew her close. She clung to his broad shoulders. They kissed until they were breathless, but even then, it wasn't enough. When he slowly pulled away and lifted his head, she whimpered in disappointment.

He smiled at her tenderly. "Hey, it's okay. We have all night."

"I thought you booked a hotel room?"

He shrugged. "Do you think I'm going to need it?"

The air between them suddenly became charged with tension. She understood the significance of this moment. He didn't know she was a virgin. How would he? And yet, he was leaving the decision about whether they slept together in her hands.

"I'm in love with you, Cayd Fairfax, but before things go any further, there's something I want you to know." She lifted head and captured his gaze. "I'm a virgin."

Surprise flared brightly in his eyes. "But you were engaged. Were you saving yourself for marriage?"

She shrugged and looked away, suddenly embarrassed. "No. Alex wanted to wait. I was happy to accede to his request. I didn't put much thought into it at the time, but I think I was happy to go along with it because it gave me an excuse not to get fully intimate with him. Now I'm pretty sure my reluctance to take our relationship to that level was my subconscious trying to tell me I was with the wrong guy."

Cayd reached out and tenderly cupped her cheek. "How do you feel now?"

She grinned. "Like I want to tear your clothes off and make love to you all night long."

His face beamed with relief and love. He whooped and grabbed her around the waist and swung her off her feet. She squealed.

"Let's get to it," he said. "We've already wasted enough time."

Lily took his hand and led him to her bedroom. She was relieved she'd made the bed when she'd climbed out of it earlier that morning. Cayd didn't appear to pay too much attention to the decor. He went straight to the bed and sat and drew her down beside him. Nerves flared in her stomach, but she needn't have worried. Slowly, tenderly, he bent his head and captured her mouth in a sweet and sexy kiss.

Until Cayd, she'd never realized plain old kissing could be so erotic. It had never been that way with Alex. Refusing to let thoughts of her ex-fiancé intrude on this magical moment, she opened her mouth and allowed Cayd's tongue to sweep inside. He stroked and tasted and sipped from her mouth, and the whole time, liquid heat grew in her core. Her arms snuck around his neck, holding him tightly. He adjusted their position until they were chest to chest.

Then, slowly, his hand crept down and cupped one of her breasts. When his fingernails gently scraped over her nipple, she shivered on a wave of desire and arched into him, silently begging for more.

"Do you like that?" he whispered, his voice hoarse with need.

"Yes. I'd like you to do it again."

He complied and then gave her other breast the same attention. Her nipples were now both hard little nubs beneath his fingers. She yearned to be skin to skin.

"Can I take your shirt off?" she asked.

"Be my guest. Can I take off your dress?"

She grinned. "Be my guest."

Together, they worked on each other's buttons until his shirt and her sundress were on the floor. Cayd's hands went around her back to the clasp of her bra. Before he took the next step, he sought permission with his eyes.

"Yes. Take it off," she murmured, splaying her hands on his bare chest.

Cayd did as she asked and a moment later, they were lying on their sides facing each other, touching as much of each other as possible.

"Your skin is like silk," he rasped, trailing his fingers over her belly.

Her stomach muscles clenched under his touch. She reached out and did the same thing to him. His impressive pectorals were firm beneath her fingers. His stomach was as flat as a board. A thin line of dark hair led from his bellybutton and disappeared beneath the waistband of his jeans.

Another surge of nervousness went through her at what lay ahead, but at the same time, she was inquisitive, and her heart pounded with need.

"Can I touch you?" she asked.

"Please."

He helped her by loosening his belt and unbuttoning his jeans. He slid the zipper down and then left the rest to her. Shyly, curiously, she dipped her hand inside his silk boxers and encircled his erection with her fingers. It was harder and thicker than she'd imagined, and having his cock in her hand filled her core with fire. She tightened her hand reflexively and heard Cayd's sharp intake of breath.

"Are you okay? Did I hurt you?"

"Hell, no. To the contrary. That feels so good."

"Oh. Okay." She relaxed and did it again. This time, Cayd let out a groan.

"We might need to leave more of that for another time," he said. "If you keep that up, this will be over before we've started."

She blushed as the implication of his words sank in. Turning her gently onto her back, he shifted until he was above her and slowly lowered his head. He took one nipple and then the other into his mouth. White-hot heat seared through her, bringing her off the bed.

"Cayd! Oh my goodness!"

"Does that feel good?"

"That feels amazing!"

He continued to suckle and then eased his way lower, kissing his way across her rib cage, her stomach, until he reached the satin edge of her panties. There, he paused and lifted his head, once again seeking her permission.

"Yes, please," she breathed.

Slowly, he inched down her panties. Though her heart pounded with nerves and excitement, she lifted her hips to assist him. He'd dragged her panties all the way down her legs and over her feet and then tossed them over his shoulder as if they were no longer of any consequence. She stifled a giggle.

Then he buried his face against her femininity. She squeaked in surprise, but was soon writhing against him in need. He wielded his tongue like a master, stroking, licking, tasting, sucking until she was consumed with the desire to have him inside her.

Tugging at his head, she drew him up against her. His cock pressed insistently against her stomach, reminding her of what they were about to do.

"Do you have a condom?" she asked, her face flaming.

He shucked off his jeans and underwear then dug into one of the pockets for his wallet. He quickly sheathed himself and then returned to position himself between her thighs. As his cock nudged at her entrance, he bent his head and captured her mouth in his. While she was distracted with another powerfully erotic kiss, he eased himself inside her.

A moment of resistance, a flash of pain, and then he was deep inside her. She gasped at the impact of it, stretching and filling her in a way she'd never been. As their lips remained fused, so were their bodies. Slowly, slowly, Cayd began to move.

The muscles in his shoulders bunched beneath her fingers. As he slowly thrust in and out of her, desire rekindled and grew. As the fire burned hotter, she clung to him, building up to a moment of anticipation like never before. When she reached the peak and climaxed, the world tilted on its axis. There was no other way to describe the earth-shattering moment.

As her inner muscles contracted around him, Cayd increased his pace. His thrusts became harder, faster, less controlled, until he too, was at the crest. On a shout of triumph and relief, he collapsed against her, breathing hard.

She held him close, loving the weight of him against her. Then he rolled to one side and gathered her in against him.

"That was amazing," she whispered.

He smiled tenderly. "That was your first time. I wanted it to last longer, but I let myself down. You felt too good. I couldn't wait. The next time will be better, I promise."

She snuggled in against him and pressed a kiss against his chest. "That was everything I could have hoped for. I can't wait to see what else you have in store."

He chuckled and tightened his arm around her. She'd never felt so safe, so secure, so loved. As if he could read her mind, he whispered against her hair.

"I love you, Lily Calimeris. I'm so glad you came into my life. Will you be my outback bride?"

A surge of joy went through her. She'd never been so happy in her life. She tilted her head backward until she could see his beloved face and beamed. "I love you too. As to your question…" She deliberately drew out a pause and then responded. "I thought you'd never ask."

THE END

Get a free book when you sign up for Chris Taylor's newsletter at: https://christaylorauthor.com.au/

If you enjoyed Cayd and Lily's story, don't forget to leave a review at your favorite digital retailer. Every review is greatly appreciated and will help other readers find my books.

A Cattleman's Daughter is the next book in this series. Keep reading for a sneak peek:

CHAPTER ONE

Maggie Fairfax glared at the approaching vehicle with a mixture of anger and dread. The 4WD was nothing more than a speck in the distance, surrounded by a cloud of red dust, but she was in no doubt that when her unwelcome visitor arrived, her life as she knew it would change forever. She cursed under her breath.

Stop being so melodramatic. There's always the chance he'll fall in love with the place. After all, it's his birthright.

Yeah, right. According to the estate lawyer, Rafael Hetherington was a city slicker. He was thirty years of age and had never set foot on his uncle's farm. Until now. No doubt he'd be there only for as long as it took him to look around and assess the value of the place so that he could put Hetherington Station on the market. The lawyer had already intimated as much. She was certain the nephew wouldn't have any interest in a cattle station. Even less interest in the people who lived out there and who relied on the station for their livelihood. People like her.

She'd managed the large and prosperous station for the past three years. At the ripe old age of twenty-five, she'd taken on the challenge of overseeing nearly one hundred and fifty thousand acres of prime beef cattle land in the heart of the outback. Central Queensland was famous for its heat and dust and its long dry summers, but Maggie had been born on the neighbouring station. The outback was in her blood. She couldn't imagine being anywhere else. She'd loved every moment of the past three years, battling the elements, making bargains with God over the weather, and getting the most out of every acre of land and station hand she was responsible for.

Now that life and the bright future she'd almost taken for granted was in jeopardy. Arthur Hetherington had died. His sole beneficiary was minutes away from arriving to claim his inheritance. There was a very real possibility that her time on

Hetherington Station was about to come to an abrupt end. She intended to make it as messy as possible.

A humorless smile tilted her lips upward. She didn't know what kind of man Rafael Hetherington was, but with a name like that, she was sure he wouldn't stand a chance against her. There wasn't a man within a hundred miles who would take on Maggie Fairfax. When she set her mind to achieving something, there wasn't anything or anyone who could deter her from her goal.

Okay, so ownership of the station had passed into the hands of a man who couldn't ever hope to understand the love someone could have for the land, but she sure as hell intended to do everything in her power to make him see that selling the station would be the worst thing he could do.

The cloud of dust grew bigger, until finally a once-white Land Cruiser emerged and came to a halt a few yards away from where she stood outside the homestead fence.

At least he had the sense to hire a 4WD. Not like the city lawyer who turned up in a Mercedes coup...

Her thoughts were interrupted when the driver's door came open and a tall, imposing and sinfully good-looking man climbed out.

Her stomach took a nosedive, and the sudden rush of nerves immediately irritated her.

Of course he's good looking. No doubt he's rich and powerful too. His uncle owned one of the largest cattle stations in Central

Queensland. I shouldn't be surprised that money runs in the family.

The newcomer took a moment to brush invisible dust off his designer jeans. Maggie took the time to inventory his physical appearance. Tall, well over six foot. Chocolate-brown hair with the slightest wave that had been tamed by an over-zealous barber who'd made sure the man had gotten his money's worth. Military short around the sides and back, though not a buzz cut, it wasn't far from it. The only glimpse of personality that remained in the stranger's hair was in the wave of fringe that had been left to fall at a rakish angle over his right eye.

Blue eyes, almost as bright as hers, fringed by dark lashes, stared at her with a mixture of friendliness and wariness. It was obvious he wasn't quite certain of his welcome.

Yes, you should be nervous.

Maggie chuckled silently in anticipation and then quickly rearranged her expression as the stranger strode up to her with a smile.

"You must be Maggie Fairfax. I'm Raf Hetherington." He held out his hand toward her.

"Nice to meet you." She forced herself to complete the handshake. Her mind distantly catalogued the warmth of his skin and the rough calluses on his palm. She frowned. She'd expected him to have hands that were soft from office work.

Maybe the calluses are from lifting weights at the gym...

Yes, that was more likely. There was no way a man who looked like Raf Hetherington did manual labor for a living.

To her consternation, he was even more good looking up close. His teeth were straight and white. Laugh lines were visible around his eyes. His olive skin was tanned and glowing, like he'd spent plenty of time in the sun. Either that, or he'd had a spray tan.

She'd heard there were men who liked to get a tan like that. It was safer than sunbaking, but in her world, there was something wrong about a man who paid for a tan. She could just imagine the way her brothers would react if they heard about something like that. All six of them would be in hysterics. Her three younger sisters would be equally amused.

"My uncle always spoke highly of you," the stranger continued. "On his behalf, I'd like to thank you for everything you've done for the place. You've battled some hard years recently. Droughts and floods and fluctuating cattle prices. It's a tough life."

"Yes, it is, but I wouldn't want to live anywhere else."

She was silently impressed that he appeared to know at least something about the station. She was also quietly impressed with his good manners. She frowned. She didn't want to find anything she liked about him. Right now, he was enemy number one.

A fly buzzed around his face. He brushed it away and looked around at the red dirt and the dust that had finally settled. He grimaced. "If you say so. All I see is dirt and dust."

Her stomach dipped. It was obvious he had no affinity for the place, and how could he? He'd been there less than five minutes. He had no idea how beautiful the station looked during a summer storm, when blue-black clouds gathered on the horizon and the rain washed everything clean. Or how the colors of the sunset in the evening were breathtaking – all reds and oranges and purples. Or the amazing native wildlife – kangaroos, wallabies, emus, birds of every description.

I'll just have to show him that this place is worth keeping. I also need to convince him that no one's expecting him to stay. I'm more than capable of running this place without him. In fact, I'd prefer it that way...

Raf had made his way to the back of the Land Cruiser and now retrieved two large suitcases. Spying them, Maggie had another moment of concern.

"How long are you staying?" she asked, striving to keep her tone neutral.

"Oh, I haven't decided. A week or two. Maybe longer. It depends."

Her stomach lurched in alarm. *A week or two?* "What does it depend on?"

He shrugged nonchalantly. "I don't know. I'll see how long it takes me to get bored."

His easy certainty that it was only a matter of time before he'd be bored irritated her no end, but she supposed she ought to be grateful that he was not inclined to stay indefinitely. Having him around would be annoying. It would slow her down and interfere with her work. Heaven forbid if he actually expected her to babysit him.

Then another thought occurred to her. The more time she spent with him, the greater the probability that she'd manage to persuade him not to sell. She had to show him such a great time that he'd want to return over and over again. As the beginnings of a plan bubbled beneath the surface, she shot him a winning smile.

"Well, we're very pleased to have you here for as long as you care to stay. Two weeks won't be nearly enough to show you all the sights, but I'll personally ensure you experience as much of the authentic station life as you can while you're here."

He quirked a dark eyebrow upward in surprise. "That would be very nice of you. I must admit, I didn't expect to receive quite such an hospitable welcome."

She pretended confusion. "Whyever not?"

He shrugged. "I guess I thought you might be concerned about my plans for the place. How long I intend to keep it. That kind of thing."

She forced herself to keep her tone neutral. "You're the new owner. It's yours to do as you please."

He picked up his suitcases and started toward her. "You're right."

His dismissive tone set her teeth on edge. It was all she could do not to bark out a retort.

I need to hold my tongue. I need to keep him on side, remember?

With an effort, she controlled her temper and smiled sweetly. "If there's anything I can do to make your stay more comfortable, just let me know."

He came to a halt beside her. "Good of you to offer. You can start by showing me to my lodgings."

Maggie felt a moment of panic. The guest cottage had stood derelict for years and the dongas were being utilized by the station hands. The only available "lodgings" were in the homestead and that was currently occupied by her.

"I-I'm sorry," she stammered. "There's only the homestead…"

"Great. That will do nicely."

He turned and strode off in the direction of the house. Panic surged through her veins. She was pretty sure he didn't have a clue that she'd been living in the homestead since she arrived there. The former owner hadn't cared. He rarely visited anyway and on those rare occasions when he did, he was only there for a few hours before he flew back to Brisbane again. He'd never stayed overnight.

But Arthur's nephew had just announced he was staying a couple of weeks. Maybe more. She had to let him know that he'd be sharing those lodgings. Heat flared in her cheeks. She cursed under her breath. She had nothing to be embarrassed about. She'd done nothing wrong. Try telling that to her conscience. She felt like a kid who'd been caught with her hand in the cookie jar.

Oh, hell. How did I get here? I have to come clean.

The stranger was halfway across the front yard when she called out to him again.

"Ah, Mr Hetherington?"

He stopped and turned to face her. "Please, call me Raf."

"Ah, Raf. Yes. Well, see. The thing is, you should know that I live in the homestead."

Once again, he raised a single dark brow. "You live in the homestead? The same homestead where I'm headed?"

She refused to look away. "Yes."

"I see. Was my uncle aware of that?"

Anger rushed through her at his implication. "Of course he was! What do you think? That I snuck in there and set up house and didn't even ask?"

He gave an infuriating shrug that neither confirmed nor denied. She ground her teeth together and prayed for patience. The last thing she needed was to lose her temper and get him off side.

"Living in the homestead was included in my employment package. It's never been a problem. I hope it won't be a problem now." She forced a smile.

He gazed at her a moment and then shrugged again. "Whatever. As long as I have my own bed and bathroom, we'll be fine." He turned his back on her and continued toward the house.

A fresh wave of embarrassment heated her cheeks. "Ah, Raf?"

He stopped and kept his back to her for a moment before slowly turning around. "Yes?"

"Um… There's only one bathroom."

He shook his head in disbelief. "Only one bathroom? What is this? The dark ages?"

"No. But you're staying in a homestead that's been here for more than a hundred years. It's had some updates over the years, like indoor plumbing and electricity—"

"Hallelujah for that." His voice was as dry as the desert.

"But I'm afraid there isn't an ensuite."

He compressed his lips and slowly nodded his head. "Okay. So that means we're sharing." He gave her a thorough once-over that left a trail of heat in its wake. "I guess I can live with that."

A Cattleman's Daughter is due for release in 2024.

Other books by Chris Taylor

The Munro Family Series
(in order)

The Profiler
The Investigator
The Predator
The Betrayal
The Deception
The Negotiator
The Christmas Vigil (A novella)
The Ransom
The Defendant
The Shooting

CHRIS TAYLOR

The Maker

The Sydney Harbour Hospital Series (in order)

The Perfect Husband
The Body Thief
The Baby Snatchers
The Final Bullet
The Debt Collector
The Lab Test
The Stolen Identity
The Cliff-top Killer
The Likeable Fraudster

The Sydney Legal Series
(in order)

An Accidental Murderer
At the Hand of her Father
A Woman Scorned
Lies and Deception
Ordinary Evil
The Ties that Bind
The Perfect Crime
A Toxic Inheritance
Malicious Love

A CATTLEMAN'S QUEST

The Craigdon Family Series
(in order)

Callum
Joel
Isabella
Nicholas
Sophia
Flynn
Noah
Logan
Elizabeth

The Barrington Family Series
(in order)

Broken Lives
Broken Promises
Broken Bonds
Broken Spirits
Broken Minds
Broken Vows
Broken Hearts
Broken Dreams
Broken Homes

The Fairfax Family Series (in order)

CHRIS TAYLOR

A Cattleman in Disguise
A Cattleman's Quest
A Cattleman's Daughter
A Cattleman's Secret Baby
To Catch a Cattleman
The Doctor and the Cattleman
To Rescue a Cattleman
A Cattleman's Heart
For the Love of a Cattleman

Bachelors and Brides Series (in order)

Matilda
Austin
Farrah
Benjamin
Verity
Denver
Ebony
Tyrone
Willow

Books by Chris Taylor
Writing as
Bella
Christian

This Is Where It Ends Series
(in order)

Jessie's Story
Ryan's Story
Holly's Story
Sarah's Story
Veronica's Story

Love audiobooks? Check out Chris Taylor Books on audio
iTunes   Amazon   Audible   Spotify

Join Chris Taylor's Facebook reader group/fan page and be among the
first to receive news of book releases, read and review books
prior to release
and other amazing offers.

Join Now!

Acknowledgments

As usual, no book comes into being without a lot of help and support by my friends and family. A world of thanks must go to my editor, Linda Ingmasson. Thank you for everything that you do to make my stories even more amazing than I could ever dare to dream. To former Detective Superintendent Michael Kilfoyle, thank you for lending my story credibility. Any mistakes are wholly my own.

To all the team at 100 Covers, thank you for the fantastic book cover. To my sister, Nicole Guihot, thank you for your excellent editorial comments, proof reading skills and suggestions. I hope you like the final result.

To the fantastic writer organizations such as Romance Writers of Australia, Romance Writers of America and Romance Writers of New Zealand for all the help, support and encouragement they offer new and aspiring writers, including me.

To my readers, thank you for your support and love for my stories. Your encouragement and enjoyment make this journey all worthwhile.

And lastly, to my friends and family, especially my husband and children. Thank you for putting up with late dinners and even later conversations as I've emerged day after day from the sometimes scary but always enthralling world I've created on my computer.

About the Author

Chris Taylor grew up on a farm in north-west New South Wales, Australia. She always had a thirst for stories and recalls writing her first book at the ripe old age of eight. Always a lover of romance and happily-ever-afters, a career in criminal law sparked her interest in intrigue and suspense. For Chris to be able to combine romance with suspense in her books is a dream come true.

Chris is married to Linden and is the mother of five children. If not behind her computer, you can find her doing the school run, taxiing children to swimming lessons, piano lessons, football, and cricket. In her spare time, Chris loves to read her favorite authors who include Richard North Patterson, Sandra Brown, Kathleen E Woodiwiss and Jude Devereaux.

You can find out more about Chris and get a free book when you sign up for her newsletter at her website:
http://www.christaylorauthor.com.au

Join Chris on Facebook at:
https://www.facebook.com/christaylo-rauthor/